Little Valkyrie

Philip Grimes

Volki

Contents

1. CARAVANS

On hollow Krausenstraße the new dogs bark in Russian. Otto wears a greatcoat listening to the Duke, with chicken wire and flour beside him; tomorrow we fix a wall against icing Berlin.

I lift my arm in the mirror - slight swelling, probably nothing. My breasts, scoops at best, are smaller. All that testifies to muscle are my calves. Eyes sallowed by hep and chest aflame with typhus, these recovered - I am bone-stretched but me - while my curly hair bounces with insulting health. Down to the mound, over which are the giveaways: livid purple bruising.

How dared they. I touch the painless marks. We bear this scar between us - unless it's divisible; allocated - reaching past the exodus and Blitzkrieg, the earliest ghetto, for clear flesh.

They appeared two days after I'd filled the racial heredity form, a cover to stamp me as Recidivist. The guards stood behind a screen which made me fearful - was I animal, had I contracted something? Zyklon B for Hoagy C, it seemed so improbable.

The nib scratched the form. I waited, occasionally looked up. Two of the three guards chatted, arms folded, the third peered into something on the desk. And nothing happened.

I completed the form, nodded through the glass and the door opened. ...Something had happened.

☆

My name is Angela. And with the onset of winter 1944 an execution squad arrived at Uckermark juvenile camp. I didn't know them as such - Conrad, Moll, Höss - but Marianne the Sintesa said Conrad was a neck-shooter, Moll a gasser and Höss a user of pesticides; all gleaned from the adults at Ravensbrück. It was also winter '44, after three years of drudgery and diseases that floored - the pale lottery of each dawn - that I thought about escape; not as the stuff of night sweats, but a reality.

As evening came I'd look over the Lagerstraße to a clutch of staff buildings, spiked by their grey tower, for the arrival of Sabine Keller in an unmarked van. Not quite unmarked, it had the faded cross of re-purposing from the ICRC. In dirt, playing three-card Monte with Marianne, Sabine was a reminder of something beyond Germany.

I was returning from the Siemens factory with a gashed palm (I'd napped upright at a lathe) as the squad stood steaming, pointing at blocks being cleared for their work; a last delusion in the Reich's executors.

My name was barked. "Schmidt!"

It was Aufseherin Horn, known as 'Polar Bear' since we believed she alone would kill for food. My eyes rolled in my lids - why now - I'd a cup of blood in the waist of my trousers.

Reflexively I felt it, smoothing the front of my jacket with the other hand.

"I cannot find Chlebek, your Blockova. Several times now. She may be returned to you for... as you see fit."

"Yes Aufseherin." --She alluded to the practice of punching and kicking a Blockova to death once redundant.

Horn must have been a neglected or least-favourite child, beyond bland into dangerously overlooked - her huge blue eyes adding layers of violence to the world. Hair drawn tight to her scalp, maybe it was last night's red wine I saw on her chewed lips.

"You'll organise your block for another roll-call tonight."

I nodded.

"You are moving."

I nodded but also inclined my head; safest.

"They needn't discuss it. Each destination was reviewed on merit."

Horn, like all Aufseherinnen as '45 set in, was beset by desperation, trying to order an unyielding hell as all else collapsed. We were still a remedial centre by name, and bitterness held everything like a claw - ice for the girls and the onslaught of inner Germany for her. Horn's eyes scratched my face, quick as a seismograph. "Have them in the yard at nine."

In block I lifted my cup from a pouch meant for a Wehrmacht rucksack, and wrapped my hand with Gosia's coat lining - remarkable she still had it. I took a last strip from the armpit and spat on it to cool the burning, carefully pouring the blood with the rest in a vinegar bottle. It occurred to me our fates had outlived brutal; we were admin in the abattoir of Europe now.

Marianne did her rounds and I was glad, I needed a favour from an eight year old.

"Cigarettes and matches."

I took five dry cigarettes from her palm - carefully keeping them lateral as the guards were smoking twig dust - and a kindling of matches. Gave her a sanding disc and razor.

"Where you've got blades now?"

"Never mind."

Marianne traced an exploratory trail up my arm, between red slices and craters; my morse, plus the new gash. Her eyes were percolating. "Is lapin?"

"No," I shook my head, but she must've created that idea in mind - a process of infecting the arms, not legs. As Albert Speer increased arms output, so the less healthy or pure were escaping infection.

Marianne was known from the reaches of Ravensbrück, past inroads to Uckermark via a rend in the wire few weasels would use. Why an orphan was with adults while I - twenty-two now, without trace of my parents in Hamburg - remained in juvenile, is not worth figuring.

And my sins won't detain us... I'll write those at length come the Red morning. I aborted a 'Lebensborn' - but Otto and I had long been watched, corrupting Hamburg's sucklings with polka dots and oboes. *Swingjugend*. For now I wish only to write myself out. I liked history, god knows why - nobody said it might stop - and I used to read from the Thirty Years War to Bismarck's unification. When Otto and I swam the lakes, under the nose of Triton and Neriede, only then did

4

I really feel loose from time, its pendulum and dry churn. I will say this though: the world was full of many things - cat gut, pasta, fabergé eggs - but a boy was asked 'what do you dream of?' and he must have replied death and sterility.

I suspect Marianne, asocial by birth, was marked for euthanasia on 14f13 and missed her party. Mistakes do happen, and the other way too (asocial Schmidt meet Jehovah Schmid. Oh...). At Lackenbach Marianne collected firewood for officers on the Esterhazy estate; which helped. Though not her uncle Bijan, who's face was pushed in shit for clowning before he was shot. Some stay where they're put - it's where they were put - while others are moved to sanitariums, subcamps born of weapons firms; it's Ravensbrück, the heavy architecture.

But I fear for Marianne. She's the age where eyes are frightless but hers have seen so much, yet she's as bold as the devil. Where does that come from?

"We're getting out, Marianne."

"Is for Hartheim?"

"No. Just you and me. Gosia if she'll come."

"For..." She tailed off, brow clenching.

She gazed over the womens' camp to the crematorium, whose smoke pulsed without schedule - a greasy black lullaby; the lagers and slit-eyed barracks like pimps in low hats. Was she forlorn? - one gets used to anything. The only sign of Blockführers and SS right now was trim and feldgrau in the distance. We sat there with our mammal wrists, as the new 'wash room' sat beautifully painted and sealed with mastic.

Marianne's scurry ditch is south-east by the knitting block - it's electrified wire but she can avoid it - over bare ground to the Siemens staff blocks, where civilian foremen get her back in. Not all devils. Only dogs make Marianne vanish, which the cleared trees hinder. She's a ghost - a barter ghost - with sandy hair from an Austro-Sinti love affair over olive skin. Borrows like the Zigeuner she is and where she can't, bribes.

But the lower half of her nose had been ripped by an Alsation. Flesh regathers, within reason, only the cherub had two dark holes in her face.

In a few days, juvenile camp will shut - so it looks - and factory workers are confined to barracks, which would land me in the adult camp - workless. Luxuries like Marianne will be buried, I know it. Over the rooves, heavy plant rises on chains to Havel barges. It's impossible to construct logical destiny.

"So is... you see Russians?"

I shook my head. "Do you ever get caught?" I asked. I'd become nervous with my scheme - it wasn't foolproof. "Other than this I mean," I indicated my face, where my nose still was.

She yanked her trousers to webbed white and pink, and smiled. "Is depend who catch. Was boiling water, for... summer '43."

"Oh god but y--"

"Usual is fine," She returned the stripes over her thigh. "Aufseherin Brinck told is the deal." She rubbed her fingers.

I lit my cigarette with careful lips, headed to shade by the barracks. "Could you get in here five to eight?" --I gouged a clock in dirt and sand, hands pointing, jabbed at the minute hand repeatedly. "Just before, yes? For Sabine."

She nodded.

"You'll have a mouthful of blood."

"Okis," Marianne shrugged.

She hardly seemed curious, so: "This is what we'll do…"

I hunched as shells cracked in unseen fields - Katyushas I hoped from the woken bear. We played Monte here in dust or frost, and Marianne had figured out what hardened bookies know: that if people always lose they stop playing. It applies to fun as much as extortion. She pinched her mouth sitting; all for schemes. I don't know what Marianne thinks of me - the hateful tapestry of her childhood - but she likes secrets.

Since the Red Cross was banned, but for Theresienstadt and a few model blocks, it's Sabine Keller who's our artery - nurse, telegraph and parcelist - and her mind must bulge with lists from some Genevan office. Her lawyer father was arrested in France for Red memories - house-arrested she said, they're Swiss - dug out by careering Vichy-ites. And Sabine's our ticket. I shouldn't call her a ticket but she'd support it. Slender in the old sense - graceful, not starved - she rolls her chemise when it warms, even wears an engagement ring. Her fair hair floats grey a little and she's firm with medics and führers alike.

And yes… I do credit this 'silver spoon'; she comes on her own in whipping snow, bolstered on the wind like an iron wren. She's as thin and blue as we are, but still wears a stole. Keller's not Red Cross but they've ridden her coattails back in, since the ban became a burp in chaos. Her oval face will be in a van after dark, searching, memorising.

These arms of raw red; I'm no masochist. Blood to the living is gold and letting it couldn't be easier. Bottles however, are harder to find and conceal. And blood doesn't keep. I tried to let Otto know this as I've thought of escape for a year, but I felt mad scrawling my news to Moringen. I probably am, but I'd need a frame of reference.

With the cycles of SS prohibition and mercy, you need a name to send anything, so Keller devised a system. Family and friends must address a parcel with a number, name and nationality if it's arriving anywhere. Dreamt up by Himmler so the world can't fully condemn us, it's impossible to actually receive anything. To know a name needing food, you'd need to know they haven't been shot in the head - common sense really.

As long as Sabine has one name, she bundles a food parcel on that with a stack of imaginary ones - fantasy scribble (and guards of all people know they may've died yesterday; they're cutting in regardless). So the French addressee 'ensures the others get them'. It's got easier by wear and tear.

"Is blood, eight o'clock," says Marianne, reminding me she's still there. I'd drifted, dizzy.

"Five to, five to," I say, toeing the ground marks.

"You want I'm..." She drops her head aside, shutting her eyes, "so I'll blackout?"

"Yes groaning. I'll carry you."

It hinges on Schuster's aversion to blood - I've watched his face lose its own when he sees some - and those nearing Katyushas help. At the moment I can see him. He's made an appearance at his post by the tower, and I know Bohm has gone to Siemens to aid clearance; I saw him by the stolen goods depot. Some underlings are by an SS barrack where they keep the dogs (not the mother that bit Marianne, its litter: all jet with tawny snouts). One guard's throwing up his hands regularly over lists. Poor man's confused, look.

Something orange waves in my eye. Marianne's produced a couple of husky orange segments - pre-sucked I believe, which beats potato water. Her smiles often seem detached, like some freakish Cheshire Cat.

I was terrified suddenly, surveying in quiet: a last chance. I chewed the orange, with a sense the chamber was loaded, and I was rattling like a marble tin. 'Appell' should be that, a call to roles, but it's our black-capped magistrate. I strain to see any shift-swap and arrivals, through the gate where staff mill. We don't see Braach or Horn much except at roll-call - and the guards are sorting things for themselves. Fresh faces offload on machine-gun avenue - hardly fresh, like soiled lassoos but fresh here. They haven't changed a few days: Schuster and Bohm, who licence Marianne's rounds.

Girls grow bold. Slovenians, Ukrainians, they leave hand-drawn maps of camp by the guards, lists of Blockführer names to spook them, as the Red Army cracks afar. But they don't know. I refasten the lining over my palm, breathe with that quiver I hate. They don't realise.

Marianne thought about taking my cigarette but turned to leave. I didn't say what, if we failed... Watched her shoulders prowl on the Lagerstraße for the wire, that tense chin and neck in caramel hair; her head is always on the move, predator or prey I don't know. Context is all. I feel it. Ravensbrück will finish its work.

One more hour, thick as glue. Time is dreadful. All there is to do is count blisters and fan my palm, wait for Gosia and scan the sky.

Adolf's scorched earth hara-kiri isn't supported by his Reich. In the same way one humours a lunatic asking you to burn his asylum (Certainly we shall, don't you worry). I mean, I know this, everyone discusses it at broth-party, or overhears the guards' considered view of Hitler now. It's said that Albert Speer disobeys him when he's out and about - and has done since he saw the Dora mine. It's speculation - we are our own tabloid, with gossiping chins writing biographies of these people; obituaries. We are a little weltanschauung. The irony of 'Arbeit macht frei' was: it was either duplicity or a sick joke. Now it's more so as we've none. Speer - if he is undermining Adolf, and his watchful hippo Göring - has given us a punchline, as the sky thickens with machinery. 'No work makes you even freer'.

A state of mind - I've wondered how Sabine does it, spotting her with arcs of morning sun, brassy on her Lesage coat and imperishable face. We all think we are that, and must live accordingly. If fate should take us, we'll at least have ignored it until it did.

The time was nearing. I'd gone to press potato cakes into shabby knickers at my buk and find Gosia, ready her, but her legs are mending from a bacterial incision - it's maybe not so good, they take more care of machines (in treeless mist, we look like a meat-packing plant). I've not saved much food - what I have is from Sabine - so we'll rob outhouses in Fürstenberg. When I found Gosia she'd returned from the crafts hut making dolls for fallen Germans.

She had been more attractive in glasses. A foggy distance in her eyes clashed with her close, secretive smile. When her specs smashed her eyes went absent, or perhaps they would've anyway. I told her to stuff her knickers. She shook her head violently and backed off, "You go."

"You'll be marched to Czechoslovakia."

"You go, you go!" she yelled. She made noises like she was going to bark, so I backed away too.

Saboteurs from Szczecin, her and her brother, who was shot in the head as a terrorist as she was put here: 'ineducable'. I'm that too, in so far as I read books and know jazz. She's ineducable in the sense of not stuffing Luftwaffe wings with sand and rags; so their fuel pipes block and they fall from the sky. We're all ineducable, though one girl alone knows more than a hundred Reichsministers.

Hothead Gosia, broken nationalist. She'd probably get through the racial deep-clean, but Horn was getting zealous on asocials.

"They'll get here," I said. "Draw your head in."

I felt my stomach lurch, leaving her in these groaning slats to make dolls - the same Marianne swaps back for cigarettes from Red Cross parcels. It's a bearable lot.

I'd an eye on Marianne's spot, the other flicking at the entrance. Two fence lights stand over it and Polar Bear suddenly emerged being driven to the woods, disappearing in threadbare haste. No blockführers shot the breeze - some were finishing lists, burning evidence, Brinck I expect was fawning over Bolsheviks. All life is arbitrary.

There was a chance Sabine Keller wouldn't come, to Uckermark tonight, sometimes she didn't.

She's also under house arrest, but got a train to Theresienstadt in '42, indignant, then Mauthausen the same year and now us, without hindrance. She says bad German got her in: mispronouncing 'Sacred Heart' they thought she was clergy. A year ago she'd arrive before officers' mess while they Pavlov'd on drool. Now as skeletons they're as brusque, but on clanging bellies. And it made my stomach drop and palms sweat - the pendulum to Appell - a mortal reckoning and a dark bus, Time and Luck joining hands.

She will come down the road at eight, bumping tin, done with adults: a van with a cross's outline. Or maybe she'll be late - nothing is reliable here but chance.

The sky burned over Marienwerder, I thought - a fuselage squirting black in a knotted dogfight - maybe further, Seelow. I wondered what was Yak and what Messerschmitt as something plunged on death's roll. Gramma lives at Marienwerder and I'd thought... stupid at my age... thought me and Otto might end up there, eating home-grown spri--

Christ, there was Marianne, waving me down. Please Sabine, hurry.

I stayed put to see the drive. Bohm is calling Schuster to the gym flapping some scrawled sheets he's found. Schuster heads, but on walking back he'd see us. I can't afford medical questions, I'll tell Sabine whatever and she'll fend off.

There was a glint on the road, a revving - it couldn't be Polar Bear's return. I pushed off the washroom and trotted for the crafts block, kicking aside my clogs. Enough buddleia grows to hide a belly-bound child. But I'm no longer the circus strongman people imagine: thirty yards and I'd not thought of carrying her. Never thought of carrying her, she's not the sort of person you carry.

And it was Sabine, stopped and quiet now at the tower, talking to SS.

"Say nothing," I said, as Marianne hopped up on my sparrow arms. "And don't cough it all at once."

She poured in the bottle, and the good tyke didn't grimace. I spread the rest on my jacket and chin.

We set off groaning, me genuinely. I'd show my hand if they asked and mutter 'septic', and anyway I was carrying a girl with TB and half a face.

We were stumbling towards the administration buildings and watchtower, along the drive. I'd started to shout 'Sabine! Aidez nous!' and her head tilted up from a crate.

"Stop, you two," Schuster approached, waving us down. His arm still cocked at the lapel as if still supporting a gun he'd long lost. His miserable, cynical eyes flipped between Sabine's hands, my drooping arms and Marianne hanging in the air.

Marianne started to cough, dribbling blood. She'd smeared some down her jacket. Schuster's eyes narrowed at the dribble, the watery smears, scanning for a cut. He slowly shook his head, wagged his finger away from the van.

"She needs attention. Tuberculosis."

Again, the eyes are looking, squinting in disgust. I figured now was the time to stick Marianne right in his face. I walked at him. "Consumption, very bad."

Marianne pushed out another globule.

Schuster backed a little, shaking his head. But then he stopped and the head shake became firmer.

"Back to block. Where is the Zigeuner from?"

You know where's she's from, you bastard.

Sabine had hurried over. "Girls. What's happening. Is she coughing blood?"

I don't know if Sabine believed it and I was going to drop Marianne any second. She flattened her blouse like a smock and waved us. "I will make a decision in the truck. I cannot do it here, you have no X-ray or.. swabs... anything."

"They cannot leave, Fraulein."

It was absurd, the sky behind was scarlet, Soviet crimson, a broken and bloody dawn in the night. His leader was in a deranged bunker shouting at cats.

"Leave us," I shouted. "LEAVE US!"

He glanced around awkwardly at my raised voice, wincing, maybe in shame or actual pity. He nodded imperceptibly and waved us to the truck.

I couldn't yet breathe a sigh of relief but Sabine, grasping my shoulders and taking Marianne, seemed to exhale for me. She spoke rapidly in French - we're fluent - and Marianne remained loose and airborne. Inside the truck, she asked how long Marianne was like this, and I said, 'three and a half minutes', smiling. She got out to join the driver, but as the door was closing...

"Wait." A voice reached in, senior and male. Marianne was lain with her eyes half-closed, as though drifting near unconscious. I squeezed her wrist on her stomach and faced him.

He had very bright lips and a fixed smile, as though painted on a dummy, pulleys working it. A bloody new one.

"Who is this?"

"Marianne, an orphan girl" I said, "she's bleeding badly."

"Where is she going? Revier is out of action, infirmary full. No, no."

"That's why." --I was insistent. "Fraulein Keller will see to us."

Behind him, some male interns were stumbling back to Ravensbrück - this Kommandant had arrived from a 'new build'.

"She is very infectious," I said.

"Really?"

"Isn't that so, Sabine. It's infectious isn't it." I added hopefully-- "I've been carrying her, look," and held up my blood-soaked hand.

"I suppose it would be infectious," he sighed, tipping back his SS peak. "So, better treat it like a genie."

Sabine's brow bunched in. "I'm not sure what you mean, we should get them out now."

"Keep it in a bottle like a genie, no?"

The Kommandant held up my vinegar bottle with the blood remnants in it. It must have fallen from Marianne's trousers.

"Out. Both."

I felt the rise of the slow guillotine - to sit and await a Czechoslovak march, a sanitarium, the 'washroom'. So be it. My limbs went numb, but Marianne was still in character, groaning and rolling. It angered the new Kommandant, and he stepped in, pulled her roughly by the hair so she span on her own buttocks and fell to the floor. He dragged her from the truck. I yelled at him - 'please, she is sick.'

"You're all sick," he said, and took Marianne's elbow to march her.

She didn't scream like a child, she slapped and shouted in his face like a Bolshie. Fell to the ground so my blood on her face was stuck with dust. She'd normally haggle or charm but this guard knew nothing. She wrenched her elbow free and squirmed when he picked her up. I thought she'd spit in his face and prayed not. Just stood, my heart bursting and veins pushing acid as they wriggled, getting smaller, kicking dust to the sky.

I ran into the shade and cried and shook. The minutes fell in private terror, the barrack pressing in, slats of my waiting. I felt so stupid... Should have tried earlier than this, I'm no coward, why not *earlier* than this?

I was wrapped in a blanket, imagining something terrible. She'd known, always, her fate was an officer's whim - I'd seen a great whack across her head from heavy German hands, shocked a guard's own pals; the boiled water and dog bite. Should have done this bloody hoax alone but... I thought I'd help her; my vision of the end of this place. I look through their eyes and see the clearance; the man walking backwards with a syringe and a mop, a can of petrol. I cried until Appell.

9pm. The yard held the feet of teenaged girls in wooden clogs. Hardness against hardness. Winter against blue flesh.

"When your name is called, move to the designated area."

She'd a crumpled and much crossed list. Paint had drawn lines of confinement.

"Area A. Beckers Alys and Ernesta. Dietrich, Groß, Hahn... Area B..."

Chief Warden Neudeck stood to one side, off whose block the Polar Bear was chipped. Being attractive was banned long ago, as stringently in staff as interns.

"...Schmidt Angela..."

I went to stand with a paltry group of mutterers and rockers. That terrified me most. Action T4. Strychnine.

There was a habit, maybe more pronounced in Ravensbrück, of breast envy. It was our petty way to damn. The fuller the breast the luckier and perhaps... more cooperative the inmate. Mine were sullen pancakes. Blisters on an alien from a sunless universe. Johanna Braach came to collect my group.

People vanish in handfuls to Dallgow-Döberitz transit camp. The most terrifying journey is the circular one: filtered back to Ravensbrück, from where the sick or incapable arrive here again, where barracks are 'facilities'.

It's a bureaucracy of flesh, where rumour sucks on bone. Rumour sucks on all life beyond these bow-headed fences and their clasped wire.

We dissolve, thoughts fading and friendships wrenched as twine. The Red Army is a few hundred miles east - they've opened Majdanek and Auschwitz - and the Yanks have burst the Bulge.

Marianne said that in Ravensbrück the adults prayed to avoid -20 degree rollcall and illness just a few weeks more; sniffing freedom like Baltic brine. We were yearning: hope was gnawing at terror from the inside out.

"Self-harm," said Johanna Braach. "Challenging authority, high IQ, suicide attempts..."

"You must know it's over." I kept my arms behind me.

"...black-marketing, hatred of the Reich, entrenched denial...."

"You must do."

"...consorts with gypsies and resistance, tends to socialism and of course negro music..."

With chain-gang rhythm, I tried again: "I said you kn--"

Braach threw my manilla file at my face, and stood up. "Gropius hospital can decide if you're an educable German."

On that, her eyes met mine. I wanted to repeat again, but I saw her desperation.

"You could let them out."

"Zoglinge?"

"To the woods."

"Gropius. Psychiatrist. Be on the Lagerstraße tomorrow at 7am. I don't know which belongings you'll find necessary to collect. You may go."

I lurched to the door. *Belongings necessary*?... But I might as well: "Could you see nothing after this?"

Braach hardly bounced my eye with a glance. "Imagine a choice, Pretty."

So, Reich. If you know it's over, the cuticle crushed, why complete the design? Into scorched earth the cleansed will tumble again, with luggage and suitcases; this ruined green.

I stood by the Krankentransport in my clogs, with the blanket and sack that covered my buk. The snub-nosed Mercedes in the clearing was ugly as a 109 is ugly (as a Mustang isn't) pulling its high and special curves.

Besides me Chloris and Ida will go, for Gropius to declare our viability. Their names followed mine in the repainted yard but they must be late - the tall-headed mute and childlike rocker - and so rude, to be late for your own mercy killing.

I should tell you the irony of Chloris. That she's here at all. Her brother was a Youth veteran from Hamburg, Reinhard (a neophyte then but a veteran now I suppose, still only half-shaving if he's alive). It was Reinhard Inquart scented our plate-nights - our vile jazz proclivities - and stuck to us like a steroid-rat until his seniors, the ones without milk teeth, brought us down by the neck.

We were just a detail in the slide of Germany. I've long got over it and I've no idea where Reinhard is now (the world has changed shape) - a boot polisher or Death's Head Squad - but Chloris was bundled from public sight in 1932, privately into the Inquart household first. But then her vanishing - to the Swingsters of St. Pauli - seemed as suspect as all that was to follow. Strange, that what we called 'sinister' or 'criminal' then was a mere sniffle, the raw throat in a flu up ahead. When I laid eyes on Chloris in '43 - her serene, unpredictable face marched past the knitting block - I guessed it was Kaspar Inquart's pact: between a daughter who was irretrievably 'mystic' and a devil in SS clips.

So there you have it - the Nazi shows great strength, to turn his own offspring in; cut off his arm should it wither.

Her profile is strange like a curly bracket or ancient vase: her hairline levels with the bridge of her nose, yet she's striking and saucer-eyed. Most of the time Chloris is as tranquil as a painted lake - Raphaelite you'd say, and were I a tribe bumping into her I'd think her sacred, worthy of a dias and heaped flowers; perhaps a plinth.

Of us all, the truly ill-in-mind may suffer least so I'll not pray for her (here she comes now, unhandled, unclasped, only herded from a distance like a one-woman flock). Nor think long on what we'll lose. What memories, for example, does she keep? ...Bliss or omniscience? Maybe her muteness besides the shrieking outbreaks was due to wanting nothing, no baubles no beads, only kicking a stink if her personal nothing was threatened.

And Ida. Her mystic pal. I've no idea where she came from, maybe equally divine in Bremen or Hannover - Chloris and she are only inseparable via a telepathic cord which makes sound if broken. And such a shriek - I mustn't laugh - but neither SS nor Aufseherinnen have the energy to deal with it. A kink in the weft that these two survived. Or her father Kaspar tugged a connection, a benevolent string. I can imagine it - *she can live Kaspar, but you explain it to the SS-TV*.

Well poor Chloris is as alive as I am for a bit.

The driver was a skin-headed orderly. With an SS guard: the first I'd seen whose face registered doubt. He was porcine, and spent too long staring at the ringing German earth with unfocused eyes. Confusion, gloom and fear.

While Ida and Chloris were escorted down the path, I heard a boom. Followed by another then a barrage, though distant like someone else's storm. Did I imagine in the silence a snapey *rat-tat* of guns on the breeze?

Ida and Chloris were put on. I took a look at Uckermark. Another bus unloaded for south barracks. Most had greying hair: over 52s. The remainder, well, you'd know - dark skin, a slender hooking in certain lights, so cadaverous as to be unable to undertake 'exhaustive labour in its realist sense'.

Come on you freezing Commies! You weren't beaten. So bring your vicious sacrifice; swarm over Ukraine and Poland like a million Genghis Khans! Lay your lives on Europe's altar.

Boom. It came again, but this time with dawn in the sky fading its strength.

I turned to the absorbed SS guard. "Heil Stalin!"

"If that is what you want."

I sat looking out. We passed a little lane to a new Jugendlager, fabricated and abandoned; there'd been a rumour of extra soup and no roll-call. It was a cover story for the extermination we had become. We were the youth camp; the last scintilla of humanity extinguished for transit. Cold for so long, I forgot to shiver.

An open-topped SS car speeding the other way forced the bus aside - I lurched into chrome - and abruptly we'd stopped, the front axle in a ditch, wheel overhanging. I looked at my SS guard who'd jolted from reverie, now at the cabin window shouting. Chloris had fallen on the floor but was looking upward, smiling.

I wrenched the back-door's latch and ran for bushes. From there to open ground and a patch of undergrowth again. I rushed on the uneven ground and heard no shots, only shouts. And among rhododendrons I sprinted as fast as cabbage legs can, feeling the line of fire behind, traced up my back like an itch. Swiping leaves behind, boot-clumps like hooves.

I stopped and looked back - all open. Ran for the fattest oak, and as I arrived foetal in its roots, I saw an imprint lagging on my retina: a hollow above my head.

I craned round, and clambered in.

They will shoot me. They will shoot me.

I could hear voices, but the acoustics were so strange in the brown stillness.

"Sie ist hier irgendwo."

"Die anderen?"

"Sie gehen nirgendwo hin, oder."

They went quiet. I put my head in my arms, pulled in my scratched toes, clogless, now written with blood. It was quiet but for a snip of twigs.

Sometimes I agree with it, you know... The intolerance, the killing, the unwanted. We turn inward without direction - we geniuses, we massed peoples - and there find extremes. There's no way to husband this thing, this 'humanity', without a strait jacket. It will scratch itself to death or flatten all in its stampede.

When all seemed quiet as could be, I raised my face from my arms. Two faces watched, the driver and the SS guard. Stubborn, awful, always there... What they'd sold to this country they sold with guarantees.

I'm Otto. In 1945 the surest way across north Germany (of whose cattle stench and torn skies, more later) was by the grace of Allied movement. Moringen's chaotic opening had given us... everyone I suppose... the idea that something might remain, however meagre or stertorous its breath. Finding it was everything.

Papa was gone - he'd overseen my letters that stopped as abruptly as he did, in or around *Blohm & Voss* when the bombs hit his meeting with Speer's associates (not Albert himself and not, I think, Rudi Wolters) - but Mama remained, even if she were miles from the living. It was possible Ange's folks survived too - my half-brother Günter no-one knew - but the angst for the living was so much worse.

Our treatment swung wildly from place to place. The Yanks and Brits, considering, were upstanding about the last six years, the French less so but reined in by their officers. Cursed us and swung the odd rifle butt, shaved collaborators and worse, but... I knew things were different in the east, Ange's last whereabouts. Real vengeance was a mauled Soviet's privilege.

In camp I'd classified myself, not to remain apart but to keep a sense of self - jazz aficionado, musician, juvenile; out here we were all the same, the only variable was Nazi, common criminal or shoeless victim. Our ethnicity was recognised in the new transit camps, but little else. We were a sea of insolent, angry faces.

I spent the day by Mama's year-long coma in Hamburg-Eppendorf General, her sojourn from a collapsing world. It still functioned, albeit in an unwired sense, any clinical green poking from rubble, reminding spent staff of a sterilised past. And with all my family masonry foraged, the double-fired bricks and fallen lintels in lush Winterhude - Angela's too - I had to face some facts, of displacement; vagabonds adrift without ownership or burial.

I headed through the rubble to Stadtpark - rust and green and coated in dust. Triton and Nereide stood above the acrid water, two oxidising centaurs.

These guardians had failed. It was unbelievable they'd survived that swine Harris. I remember back before, bathing in innocence when none of it was possible: grass bright and kids splashing. I still don't know how National Socialism lured one solitary disciple. Even as we were threatened - truly in terrible danger - it was comic. They were comic, po-faced clowns with big shoes at a remove from us. What's more... *I felt a terrible laughter rising*... they were dull; a drag with their folders and stamps and dreams of vulpine castles. Some discarded boy, mulling revenge as he shops for manilla. Obscured by the hours and days now, I remember thinking as they bulldozed joy, I hope Hell's had a run on stationery.

Into this, Gomorrah.

The signs we were being trashed were long coming - everyone knows it - but the personal signs, of one's own danger, weren't so clear. Reinhard Inquart was my first figment, in shorts and vest: Unit Leader of the Dammtor Youth. He was the first inkling I had that maybe the national was personal. One cannot know what scenery will break free and attack, you dig that? I wondered what happened to him, if he died under rock or tortured scores of Hebrews, or... maybe he was helping now, rounding up his proteges. My age, twenty-one. Maybe I'd visit a missing persons' bureau, just for old times. I got up - with a sudden sob I wasn't ready for; it weltered through - to say goodbye to Hamburg.

German railways were destroyed or had no locomotives, so I got a lift outside Ebert-Kaserne barracks to Wöbbelin; halfway to Uckermark.

"Dein name?"

"Otto. I speak English."

"Dwight. Hop in."

Dwight was a Yank photo-journalist documenting the camps for a ravenous world press - by which I largely mean the lens of America.

Crossing to the Soviet Zone our trucks stopped at Wittenberg. We sat in Cafe Marktplatz under a double belfry, with Red Army troops in the square; some in our cafe. They kept raising glasses to the Brits, and each time the levity was more forced: watery-eyed with heavy back slaps.

In the cafe opposite an auburn girl in a midnight dress danced to *I'm just a lucky so-and-so*. Causing a drunk Red to head for that cafe and pull the now-reseated girl from her chair by the arm.

"Tantsuy so mnoy!" He tugged at her hips. Her companions looked nervously at an attentive square. "Dance German, for freedom. Like a bear!"

I looked between cafes. The Brits were drinking but restrained. The soldier's companions clapped and raised their glasses, screeched their chairs and went to join the forced dance. Brits headed over as though they might, perhaps, supervise Stalin's million-man fodder. The other end of the square cheered but those Reds weren't drunk; on duty in personnel vehicles, sober as sunlight.

"This isn't good," I said to Dwight.

It was just us left in the cafe and the throng over the road jostled. A Brit stepped in to uncouple the Russian from the underdressed girl, and was pincered by two Soviets immediately. Pushed back. Then pushed again heavily in the chest. Another Brit stepped up to stop him doing it a third time, and in pushing his incoming arm from the side sent the soldier into a lateral spin landing on the floor.

A couple laughed, but then a Red officer with stripes slapped the Brit across the face so hard it silenced everyone.

The Englishman said, "She's too young for reparations."

The commander's eyes wandered over him. "You know about this? When butchers take your land?"

"They tried and failed."

"Brave Winston," he sneered.

Dwight rummaged behind him, and pulled his flashgunned camera.

"What are you doing?"

"Childcare," he darted off with the camera by his leg. I heard... "Guys." Dwight flailed his camera-free arm, and walked up to the striped Red officer. He held out his hand to shake.

"Dwight Westwood, Associated Press." He pulled a badge from his pocket. "Listen, this is a photo op, right? We got the liberating Red Army, the Brits liaising with the Soviets, all helping rebuild a country. I mean it's ideal right? What do you say to a snap? For the NYT front cover?"

The bull steam seemed to clear a little.

"And we'll, er... get you Germans out front here. Except... we'll need some indication you're German of course. Ha ha."

A Red soldier lighting a cigarette tossed a souvenir swastika armband at the group of Germans.

I buried my forehead, fearing it would kick off again. But there was singing above my head, from the rooftop. The Internationale. One of the Reds in our cafe had found his way to the roof, and was swigging from a bottle of clear spirit, now proudly singing his anthem.

"Valery! He changed it you fool!" shouted a comrade, and they laughed.

The man slipped on the tiles and a couple of silent seconds later, landed with a crack and burst like a sack. His blood watermeloned in grey seams, pooling behind his staring head.

You'll understand perhaps, sudden peace asked questions of the living for which we'd no answers.

"How do you feel?"

"I can't think. My memory. Just dreams. What's that?"

A crack less like thunder and more like god rattled the window.

"Dr. Neumann is stabilising you. Try not to worry. He can change your medication."

"What am I?"

"You're on antipsychotics and a sedative. To help you sleep."

"What time are we?"

"It's five. Late afternoon."

"What time are *we*?"

"Try to relax Fraulein Schmidt. Eginhardt has put matters in hand, given..." the nurse nodded outside, where it sounded like volcanoes were errupting along the Oder-Niesse. "There will be no more talk of T4, euthanasia and so on." She smoothed her blue smock. "You were lucky."

"Yes?"

"We are a clinical facility," she said. "And since Triete and Mennecke evacuated, we've reverted to that. Try to forget and look to the fu---"

The boom was enormous this time, and the window at the end of the ward shattered.

"Red vengeance," she murmured, flattened the sheets over me and left the ward.

You remember Hanseatic skies? How they polished the ponds. My hands await your chest's chamber, monstrous male. Your laughter bubbles in my ears.

That serious brow. What moved you, me or rebellion? ...Privileged beasts. I thought of others while with you, briefly. Dragged your heart through my dirt, but something turned my light on you.

In oblong moon sits Hofner boy. Lanky lover. Monstrous male. Strummer.

Picker.

What?

Picker, not strummer.

Find us.

"Why you headed east?" Dwight said. "Don't go believing all is forgiven."

I sat thinking about it, moving further into the darkness. "My girl's missing at Uckermark. Might be starving in a forest for all I know, lost her marbles." After a while I added: "I don't blame her. It's the harrowing of hell."

"It's not hopeless Otto." Dwight was older, but young enough to enjoy confidences. "I'm privy to stuff."

"Yeah? What."

"The big knobs are already talking about how to unite the nations. Truman's on it, put an end to this shit. And a big case down in Nuremberg, where it all kicked off." He tapped his camera, always in arm's reach. "This'll get used."

What neither of us knew was the bitter winters of '45-7 accompanying the trials would be trials in themselves. No food, water, housing; the Great Nothing.

"Uckermark's part of Ravensbrück, right?"

"Yeah, auxiliary."

"It's on my list. Wait a day at Wöbbelin and I'll shift stuff. I can use your testimony when I file copy."

I glanced over amber fields; kids traipsing with clean faces at odds with rumpled rags, a continent without order, possessions bagged. Where trains stopped, out of oil or usable track, migrants clung to the tracks anyway like arrows to the future. Sleepers had been ripped up by an iron hook - a schwellenpflug - to piss petulantly on the retreat.

"Well old chap," I slumped in the dusk. "A Yank might save me a Russian lynching."

"Good man, I speak a bit."

In this wing the silence makes birdsong audible; the colour in the unthinking cherry trees deep and vibrant. The odd patient on accompanied walk in the grounds pierces the afternoon with unwanted bulletins.

Now my hands speak. I crave this peace because there's a war on - isn't there? Men against helmeted men. Turret versus muzzle. Sky-thunder versus ground-lightning. Except it seems to have stopped or become puddles. At night there's a drone from roads far away. The sky flares with local lightening, cracking off the sky like clapboard.

An army arrived at my new home one morning, and we were ushered out of our wards and huddled in the day room, pressed against each other.

Outside, the personnel carriers had red stars and Slavic chatter. Among them were civilian vehicles and removal vans. After a while, we were led past the troops. Some were bandaged and bloody, some whistled, some smoked bent cigarettes and laughed and pointed.

A soldier with a blank white eye and a shiny weal through it looked at me with his remaining pupil. There were things in there I didn't want to know. Why'd he picked me to follow with his scorched mind? If there was any desire it had grown a carapace.

We traipsed out of the old Krankenhaus grounds and through a new gate, towards smaller or prefab buildings in clusters. The eye burned my back until bushes concealed us.

I'd no desire to see this Wöbbelin - Neuengamme's overspill - and sat half a day in a truck picking nails. The place was overrun with 8th and 82nd; Yanks. Eventually loneliness overtook me so I went to find Dwight. I was told he was in the woods photographing eight hundred shallow-buried victims of starvation.

"No gas chambers," I said when I found him.

There wasn't birdsong here; just leaf-litter, intermittent birch light and the high-contrast of black earth and flesh.

"They were PoWs. How would you rather go? ...I'll get supplies for here on."

I waited at the camp gate and Dwight roared out in a confusing American Jeep with red stars. He'd stacked the trunk.

"Jeez you're connected. What's that?"

"Lend-lease. We lend, I reclaim."

"And the food?"

"Yeah, we'll have to protect that."

We span into the woods, heading east in the flicker and breeze. I think we both enjoyed the lack of displacement here.

"Why are you allowed in the Soviet Zone?"

"The bulk of the PoW camps are east. They won't entertain us long."

"Is that what you were discussing with the Commandant?"

"Eh?" He was struggling with the heavy gears.

"You and the Commandant."

"I'll really be needing that testimony, OK?"

"Sure."

"Before I lose you. We'll bag it at Ravensbrück."

"Sure."

"Are you listening?"

"What do you want to know?" I snapped into focus and looked at him.

"It's war trials, man. You may want to prepare something."

"I don't care about retribution," I said, but my mind was elsewhere. "You've seen the place, it's all retribution."

Yeah-- familiar with the Commandant, and I was fairly sure he'd passed some discreet papers.

"OK," Dwight joined a main road. "You've got other things on your mind, matters of the heart. We'll park it. But I need it."

"Sure."

"No fucking around." Dwight eyed me levelly. He didn't look much like a journalist then.

A scream in the night became muffled. Harshly whispered Slav then bad German, "Keep quiet, slut."

I sat up, straining to listen. There were footfalls around the building, undisguised heavy boots. Flashlights slipping under doorways. I started to tremble and my lips mouthed 'Leo' and then muttered again, "Leo where are you?"

While saying it I felt betrayal. The North German beach; the wind-sharp sand and thorny gorse against my flesh. I pushed my face in the pillow and screamed "Leoooo!"

I heard the door open but couldn't look. The flashlight moved around the ward, highlighting iron bedsteads and rumpled patients. The beam travelled over my back. I tried to make my shape comatose. The beam stayed put. The boots moved slowly. By the time the owner could focus in it - safe in his uniform - I'd figured I pull a grotesque expression it might revulse him. Drooling, misshapen.

The torch shone in my face, then retracted slightly. The face itself came into the beam. The beam moved down the sheets. Then it moved to the next bed.

Five a.m., the curtains greying, and the ward door opened. A sliver of hall light outlined a shape. My initial panic subsided as there were no boots: female.

She shut the door quietly and went round the ward handpicking from eight occupied beds who to rouse and hush, "Shhh, deadly quiet. Make your way to the door with anything you want with you."

We could count our possessions on one hand. I recognised Nurse Wagner's voice, and when she reached me, "I'm awake," I said. "I'll be at the door."

I was the last. Three were left on the ward, either asleep or catatonic.

Wagner opened the door, poked her head out, listened and went into the corridor, waving us on with her finger to her mouth. We shuffled over the sheen in our pajamas, reached the door, which you couldn't open without a hell of a racket.

She gathered us, "Walk quickly and quietly to that truck, no sound. No discussion."

"Where are we going?" I whispered.

"Berlin," she said.

"What's in Berlin?"

"Not this." She opened the door with a metal clank and judder like thunder and we headed, some running barefoot on the gravel.

I was last in and got half a buttock space on the benches along the walls. There were twenty ghostly, frightened faces.

The driver door opened and Nurse Wagner clambered up. "Angela, pull the door." She started the truck, with a loud diesel gurgle and spun over the lawn, a short run to a country lane, in which she crunched the gearstick and got up to speed.

I looked out the rear slit window. Branches fuzzed and meshed what was behind, but I thought lights went on in the main building.

We joined a better road through forest, and Nurse Wagner floored the truck on the straight. She started to relax a little. "Alright in the back?"

A murmur of assent.

"We're out of hell, purgatory next," but her voice suddenly dipped, and a hand rose to her face. I knew what it was, I think. The unchosen. The stupored.

Pine-clad country fell behind as I drove Dwight's Jeep into Ravenbrück's interior. Armament works and SS quarters to my right, warehouses and roll-call yard. Bearing left I could see Siemens disappearing to the south-west.

Pulling up at the gate in a Soviet-starred Jeep, with unruly hair and civvies, confused the guard.

"Kakoye delo?"

"Ne Russkiy."

"American?"

"German." Like everywhere the concrete pillars were bent in at the top, wire unwound in the maniac's cordoned dream. "Anyone speak German?"

"There," he pointed to a small hut which must be a reception for the new ghoulish. I accelerated in dry ruts, parked and went in. A soldier in the hut seemed to have no real business, just gassing.

The grounds weren't different to Moringen. White huts, inner fences and workhouses.

"You speak German?"

"Yes," she said, and the hovering Russian backed off a bit.

I tidied myself, flattened my hair. "Looking for a former inmate."

"There's nobody here now."

"No-one?"

"Five people could not be moved. Everyone else via Dallgow-Döberitz, or a truck-ride north, south, east..."

"Who are the five?"

"And you?"

"My girlfriend was interned."

"She will have taken a ride."

"But do you know the names of the remaining?"

She pressed her uniform. "This is not automatic German business, so please remain calm and polite..." She nodded beyond the cabin, and I realised the hovering Russian hadn't quite left, leaning at the door. "...I look after in here. He looks after out there."

"Her name's Angela Schmidt." I tried a half-smile.

"Details?"

I fumbled in my trousers, pulled my wallet and fiddled it. She watched me as a sea-fixed rock watches spume. I prised the photo out. She looked at it for a while, in different lights, far and near. "She's young."

I was about to say something about juvenile camps but I'd nailed this Soviet thing. It's mainly: shut the fuck up.

"We were interned."

"What for?" she said.

"Dissidents, anti-social, jazz."

"Like your Basie and... Gillespie? Like that?"

"Exactly that." She'd drawn out Gillespie like it was a poem itself. *Geel'eyish'bee.*

"She won't be here," she said with a sad sweep. "Rodion will check but..." *Softening.* "Chto!"

"Voz'mi eto i posmotri, ne zdes' li ona."

Rodion took the photo with a questioning huff. But he left the building. I watched him in mud between huts. The desk-officer stood waiting, as though buses of tourists were due. I stood. She stood.

"Thanks," I said.

"I'm Warrant Officer Zhvikov. Where will you look?" she said, with crossed arms.

"There's a clinic," I said. "And an asylum down the road."

She nodded. "Salt-heart?"

"Sorry?"

"Your salt-heart?"

"Salt-h... you mean sweetheart?" I smiled.

"Sweet, sladkiy? No not povarennaya sol'."

"Salt is..." I rubbed my fingers together and made a cat-face. She covered her mouth in laughter. "Not salt. Sweetheart, yes."

I nodded. "You have one?"

"Sure. I got a saltheart!" Zhvikov found this tremendously funny, and electric mirth continued over her face. After a while she eyed me again. "Gropius Krankenhaus."

"Yes?"

"Is Red Army General Hospital. Now."

"And the inmates?"

She shrugged. "You wait twenty-five minutes and I'm relieved. When Rodion comes back, we take the photo." She nodded in place of my answer. It was decided. "You have transport."

I nodded. "Can I look around?"

She shook her head.

"I won't go far."

She sighed and waved me out.

God knows why. I closed the door onto the crusted mud. Little here but barracks. They separated the youth for night dormitory only perhaps, traipsing to the Ravensbrück machine in the day. Sitting west was a chimney now quiet; perhaps it had churned munition exhaust, not flesh. Perhaps.

Except I knew Ravensbrück hosted female holocaust, why not Uckermark? Lapins. Injected sulfonamides and gonorrhoea. The bodies from bad scientific ideas and eugenic bunkum tossed into soil like rags.

I was liberated at twenty-one. Ange's last letter Jan '45; twenty-two.

I heard the ghosts of girls giggling in a hut, closed my eyes. Savouring some prized moment. The sound of unextinguished friendship.

Women perhaps, touch more than men. An idea conveyed through the brush of an arm, or the osmosis of shoulder-to-shoulder, is an idea that won't get lost.

☆

We were behind the Russian artillery but nurse Wagner kept driving the ICRC van to head off the extending Reds north of Marzahn. A shell exploded yards away, from a jeep-drawn German gun. Tarmac and dust and air shunted the van and she had to reverse out again: a defunct tram had been dragged across the street and filled with rubble. Buildings flapped fire like intense orange flags.

Behind them, in the distance dark stick men stood on civic rooves, hoisting Soviet flags as desperate men shot in the dust below. Apart from those putting the flags out, it was hard to tell who were statues - dusted gargoyles - and who were Soviet troops.

"Where are we going?" I shouted. There was moaning and sobbing back here. ...*Rat-a-tat*. Echo. *Schtum!* Showering earth, head smashing tin. *Rat-a-ta-tat-tat...* The spattered ping of bullet and daylight.

If battle wasn't raging East Berlin was dust and fire pimples. The madman had got Berliners to kill even as they were shot for nothing. It was Hitler's birthday - they said, 20 April - and his last act was to decorate the Hitler Youth protecting this greasy, mortared vanquish.

Red Army faces manned their guns: a mix of terror, rage and hate overlaid with desperate shell-shock. Some looked like heaven beckoned, in wide-eyed savagery pushing their triggers.

The truck got stuck on an intact corner of exploded building. Our angel was squeezing through a gap for a side-street. The front wheel, with much yanking and turning, got over the mortar and enough speed for the rear wheels to bump us to the floor and clear of brick. She swung wide and took us down a back street.

The gunfire and explosions waned. Dust and smoke cleared, the assault softened and we were looking at a relatively clean, clear building: Fliedner Klinik.

"Fuck," said our angel, yanking the handbrake. "It's all happening."

"I'm not going in."

"You are. I have a duty of care."

The others were traipsing into the Fliedner building.

"And I have a family."

"You're not well."

"I'm better, than Uckermark. Which made me sick."

Wagner looked around the streets. Restrained they may be, but each building was bullet-caked and we'd the surrounding thunder and breakaway clack of desperate men. "Where?"

"Hamburg."

She looked down. I could hear inbound planes. "Look at Berlin," she extended her arm. "It took this long and this is what they're doing. Try and imagine Hamburg."

Like punctuation, a whistle preceded the front of the building opposite blowing off its frame, wrapping immediate air in whoofing dust. We cowered. The next shell took something out a street away.

"You would go. Find your own."

"How would you get there?"

"The arteries. The Army."

"Hold on." Maria Wagner climbed back in the cabin, returned with a manilla folder and opened it. "Don't burn any bridges," she murmured. Then stood leafing papers a while. "Yes. Got you."

"What's that?"

"Your record. I'll file it, in case." She looked at my worried face and rolled her eyes. "In case you need us. Suppose you get to Hamburg and there's nothing. You've got a roof here."

"Ha ha!" I properly laughed - the last place in Germany losing its rooves - and shrunk my head in my collar at another whistle preceded a fiercely contained thud; a building front slid to pile.

"Is all this building yours?"

"They're not fools, the top two floors are empty. I'll get your ration cards."

"What for?"

Maria's brow forked. "Food?"

I shook my head in confusion. "Are they valid at the Allies' canteen?"

"They're valid. How else will you eat?"

"It's a couple of days only to Hamburg."

"Nonsense. Not now, best part of a week."

"Not if I keep going."

"How will you keep going?"

"By not stopping to eat. Or handing the liberators Nazi food coupons."

"Just take the cards, I want to know you're sustaining yourself. Even if it's a hedgerow eating corned beef."

"Look, I don't understand, we're here in ruins and shells. The sky in the east is red all the time. Who the hell is selling food?"

Maria simply pointed. There was a queue - bulky shadows in a line, some with improvised flak helmets - for a general store.

And I didn't get it. Ration cards for cows in the slaughterhouse? It was some city-wide delusion, hypnotised by attrition. But what did I expect of Berliners? Starve in a basement as grain was given out, butter maybe, albeit without life insurance.

She handed me a cluster of coupons. "Fill a bag before the city limits."

"In tin pan alley I saw a halo on your head."

"Balls," she smiled, wrapping me in her arms. "I'll be here."

I regretted it immediately: trading what the Klinik might afford me for these powdered streets, in which ran the decorated HJ with little high voices. The suicide man's last award.

I wasn't in my right mind: so I can blame Maria. The whispering basements called frequently; hoarsely. 'Come down here. There is water. Tea-towels.'

Excellent. Tea towels.

'Where are you getting that coat?'

I'd thumb back over my shoulder, where the quarry-town boom and pinging masonry followed. 'Dead Red.'

After Kreuzberg it became eery. All had gone to Marzahn; Mitte's rearguard were Volkssturms on barricades made of trams and railing, upheaved street, beavers atop shit with widowed helferinnen, their epaulettes clean by pouchy faces. War-riven Landser must be behind closed doors chuffing their last in a pretence of planning as young Soviets, *frontoviks*, beat inexorably through the suburbs. Quiet by comparison, the dead centre drifted smoke in the artillery damage.

You can't bare your arse in a siege, and the pincering was already done: no dour general thought the western front wasn't about to arrive in days. Shadows and clusters; vehicles speeding with bedecked Reichsministers, heading for Gatow and the Berghof or far far away. One, I swear, had gilt frames sliding from his trunk.

There was acute shouting in Charlottenberg, audible over the advancing cannons. But from what I could make out from the shouts, and emblems star-wise, they weren't US Shermans coming.

"Fraulein. Fraulein! Komme!"

It was just a splintered fog, over which uniformed shapes moved or ducked in the cannon recoil, the strain of diesel lumbering over fallen buildings. Some scurried or fell, but the frequent sight was raised hands, clutches of us, stumbling to put weapons down. The ghost was giving up.

"Komme!" --a man with a white moustache and buckled cheeks was beckoning from brick. He was in shadow in the collapsed department store, its roof unicorning a vast old Lancaster tail. His eyes glinted, moustache waggling.

"Do not worry about Bolsheviks, they are despoilers, I will protect you. Some things won't be breached!"

I said nothing, mouth agape, and he took my arm gently.

"I know these cellars, I inspected every sewer from here to Grunewald. We'll go beneath KaDeWe, far from the line... the east line."

He dislodged a post with a clumsy slip on rubble and sent hardcore scratching into the dust and darkness. As it cleared, I could hear a screeching, a rug of screeching, and the puddles started to splash and reflect. I feared bats from the noise. But the shrieks surrounded and my ankles teemed.

"Jesus god!" I yelled.

"Just a fireball sending them back. Don't panic, stand still."

I did, stock still. And over the sheet of rat noise this sunken codger, someone's uncle, said: "This is what our Führer fought. This is how they come. No other nation understands but us." And as an afterthought he raised a *Heil*'ing arm.

"You fear a Red life?"

"Life! Come along girl, where are you from? Why are you out in this, send menfolk."

Like it was a weather apocalypse. Moving further into darkness, the circular vaults, I heard a yell and looked back expecting shots or troops, but moustachio was half-supine, tugging his leg. "I'm..." he cleared his throat-- "well yes, I'm stuck. You go through there, through that arch is a ramp, you'll be on Wittenbergplatz, don't go south, there's just a road open in the Bayerischer Wald, it will close."

"I'll pull you," I said, and hopped in semi-blindness to his form. But even I could see he'd gritted teeth, and his shin was the wrong slant to his body, this man who knew every sewer. I must have mistaken the snap for a splash.

"Go. The Reds won't rape me, I've a surprise. Keep going on, fraulein."

A die-hard, with bulgy German eyes quite kind in the gloom. As I left him pulling myself through darker pitch and splashes, ankles growing scratches from the brick I hoped, I wondered what his surprise was - a found grenade?

Fireballs, sending rats the other way. Well and good but he'd brought me here and left me. I didn't want to go by incineration but pushed carefully on, in the angular gloom. And with an afterburn of rats in my ears subsiding, a heavy scuffle arose, further into the silver umbra where the duct bent. A flash of high-ranking stripes, elbowing in the filth towards me or fleeing.

I pressed against the wall, concave in the shadow, and figured how soon a crawling man passed - maybe just the first - how long I could hold my breath, but the jet eyes locking mine were in a face too small... it sploshed on, a badger! Two, soaked and lumbering badgers. For accuracy, a family of fucking badgers and they didn't look happy, but they don't do they - their misery pre-dates the war. I ran past in hysteria, keeping my ankles clear of nips and saw the top of the ramp.

But blinking onto Wittenbergplatz a fervent Youth stopped me. "Fraulein, what is your destination?" He looked at my partial nightwear: his pimply face a bureaucrat's.

"I'm taking a walk in my country."

"You must return home."

"That too."

Still in the spillage of KaDaWe, its gabled mineshafts on the street, a man called this reccying Youth back. Too late.

Where my skinny frame was caged by a fire escape, my all-important spine against a wall, his wasn't. A shell in the street, the boy ripped open. Blood and bone and wind in my face, gristle slapping air; a piece of blockade with an iron centre struck my feeble chest.

I don't want to talk about the boy's head. I was thrown into dustbins. I'd have lain there forever in shock, but something wriggled under my bum in paper. A rat or freed lapdog - I rolled away.

His comrade watched as I took the Swastika armband and removed the child's boots, scattering ration cards hidden within.

He came running, but I stood up straight. I'd have to be fearless.

"Robbing the dead!" he cried.

I smirked badly, and continued pulling his boot. *Oh god*, there aren't many things which stop time - heart attacks, poems, bombs - but that moment in the kid's face is preserved; a flapping projector reel or unwanted heirloom.

At night the Yank drone was constant - the sudden roar and flash bore no relation to its carpet in the sky - and by day those imagined trajectories were at street level, like steel comperes eliciting their gouts and groans. What would happen when the flying carpet met the scarlet wave. They couldn't bomb their own.

Gouting pity. How can one feel pity? Imagination's on vacation; empathy is dodging falling walls.

"What's that?"
  "Dictaphone."
  "Like... recording?"

"Yeah, magnetic tape. Quicker than shorthand. Someone can type it later."

"Right." I felt nervous.

"Just answer the questions as you recall."

"How will you use it?"

"You were in a camp on munitions, so we prove that your protective custody became slave labour. As a Kapo you were tortured, right? Testimony."

"Maybe this isn't a good idea."

Think they'll come after you? No-one will get less than life."

"What if there's further questions?"

"Be available."

"Who are the big defendants, do you know?

"Anyone who didn't shoot or poison themselves." Dwight smiled. "The rats alive. Let's make a start. If you're not happy the backroom boys can redact."

"Mmm."

He hit record without warning. "Name and age?"

"Otto Bebel. Twenty one."

"You were interned at Moringen Youth Correction Camp."

"Yes."

"Dates?"

"From 1940 until it was opened by the British Army in April '45."

"So... between sixteen and twenty one."

"Yes. Correct."

"You were not moved anywhere else? Never to an adult camp?"

"No, I was on munitions at the Moringen mine, to the end."

"How would you describe conditions in the camp?"

"They... deteriorated as the war..." My heart started palpitating and I felt sweat on my head. "Can we stop the tape, I don't feel prepared. My heart's haywire."

"Stopping tape, as witness is distressed." He hit the button. "I did say prepare."

The word *witness* was a blow. I ran out to be sick. I was testifying against Ritter, Krack, the whole Totenkopfverbande. How many would be imprisoned or hanged, boots twitching?

"I can't do this."

"We've a deal."

"I can't."

"You don't want justice? Five years of your life, your girlfriend's life. Making bombs, no food. Half-dead for music."

"Justice can get on without me."

Dwight looked away. He returned less easy-going. "They killed your father."

"The Allies killed my father! Any country calls a campaign Gomorrah isn't squeaky clean, is it? Doesn't have our best interests at heart."

Dwight was quiet a bit, prepped and treading calmly. "You're not testifying against the military," his voice was even, "where those reservations may be justified. Just labour camps. Crimes against humanity. The Geneva Convention."

Dwight waited a while, until I nodded. "That's not to say other people haven't committed crimes, on both sides. This is reality. Which puts people in prison or to death."

I was picking at my mouth. He didn't get it.

"They no more care about you than a fly on the sill."

"The big names," I said after a while. "Who's in the dock?"

"Hermann Göring's the trophy. Boorman, Wilhelm Frick, Jodl, Hess, Albert Speer..."

There it was and it stuck in my throat.

"...Streicher..."

"I get the picture. I need more air."

Outside I smoked and properly considered what I hadn't when Dwight said testimony. Figuring I'd just write a paragraph confirming Moringen was a shit shower. He'd been good to Papa, tried to keep me out of detention. And - from '42 - was inextricable with munitions and forced labour. What if we locked eyes in the dock? Torture alone would raise questions in this dark tribunal. *Culture is our inner life, no?*

Jesus. How did it run away from us? Sealing our minds against sympathy, like a cracked submarine closing airlocks going deeper in the trench. I smoked heavily and went back in. "OK."

Dwight hit record. "Tell me about your daily routine."

"We got weak tea or coffee and stale bread at five a.m.. Roll call took longer if work detail was being reallocated..."

Two-and-a-half days without lifts or sleep and I'll cover one-seventy miles.

Once Berlin breaks to the Havel I follow it through bird-echoed forest: a day and into evening. It's 1st May and I sleep under my Soviet coat in the cold nights and carry it in the sun. Until Havelberg and the Elbe there's flanking Reds, while SS Commandants surrender by region. Get ahead and I'll meet oncoming Yanks and Frenchies. I'd have to be a diplomat of Babel with several costume changes, to blockade my genitals and keep body and soul outside of wire.

But I speak French.

There's a telegraph pole tangled in a Sherman halted on a hedge (Otto would know which model); plundered like a giant applied a can-opener. Above it the sun's kipper-peach.

I've walked since dawn and it's hot, so I lie over a brook on a trunk, worn from secret feet. I must be on a concealed trail for Waldvolk dodging treason. What a sight we are - homing pigeons now - untidy columns weaving through smoke: the weary collapse of feudal clans. What other migratory species digs graves preparing to lynch?

Asleep in crisp leaves with midday stretching, I hear grinding gears and a bark in the lane: "Commander!"

It's American but relaxed. I'm dizzy reorienting, no longer clear where I belong. I scramble and run, across the scratching stalks of meadow, call out 'Attendez, attendez'. Among the crowns of heads above the hedgerow, several look over.

"Halt, ma'am."

I must seem a desperate anorexic crow, with a French accent and a Red coat, but I stick with it. "Est ce que aidez moi?"

"Attendez vous," An officer looks around, beckons another, slenderer of jaw. "Antoine, come over here."

Antoine joins the officer beside the Sherman. "She's French."

"Où vas tu?"

"Hamburg."

"Pourquoi?"

I shrugged. "Ville natale."

Antoine spoke quietly to the Yank in English. "The shaven head?"

"Yeah?"

"She's a collaborator."

"Non," I screamed. "Pas une collaboratrice, camp de concentration. Konzentrationslager. I can't take this."

A Red Cross worker had jumped from a white van two back, hurrying over.

"Hey peacenik, we've got this."

"You can't call her that."

The slender Frenchman strode to me, lifted the coat from my hand, flung it to ground and stood on it. He violently roughed my head. "Germans don't shave their women, and we don't shave patriots."

"Back off Antoine. We'll take her to Hohne DP. They can forward her."

I clunked in the Red Cross van, sat in shadow. At Bergen the door opened again. "Stretch your legs a bit. Don't go far."

I did stretch my legs; as fast as they would run.

Havelberg teems with Soviets and western Allies face to face at last, the one bringing its bitter socialist wind, the other chocolate. There is faux-friendship and heavy traffic. To be caught before Havelberg was unthinkable, but my acte

Français could've buried me in a ditch or in Schwerin - a thought I can't entertain.

Overlooking Hohne camp I had a choice. To rejoin the tarmac of civilisation, 'helped' behind wire - there are assistance programs - or be shadowy Waldvolk, crouched in the undergrowth.

It is unsanitised chaos down there. Thin shapes in the yard could be Lithuanian, Dutch... persistent Mischling... You can't know who's a friend. Red vs. Hun or rebel vs. Vichy: this you expect. But now we turn on our own. Germans despise each other - in my own dear Schleswig-Holstein they'd drive refugees into the North Sea.

For two weeks I sifted Hamburg's buttressed walls on mine and Ange's behalf: innards on show and the sky visible in lintels like a firestormed MGM set the actors won't leave, trying to re-people their lives.

Dust-strewn hospitals at a quarter function, grey flak towers pocked and fissured. I dug verbally with public servants and nurses, but paperwork was incinerated or in disarray.

"Excuse me," I halted a nurse in Hamburg-Eppendorf.

"You'll have to speak to Nurse Meier. I'm on rounds."

"I need to know if my mother is here."

"I'd have no way to tell. What does she look like?"

"Short grey hair, five eight. Grey-blue eyes. She has gold glasses."

"I'm sorry..."

"A scar on her chin runs to her mouth, from an operation."

The nurse glanced away and I thought she'd make a dash, but she said: "There's a woman in a coma something like that. Wegener Ward. I'm sorry if it is her. Brain stem trauma."

Searching on foot through Wegener I found my mother in her forecast coma. The corner the roof had collapsed; luckily summer was with us. She breathed without aid but her face was a blank escarpment, bandaged widely across her left cheek and eye. I felt her hand: cold. Upper arm: warm. I lay my hand on a hot brow. Her specs had been removed and she lay in a smock, vegetative or peaceful, whichever you may suppose.

I left Ma a letter and told a nurse I'd be away:

Mama,

This is your well-earned rest. We will grieve for Paps when we're back together. If you regain consciousness in the next few weeks I won't be in Hamburg.

I lost contact with Angie at Moringen and her last letter was fragile, talking of self-harm. Maybe the opening of Uckermark snapped it all away but I fear not. I hope you understand I am not sitting by your bedside as I'd feel a useless witness to your vacation.

I made contact with Adelheid whom you know lives out of harm's way. She is resigned to Günter's death, and now we are all mere 'Germans' again, perhaps we may see eye-to-eye.

We have no home so will rebuild. It will be tougher even, perhaps, than the war. But I'll find work as a translator or accountant (if money recovers), and we'll survive.

Until we speak, All my love,

Otto.

"You must be a Bebel?" The nurse was very olive-skinned; I wondered how non-fascist Latins were faring.

"This is my mother."

"You're Otto?"

"Yes. How do you know?"

"There's a letter for you care of Frau Bebel," she nodded at the cabinet on which - I'd not seen - another white envelope lay. "Hand delivered by a Herr Wolters."

I ruptured it.

Dearest Frau & Herr Bebel,

  My deep condolences regarding beloved Ernst, whom I counted among true friends. You may know I'm in the Luxembourg 'Ashcan' awaiting the trial of national beasts. If nothing else this frees me to reflect on friendships neglected but I hope unsevered. I had meant to write sooner, and it is the fault of world calamity it has taken so long.

  News of Ernst's passing reached me in drastic hours. I understand that while liaising with my colleague Friedrich at Blohm & Voss, an American bomb caused their deaths. Friedrich Graf was a good man also.

  It is important that you understand: I did everything in my power to divert our Führer's last resources to agriculture and Germany's future, not demolition, and as my testimony at Nuremberg will indicate, use my structural expertise to poison the Chancellor via the Führerbunker air-conditioning. (My desperate plans were scuppered by a chimney built on the vent into which I meant to drop cyanide. The Führer's nodding dogs had by then built impregnable security.)

I now look upon my actions, my moral choices and blindnesses, and understand my part in prolonging that bloody war. But I remain proud of sabotaging all Scorched Earth instructions until my considerable influence ran dry. Since isolation, I have become close to Hilde - my confessor - as I have never been with my other children.

I offer no excuse, only apology, for how the Reich let the wider nation down, and for the inhumanity which was concealed from high-ranking Reichsministers. And for the death of a good man, Ernst Bebel.

I hope you are rebuilding a Germany I long to rejoin. When I am permitted, I hope we can renew our friendship.

The highest regard,

Albert Speer

Minister of Armaments and War Production.

Can't climb down from office, though you are nobody now. You'll be guillotined. Or prison will rub you out. Shiny corridors and ladling queues, clinging to life like Raskolnikov's shadow.

You were supposed to save us Albert.

After overturning Ange's home in Altona, for probably-dead Lutherans, I went to *Blohm & Voss* at the docks. Gomorrah's reckless bomb-door policy was on display in heaps, still black, over which the gulls cared only for scraps. The conditions that week created vortexes of fire spreading as fast as humans run.

No record, no administration, no census of human transit.

Some rubble pyramids had white memorial crosses. I stood on the Elbe bank. The odd bit of railing poked through, protecting the calm, oil-grey estuary from us.

Defiant bird. Starling un-murmured. Ladder-necked beauty, where do you sleep?

The crater - that is to say the sudden nothing - of the stray bomb on our street was two houses away. Herr and Frau Lange would have known little.

Our ruined house was unpilfered; Papa's jars smashed in the sideway. The understairs door with the broken staircase over it and satchels and coats. The larder had collapsed like a parallelogram, with charred kitchen worksurfaces now ballast or barriered entry.

I pulled back side panels. There were tinned peaches and carrots, syrup, powdered milk and - somewhere - I suspected wurst and coffee rations.

Pulling bits of ceiling that covered my collapsed bedroom, I found my record bag. I put *Caravan* inside, filled the rest with food and what clothing I could yank from timber and plaster. I could see the splintery remains of my Hofner. About to leave, brass glinted in a flimsy cabinet. I crawled under the plaster and beams and reached for the knuckle duster.

Was testimony trading allegiance?

An American cordon of tanks dotted the roads of Nuremberg (amid rumours of Bavarian resurgence). The red-roofed Justizpalast was unscathed and reminded me of rural oompah bands. A grand failure of a complex.

Defendants were in the prison adjoining the back; which didn't stop the fear I'd bump into a senior Nazi under guard, whether staunch to the end or a blown leaf quivering. MPs dotted the sheened halls like angelic stormtroopers in white trim.

I held Flächsner's witness summons. Security directed me to a waiting room, said be on premise for two days, 10am to 5. The other occupant was Sabine Keller - an honorary legend to the Red Cross - her face asleep in her clavicle.

I kept abreast of Speer's condition via court secretaries and corridor whispers - Göring's also, caged opposite Speer with grubby pallet and blankets. The most base and venal führers - the indefensible - had killed themselves: some like Goebbels taking children with them.

But how did these two surviving opposites - these demon poles - prowl their peepholes? What esprit d'escalier might they've exchanged were Nuremberg not hovering above. The one was a bullet-riddled morphine addict running the Luftwaffe - known for astonishing arrogance and cruelty. The other an ostrich pragmatist; a head-burier who'd scaled the echelon, one hand building a purring Reich as the other oiled gears with blood... 'unknowingly'.

I'd never felt so low: this claustrophobic palace beyond good and evil.

☆

"You were detained for two weeks at Fuhlsbüttel without trial or plea."

"Yes."

"Dissident, what did that refer to?"

Albert had his temples pressed between finger and thumb. He looked gaunt before his time. Less handsome. I recall his position in the defendants' gallery: second row centre-right, chalk-striped suit. Always the civilian, when civilian suited.

"It was cumulative," I said. "Started with jazz nights. The Youth and SS shut them down and smashed our equipment and faces with batons. After several of such, I beat an HJ half to death in an alley... Then it got serious."

The ranked press and counsels tittered. Even an interpreter smiled in her booth. Lord Justice Lawrence had a new gavel and demanded order.

I was blushing hard amid these people, lights, cameras; such trivia in the witness stand, abomination in the dock. Embarrassment made me a little testier and I held Hermann Göring's cold eyes. Until he got bored and started reading.

Hans continued. "Serious in that you went to Moringen?"

"Tortured at Neuewall, then Moringen."

"Neuewall police station. With no access to counsel?"

"The legal system had collapsed by then."

The British Magistrate interjected. "What has this to do with the forced labour charge?"

"As my witness has ably pointed out, the effects of such... cumulative dissociation from authority allowed unseen crimes. Legal circumvention for one. The assault of a minor, for another."

"You are defending a specific charge, that of forced labour and inhuman working conditions."

Hans nodded. "Your testimony states," he looked down at his papers, and I heard the echoing jabber of interpreters, "through a working relationship with your father, where Albert Speer had knowledge of your detention he intervened."

I looked at the dock. Albert's eyes wouldn't rise. Instead I received Göring's icy gaze again: one that said when this travesty finishes... Beside him, Rudolph Hess the nutter looked up at the fluorescent filming lights, rocking perceptibly.

I nodded. "Yes."

"Once on munitions at Volpriehausen you remained there for the duration. Three years. Though you'd reached serving age."

"Yes."

"Did Speer try to intercede, have you released, provide habitable conditions?"

"I expect limitations were placed on his influence."

Hans flipped forward in the transcript. I eyed the gallery and thought I caught a nod from Speer's bowed figure. Albert, betrayer of party and neglector of humanity. Expedience hung round him like a gas. Family friend almost; one that either didn't know, or didn't care to know, the depths.

"You claim you were tortured by Totenkopf while in Moringen in your role as Kapo, that is, block-leader."

"It's a statement not a claim," I could hear the anger in my voice rising but it was shrill. The water was flooding back, the bursting lungs, the plaintive wish for blackout. Death's Heads playing cards and smoking as water rose. About to say more, I didn't. Eyes were boring me, the lights hot and the press murmuring.

"Who was responsible?"

"The whim of Dr. Ritter, enacted by the Death's Head Squad."

"Ritter's a psychologist, not a commandant."

"Krack was Labour Director. I've no idea who had final say on torture. I believe it was Ritter's instruction based on my insolence."

Justice Lawrence interjected. "If you're not about to sum up, can you indicate where this is heading, Counsel Flächsner?"

"I'm demonstrating, through the account of a camp intern who knew Speer, that even family connections between those in the camps and Reichsministers were severed, unknown and useless. That my defendant's claim to have no knowledge of conditions in the camps is born out. And that those who ran the camps paid no heed to humanitarian obligations or even Nazi command, instead using mob rule at ground level."

"I see. Well... You've demonstrated that in this instance."

Hans gave a perceptible nod to me. I turned a last gaze at the dock. Göring scowled with a headset flapping loosely by his right ear: this confederacy of morons. But Speer looked up quickly to the ceiling, one folded arm propping the other supporting his chin.

"Witness dismissed."

You were supposed to save us. The better Germany, the better ideal. You chose to walk in the ruins of civility in privilege.

But I realised his name was now poison in his clique.

We capitulated, yes, though it had little impact on a German in the Soviet Union. It registered as a kind of official seal on a mauled tin of shit.

In Moscow's fields behind Lunyovo factories in the barracks' splash, I'd hear chuckles, voices raised in a bolt of humour. Bare chests and braces now aren't rare. Assemblies, conferences. One sees Seydlitz, striding to meetings with his stubbled bull's head.

The warrant officer from Dubovka is here with the dorsal nose; Generál-leytenánt Vormelker. Rolled sleeves, veiny arms and fussy lips - he nags at my youth. Looks like a beaker stand clamping something invisible up ahead. Tan shirt and cigarette - a handsome fellow if he didn't dress like a writing desk.

But his christian name is Raymund. I had few friends as a child. Only one in fact, Detlef, who was also flouncy: a dreamer at his papa's theatre. Tack-sharp if a bit volcanic - he went to prison for murder in 1927. When I knew him, he was fourteen and walking out with a Josephine Baker lookalike, Missy Lehane, a starlet and all-round nice girl but some bad stuff happened in Neukölln and Detlef was embroiled. So was his *male* lover, one Raymund Vormelker. It's a common name, right? I'm homesick, finding nostalgia in weak chimes.

And in the Generál's slipstream I have... Zetkin.

"Potential." His door is closed. Zetkin's hands are swift over files. "Is what we're looking at."

...Months of leaflet vetting for Soviet accuracy - and it's true we do no work - but I'll be gone. Jonas was Vormelker's emissary, Zetkin is his adjutant.

"Repatriation at Küstrin. Wouldn't normally entrust it so early, but... time presses and Vormelker keeps an eye, as it were."

"Doing what?" I asked, knowing.

"Thinning out Werwolves, Silesian troublemakers and so on," I got his red zeal eyes. "Disruptors of the process."

"I've met Polish Nationalists."

"Good. You'll know they're shadow Nazis."

I cleared my throat. "How do you define a shadow, fanatically?"

"Pale imitations, Captain."

Pale imitations of men. So the mugshots came out: engrained, enclipped and corners tucked. Their impro uniforms and bomber eyes. Lugers-at-temples and no offspring. (I know what they believe. They're me seven years ago at a table in Hamburg, only I'd everything and they have nothing.) I nodded a lot. Waylaid at Küstrin, snow or bullet bound.

"It's probationary," Zetkin was all but pushing me, my file reconvened under my arm. "A bit rushed, but I don't think there'll be a problem with you, Bebel. If there is..." Finally a smile.

I blinked in the corridor, barracks appearing in gloom. *Spetshrupy. Denazification.*

"You'll have support. We might even swing you weekends at home."

With the stretched face of bad soap, I was driven to Khimki for Wroclaw, a Lisunov DC3 in their Yank-leased sky; a tin horse within a tin horse heading for claimed fields.

We're contained by brute force and memory now, revenge not wire. I promised myself as the things I loved got smaller I would hold on to them, not long dreams of regret. But time ran out. We've not yet returned to Time. Without resistance she sits still; looks at her belly button, waves us on. Time used to move with us, aching and maternal.

I had got to counting days in a way I'd never done at Chelyabinsk, as the Baltic swelled to the north quite empty now. Day 63, Küstrin-Neustadt. Noone gave a shit how Günter began and ended; what was in his briefcase; how he smelled or which way he parted his thin hair in the stained mirror of 188 Bleyener Weg.

After Stalingrad, I'd not believed anything could look like Stalingrad. In fairness nothing did - maybe the Dresden and Warsaw I saw in photos - but what emptied me out was that it was everything. Everything was this. Wherever humans gathered, if wire and water and commerce met it was smashed, leaving only a few cows staring in plain pasture. All Europe gone for the failed flutings of a Norse fantasy.

I'd sent four women and children back to Majdanek, where their husbands had been slaughtered; alerted SBZ authorities to nine jaded Wervolves moving west in a dreamstate; photographed two prospective 'Spetshrupy' and smelt clinging death in thousands. I'd patted the heads of countless childhoods without Heimat, dragging their salvaged toys...

And still somehow, given Sundays were free, I'd not told anyone - notably my wife - I was alive. A psychoanalyst may have plenty to say but I'll tell you I needed a trigger, to set the world back to normality; some jolt in the 'cooling off' or slap in the miasma. It duly came.

☆

"Priyti." --Zhvikov took the photo from her pocket and climbed from the Jeep. I didn't move. Easy for her; this was my last port of call. While I stayed in the Jeep all remained hopes and maybes. "Come."

I lifted my knees out and grimly walked through double-parked vehicles.

Zhvikov stood at the foyer's desk with a Red Army nurse. From body language the nurse knew everything or nothing; shaking her head periodically. Zhvikov tilted the photo in. More head shakes, a defensive posture. After a while, she pointed out the door we'd walked through, and guided a straight palm up the side of the building.

"Doesn't recognise her. All the inmates were moved to out-buildings when the army took over. But..."

I was nodding mutely.

"A nurse took some of the inmates away. Nobody knows where."

I pointed in the supposed direction of the out-buildings. "We'll... Can we?"

She nodded. Wire-glass doors and soiled sheets and plastic curtains and rocking moans like confidential poetry; the vocal record of those who *could not take* the thunder.

I held the key a while before turning the ignition, dusk melding the trees. The evening chorus was inconsiderate, the lawn daisy-bursts thoughtless. Furled buds in a new world. Don't get too cocky, joyful spring, humanity runs this place and we're scheißköpfe.

Now what? Give Dwight his Jeep and testimony, hitch back to blackened Hamburg and our house eruption. Then what? *And then what, and then what?*

"She'll be dug up in a corner of Uckermark. Some woodland glade. Her bones picked."

"Don't talk like that. She went with the nurse of course."

Was that hope or denial or their collision? Zhvikov's hand gripped my shoulder.

"She still breathes but can't swallow. She's on drips and... well, there's no eye movement when we slide her up. Fourteen months. Something in her is a survivor."

Her eyes were closed and still, vacated, as if she'd swum away untroubled beneath the skin, but I was whispering all the same.

"What can be done?" I said, teeth clenching.

"Likely nothing."

"How would it end?"

"She's not in any pain, I think."

"No."

"As her only member of family, we wanted to discuss with you..."

"Yes?"

"Taking out the drips. Letting nature take its course."

I looked at her lids - the detonation at home - difficult to know what she thought sliding off, consent or no? A tough cookie but nobody'd expected years of oil-smeared and riddled skies. Six years' stubborn, stupendous dick-swinging. Her body hung on while her humanity - her very illumination - had walked the garden path. Otherwise healthy I pictured her grey-blue irises, a bit scathing.

"OK," I said.

I picked up her gold-chained specs, carefully wrapped. She used to push them down to see Ange more clearly of a morning. The oven would wreath something basting in the house; sunshine on their newspapers and brows. Sometimes, late, with Pa and Günter arguing Bauhaus and bilge in the lounge, Angie'd prise from Mama happy tales of Weimar scrimping in the kitchen. I'd sit on the turn of the stairs with my Hofner, picking lightly enough to listen, unneeded, happy.

"I'll confirm with the doctor, and remove them."

I sat awaiting the nurse's return. She began to take the needles and drips from Mama's arm. At the quietest moment, while the sick and departing dreamt of their own plight, Angela was standing over me in stolen boots, a thin dress and her camp blanket under a Russian greatcoat, a light hand on my neck.

My dark finch had flown home.

2. SAVAGES & PARTISANS

Yes, Günter here, you see?

I'd join my smoking compatriots in the fissured dawn: 'Glib', Hans and Tomas, all pragmatists. By 10am some black bread and kulesh was available in the hut - odourless and congealed.

I returned to my post as a train had finished unloading. I was waiting to relieve underling Tomas so that he'd eat, but he was gripping a breathing bundle of clothes; some bruised pillar of laundry. The only thing that gave away life inside was a persistent cough wriggling through. This man wouldn't look at eyes. But found mine.

König.

My heart paused, then double struck.

"What is this one?" I said.

Tomas answered with absent emotion. "Papers from Poznan. Volksdeutsche." Tomas had a smudged sheaf in his hand.

I had to think quickly but I couldn't think quickly - my brain was sapped; I wrestled as Tomas watched other guards pull stragglers from the huddled stench.

"I'll take this one. He's on two lists. It could get complicated."

Tomas looked at me. König hadn't said a word - by incapacity or discretion I couldn't say. My mind saw the imprint of the side gate; the alley bathed in sun. I'd have to flee without possessions, my decision made.

"You're relieving me now, aren't you? I'll take him."

I tried to avoid König's eyes and prayed he didn't speak.

"I need to retrieve a Bandera file. Come..." I wagged a hand to where Tomas held König. The material unrumpled, and I walked with my silent shell-loader - even his whirring chest had seized up; his sheened face looked out like separating mayonnaise.

Between the rest hut and the offices was the alley; invisible to the repatriate hoards; most of whom were dead to observation. I turned to look at the border station shrinking; so far so good.

The feet of East German children - orphans until told otherwise - dangle through blown masonry, staring at us with grubby curiosity. While over the border ten year olds scour the country with PPsh tommies for limping Jews and collaborators, or each other.

This is the mainland, you see? No Leicester Square buses, no dancing in fountains or swilled cognac, no grateful polkadot dames smacking us kisses. No jazz band.

Freedom was the terror of Germany and its clashing tidal waves. I knew the routes. Trains from Kharkov connected to Poltava-Kovel. Out of Galicia and the further west they got, the more cramped and inhuman they became. By Wroclaw the piled excrement was intolerable.

I'd guarded the Sonderkommando whose lives were in danger - separated to their own slatted carriage - so in a sense,

König was nothing new - except for that whole pre-Panzer life ...thing.

It was two days walk to Berlin, accounting for concealment.

We walked through bright forest; König was absently stripping bark from a stick. He was feverish, shrinking from daylight, occasionally muttering and glad of shadow. I fell back to his pace quite naturally, limping.

"Your uniform might protect us," he said.

I shook my head. "You don't expect to see my kind on the move."

König must have seen the Wehrmacht-adorned lamposts of Ukraine, Belarus, Romania, swinging, doused and burnt. Could perhaps not countenance we were at source; the Fatherland.

The first thing I heard at sundown was the crack of rifles. Not the skirmish of unearthed fanatics; well-timed, three seconds between each shot. Someone was walking a line.

"Not every soldier accounted themselves honourably," König murmured, his pink face breached with sweat.

At night I see his symptoms, the full body rash. ...It spares only his face and palms, the rest raw. He groans at night, augmenting my sleep with oil-slick colour, and between our discreet glances by the daylight he shuns, I don't know if it's typhus or typhoid. They begin the same.

I set snares and found brooks for König to wash in. (Hard not to keep a rude distance.) In Schöneiche's skirts, we hit a band heading south. I was coming out for water with König's voice following me louder than usual. I waved a hand frantically to shut up, with movement in the rubble round the broken house. I got out of direct moonlight. Could hear harshly whispered Slav. Partisan exodus. I wasn't armed but for wood yanked from a sleeper and a hunting knife.

Two tawny heads found our derelict interesting. They listened a while, looking at the dusty basement. After a while one's arm came over his head, and I had to race down, prep König to hide.

I readied my heavy timber. Quaking with boots above I shouted, "Don't move," in German.

Boots stopped in surprise.

"Who are you hiding from?"

A brief silence. "Not hiding. Travelling," one said, in the guttural German it had paid Slavs to learn. He couldn't figure our mismatching uniforms.

"So are we. We'll do a deal."

"Not with Nazi."

"We're Wehrmacht," I looked down at my Communist lapels then, wondering what they instilled: fear, hate or likely obedience. "You want our basement?"

The air thickened. The rest were grouped at the top of the stairs. "We'll take it."

"We're travelling too. I've set snares. We'll share the basement and the catch."

The leader shouted back to the shadows above. There was some heated talk.

"You share. One night. No vengeance."

Four Slavs came down. And one did, after all, have a gun. "Where are your snares?"

"Just one, I'll show you."

"Is that potatoes?" He pointed at a sack König had disturbed.

I took the Slav back up and pointed towards the snare in a run between field and copse. He returned pretty astonished with a boar, no more than a squeaker. "Might feed five thousand. I got wild onions and blackberries."

I hesitantly asked: "Polak?"

"Czech."

The fire in the basement lit faces starved so much that suckling boar cooked in blackberries might cause convulsions. I skinned and gutted in the corner, handed the carcass to Czech no. 1 to butcher for a tin tub over the fire, then took the pelt and offal up the stairs. The faint smell of shit from us all was briefly covered.

The Czechs were watchful but smelling stew one grew talkative. "Fight Reds, or with them?"

König replied cryptically. "They're your new bosses."

"Now what?"

I piped up, "We were conscripted. Stalingrad. The dreams of madmen." I said nothing of my collar emblems, my safety.

A Slav hand passed canteens holding portions, "Play fair."

Things got primitive over the stew. There was the noise of indignant stomachs as we chewed meat to ribbons.

"You OK there, Günter?" König was grinning.

Blackberry gravy must have been drizzling down me. He pointed to his stomach, "I'm still having to reaccustom."

The Slav said, "I asked now what? ...will you do?"

"We're not decision-makers."

He jabbed a fork towards my chest. "What will *you* do."

I looked at the sharp eyes, wet in firelight, the narrow and mournful face... In truth I'd no idea.

Under my coat I dozed fitfully; possessions close. Even the word enemy's splintered from global coherence now. The charcoal dawn is no blessing but we set off into Berlin before the south-bound fleeing Czechs.

By afternoon, the stagnant troughs warm and buzz with flies and mosquitos. Decomposing blue faces and protruding hooves line the ditches where rats grow large, in the grey city, swathed in red by lowering dusk.

Nurse Wagner was surprised to see me and some of her clutched files slid out the back of her arms. "Darling, I didn't expect you."

"I'm starting over."

The other files fell to the floor and she give me a hug. "Who's the tall dark stranger?"

Otto stood watching in the grizzle outside Fliedner Klinik on Charlottenstraße.

"That's Otto. Hands off."

"Where are you staying?"

I looked at my curling feet in child Hitler Youth boots and found it hard to ask. "I hoped you'd help."

"Of course my darling. We're low on sanitation. Fine on security."

"Anything."

She became quiet and awkward. "Was anyone left?"

"Just Otto."

"From the front?"

"No, he's younger than me. Internment was a blessing."

72

"Cradle snatcher," she nudged my ribs. "Go to 16 Krausenstraße for now. It's not great, but it's not hostile and the plumbing works. They've got blankets. You can set up a room in the tenements. Grab what you need from Gertrude in the foyer."

"Thank you Maria."

"I'm glad you came."

Otto'd rolled a cigarette and stood hawkish on the kerb smoking. Besides a holdall of very few clothes and tins, he'd wrapped his record bag over himself with his one record, *Caravan*.

"Wait!" Maria gathered files and plonked them on the desk. Behind it she rifled a drawer and pulled papers describing my former psychiatric status, handed them to me. Perhaps the only record in Germany of who I was. "You'll need this. 'Especially vulnerable'."

I took the papers and kissed her cheek. Maria Wagner was brass in muck.

The only difference with 16 Krausenstraße and any other blasted building in Berlin was it remained plumbed with a little electricity if electricity happened, and granite Gertrude stopping the unwanted.

So we set up our new life in an old dining room which at least was sheltered, with a shell hole for air con and the electric corridor keeping a dim light through the door. Otto found candles in his holdall. The odd group of Reds passed.

"I can hear every footstep."

"There's a five foot hole in the wall. Want me to plaster that tonight or in the morning?"

I pulled Otto closer. He bent and rearranged, his big mitt on my rear. Beyond us were the varnished splinters of a dining table; some reminder of the original family eating during Nazi ascendence. Otto has changed; he now has a habit of quietness when I expect him vocal and reassuring.

"Are we scared?" I murmured.

"You keep good hold on those papers."

"And if I left you?"

"You'd have nothing."

"I want half your possessions. I'll fight you in any court."

"You get nothing. I worked hard for my empire."

The moon shone on his bag against the wall with its solitary record.

I dreamt a blue tractor was ploughing towards a hedge. The other side children played kegel pins. The grinning farmer looked like he wasn't stopping until some force knocked him clean off, the throttle slowed and the tractor idled.

I awoke to Otto gone, a coldness under blankets on the cushions from the settee. We'd hoarded anything comfortable to the corner where we lay for the night.

I stood at the hole in the wall, blinking at Berlin day. The streets were quiet bar Reds or kids too energetic for dereliction, and old men - too old to have changed routine even as bombs fell - walking their lumpy dogs.

Otto must've gone scavenging, though there was baseline food here. Bread, a little cheese and berry teas. *God*, a vitamin would be nice.

"Back," he murmured crashing through the door, not it seemed through urgency but clumsiness. "I got soup old girl."

"Where from?"

"The Russians dole it out. Well, the ones not looting."

"What kind?"

"Boiled horse I expect."

I shoved him. "Don't joke if I'm eating it."

"Any post? Phonecalls while I was away?"

"Stop acting the clown."

"I'm entitled, I got soup. You know that huge, smashed-up industrial block across the park? I think it's the Nazi film company for *Deutsche Wochenschau*. Dusty shambles. I bet it's got typewriters. ...Maybe printworks."

"Honey, I'm not that advanced in our domestic lifeplan."

"Why wait until they cost money? I'll recce later."

"Copy that, Captain Bebel."

"Also I was thinking, I need stuff to trade."

"For what, food?"

"Records."

"Again, you might be getting ahead of yourself."

"The airbase at Tempelhof. Yanks will have shellac and players flown in."

"It's miles away," I muttered, and to annoy him added, "And it's vinyl."

"So I was thinking..."

I smiled sweetly, enjoying Otto's manic episode.

"...I'll work at RIAS."

"Uh?"

"Radio In the American Sector. New station. Some feller in the soup queue with a radio'd tuned in. I know jazz better than anyone. I speak three languages, well two-and-a-half."

"If you're going to put the world to rights in a day, I'll get out of your way."

"Please do old girl, you're cramping my style. Now drink the horse soup before it goes cold."

He rummaged in his holdall that clanked with tins from his destroyed larder. Enamel mugs. An ornate silver jewellery box edged up, but I didn't ask. He unscrewed the jar of tepid brown broth.

Otto retrieved a *Continental* typewriter from Goebbels' shell-shocked film studios down the street. He cleared masonry from roller and ribbon and gifted me one evening with fifty sheets of paper.

I sniffed it; an exoskeleton of old inky dust with brass mandibles.

"And they love me."

"Who? I don't."

"RIAS. Reckon I'm perfect for jazz hour at midnight. They wanna flood the east with jazz, Hon. They've got the masts, and they're worried about Red spread."

"Is it a live broadcast?"

"Who cares, it's work. Maybe I'll pilfer shellac."

"Vinyl."

"We need a record player."

I glanced significantly at the night sky watching us through our hole. "No, Otto. We need a wall."

"Berlin only needs walls when the cold comes."

I could hear bin lids slipping. Crashing and laughter. Suddenly there was a racket. Drunk Russians.

"Uchebnaya strel'ba."

"Chto?"

"Sobaka."

Otto got up and went to the hole. "Fucking Soviets."

Quivering from a nightmare I joined him, holding his back.

A stray dog, buff with a black muzzle, was sniffing around a tree. The first shot hit the trunk way over its head, causing the dog's eyes to focus on the danger. The second narrowly missed its nose, and it started loping over the street. The third hit it in the body and it whined, fell gasping.

I started crying on Otto's back. Otto hung in the hole in the wall. "Fuck off," he shouted, but I heard the quaver. "It's four in the morning. Otvali!"

"You make us fuck off?" And he shot his pistol in the air.

His companion shone a torch at us. Otto covered his face with his arm. The light flipped back to his own uplit face, pale and inverse. "Remember this face!" he shouted.

"Go sleep it off," Otto yelled through the hole.

We went to the bed worried what might follow. But the laughter - Otto exhaled in relief - was moving away.

"What's got them so jolly at 3am?" Otto said.

"Alcohol," I breathed in half-sleep, "would be a guess."

The two men next door and girl opposite I was convinced were in some dodgy menage a trois. I never heard Adolfa leave the men's room or saw her enter or leave her own. They were socialists; at least from their talk. Johann was a mechanic getting extra coupons fixing trams and the older, Falke, a train driver.

Otto, having fixed our hole with reclaimed bricks bodged in, chicken wire and plaster, fixed theirs. Johann could fix it, uses his hands all day in oil and grease - maybe that's why he hadn't.

When he cursed bashing his finger I suddenly thought: "Your guitar."

"I'll get one soon enough."

A quasi-cafe sprung on Leipziger Straβe. All was barter, but we'd also get up early for the Russian queues. We were standing in the cafe with a bag of gathered mushrooms hoping for coffee. A Red soldier stood in front watching us curiously, slotting us into his index of Germans.

We drank our coffee in the corner and on leaving I heard: "Otvali?"

I only knew four Russian words: yes, no and fuck off. The last - which the Red had stuck a question mark on - clearly wasn't helpful here.

I looked at him, his loose slung Kalashnikov, hand resting on the muzzle. Then I looked at Otto, buried my head, and the pair of us moved towards home.

"Otvali? Big mouth little Nazi?"

I was scared and paranoid for Otto. Maybe those revellers weren't so drunk; the torch in his face. I occasionally flipped a glance back. His comrade, who called him Kostya, was trying to drag him from his angers.

We have the choice: clear our city voluntarily - but with empty stomachs and foraging for nettles between shallow graves - or brave Red supervision; but while they scream "Rabota!", they also give us black bread and barley soup with grease-bubbles before and after clearance.

The saddest sight for men, I can feel it, is to watch creaking trains head east with their machines buckling the floors. You rob a woman of work, she'll find something vital or trivial to fill time; take a man's machines, he is nothing more than an idle and bitter mammal.

And a sober one too, unless it's left to women to hide the damned stuff from the Red blizzard, which in itself gives twofold benefit: fewer rampant Soviet waistbands, and a pool to drown German sorrow, looking at the space where once the male Bosch had produced.

Luckily, Stalin doesn't want our trams or the S-bahn itself, so we can traipse in disconsolate idleness, back and forth in our blown quarry.

Marianne haunts me in bricks; hoves over the shattered Dom and shimmers in lintels. We've much to forget and remember, but in all that Marianne's printed - kicking legs and flailing limbs, or a reposed face.

And they're hopeful eyes - maybe just Sinti-hopeful - with the black caverns like urns beneath. Logically she's gone. No-one gets dragged off by an SS guard for dominoes. She'd made a fool of Schuster, and probably others.

We have to put a lid on things but it's hard. I expect to see old faces, schule faces - what we knew in parks and train compartments - as I round each corner, though the corners are hardened flannels. There's no sense in it, though a Cartesian would say there's perfect sense in it...

We went foraging in the woods where the Spree opens. Berries and mushrooms mostly. Anything cookable we shared downstairs at the hob.

One morning we found a tiny overgrown orchard in the trees, like a bygone memory. The trees wcrc gnarled, fruit scarce, but we began a frenzy of picking, biting and sucking the pale flesh.

"How will we carry it all?"

Otto took off his jacket, and the apples plopped in. Back at Krausenstraße Gertrude was excited.

"Wait!" She hurried to her office-quarters and came back with cinnamon and sugar. I clapped my hands in joy. That evening everyone wolfed their mains - pumpernickel, cheese and a thumb of wurst - and then sat smiling over hot stewed apple.

Two months and RIAS paid Otto. He'd leave for Winterfeldtstraße after lunch, kissing me at the Continental. I awaited his departure like a gleeful student.

> To understand Stalin's murderous hypocrisy one must understand - slowly, like a man inhabiting his own lies - the cloak of human concern and thereby respectability, by which a tyrant steals their throne.

Too abstract. I ripped the sheet out the roller and rubbed my brain.

I'd a grainy photo of Mount Mtatsminda looming over Yerevan Square; the wild east, Georgia. I'd carried it close since Hamburg, knowing it would one day be a beginning.

In 1907 Josef Stalin stood on a roof in Tiflis, Georgia watching a bank-robbery he'd organised, smiling at the carnage of dead workers and Gendarmes below through smoke and dust. It would net the Bolsheviks 341,000 roubles. His boyhood friend Kamo - who'd later rip a man's heart from his chest in Bolshevism's name - coordinated the massacre on the ground.

Better. Well pictorially, perhaps not if Soviet authorities read it.

Winter '46-7 was atrocious. Snow banked the concrete and spiralled in our hungry eyes. We'd no meat on us (even properly fed) and no radio for jazz hour: on which Otto laboured with setlists and continuity. He started nicking my Continental to type his evening's gas. Typewriter envy grew and Otto (at night so's not to bump into Reds ripping out the building's machines) took two Olivettis, knowing Falke was a pamphleteer and could use one.

After an evening's typing, I'd pop next door until Otto got home. They liked me, Falke particularly. It was certainly communal: they'd a curtain separating two matresses, meaning someone was at it with someone.

Adolfa would sit at the window aloof and autumnal, pushing her rust-yellow hair back in silence.

Otto wanted to move further west but I vetoed; intrigued by the birth of German socialism. Gradually market stalls were inhabiting the shops behind them. Everyone became a shop-fitter. The Soviet Army'd backed off a little. The previous spring the drinking water had been officially cleared of putrefaction, but now the pipes froze and burst. The city looked like a painting: 'Still life with ice explosion'.

Berlin, Hermannplatz-- Crippled walls like ravenous old men. Among the black vault-skins of department stores, stalls had been forced to life: thin soup, bread and veg. Linen, soap.

One stall had kegs we hoped were beer. Two storeys up a family sat over lunch with the side of the building blown off; in view like a doll's house.

We approached the stall dangling our potato sack, and spotted the Red Army too late. They were in a cafe in shade, drunk, and one tugged another's sleeve. Must have presented a sight, a turncoat Kraut Soviet in the company of a tramp Wehrmacht.

From the cafe came the Reds. König held up placatory hands but it was no good, the speed they were arriving, trotting and winding. We just protected ourselves. The cracking pain in the side of my head landed me in dust. I could see a gun-holder looking up and down the street shiftily. A heavy boot stomping my stomach winded me and I floundered. Then my windpipe.

Blood in the dust from my mouth and nose conjoined, and I wished they'd give up. One more boot and they did.

I couldn't move. Eventually I turned to König. Out and lifeless. I turned my head back and saw more boots ambling down the street. I twisted my pupils up. He had the emblemed red collars and blue cap of the NKVD.

It was our apparatchik from Dubovka, no longer in Dubovka. Vormelker the Generál must have the whole run of the bloc, my latest desertion reaching his hooped nose, that shinbone in the sun.

He tried to use a boot to turn me, but had to crouch and roll with his hands. He took a handkerchief from his jodhpur, spat on it, and wiped blood and dust from my face. Stared a while, said nothing, and did the same with König. Then he returned to me.

I looked at the blue sky, wondering if I believed in anything higher. Two more faces joined the leader's looming shadow.

"U vas yest' fayl?"

"Da, Generál." An underling opened a case and handed Vormelker quite thick manilla. He leafed, found a page, studied my face and looked back in the file.

"Etot," he said. I was lifted by my armpits, and half-dragged, half-stumbled back through feral lanes to a car at the end, a Russian GAZ. He opened the rear door, shovelled me in and landed softly in the seat.

"Doesn't look good."

Vormelker curled a puff of cigarette smoke. The window sucked the blue. We moved on in silence, until: "Plant 183 eh? Architect and Wehrmacht Captain. Eagerly killing Russians right to the moment you surrendered. Retrain, desert again. Does anything hold your loyalty, Bebel?"

His tone was weary, as if my particulars had always been under his fingers. Eyed me shinily, then didn't say much through Berlin, and I was too shattered to protest König's whereabouts. The car parked up in an unscathed suburb.

On Leipziger Straße Reds were overseeing Trümmerfrauen, the 'rubblewomen' clearing a block that had slumped in its own alley.

Except the women had stopped clearing and were looking at each other in fear. It was our local troop, Kostya's troop, but Kostya was not to be seen.

Ange and I stopped. Something unnatural had thickened the air.

"What's going on?" Ange murmured.

"I don't know."

There was a weak, muffled wail from the alley. "Oh god. Otto do something."

"Do what?" I felt electric cold in my back. Kalashnikov muzzles pointed at the ruined tarmac.

"Anything." Ange let go of my arm and strode towards the women. But the smoking Reds - two smiling, one deeply unhappy - blocked her path.

"Get out of my way," Ange shouted, and ducked nimbly under an outstretched arm.

I trotted to follow, but the Reds were certainly not letting me closer. My heart started beating in terror; to do *something*. Ange walked over brick and wire and stood staring at the rubblewomen. She pointed down the half-cleared alley. "What's happening?"

Silence greeted her.

"Tell me."

An imponderable quiet, broken only by another muffled groan.

"It's Greta's turn," one of the women said.

"By choice?"

The woman - eyes both hard and disappointed - shrugged as if that word had no meaning.

Ange looked at the alley shuddering, and headed for the shadow. The Reds watched over their shoulders, and I sprinted around them, to block her path.

"Stoy! Halt!" said one, raising his rifle and firing rounds into the brick over my head.

I grabbed Angie's arm forcefully. "Not you." But the shots being fired must have stopped hidden Kostya mid-hump. The alleyway was quiet, followed by rasping brick and hurried footfall. I was almost in the alley when the explosion happened.

A terrific boom and flash in front of my eyes. Smoke and dust rushing like a hurricane. My eyes went dark, my ears deadened like a sudden plunge in water, a loud ringing replaced everything. In the charcoal mist, my eyes must have seen more brick and mortar tumble into the alley as fire engulfed the ground. I felt pain in my face and the world turned sideways. I blacked out, believing I'd seen Sodom and Gomorrah in an alleyway.

Ange was over me and my sight was redawning. She was scratched and flecked with blood.

Both of our faces, once we'd realised our lives were safe, looked gobsmacked about those in the alley. Kostya, and the unknown woman.

Unexploded bombs weren't unusual, and the rubblewomen copped them. The papers reported casualties. But tended not to report the number being savagely fucked at the time.

Winter 1947 was the bleakest. Not labour camp cold; colder still.

Permanent Berliners who'd survived still had prewar suits, dresses and overcoats, while returning PoWs and interns had a mish-mash of robbed army wear and loft salvage. The girls of Charlottenburg improvised. (Those bobbysoxers: if an air-raid siren went off they'd shriek *what shall I wear*?)

I dressed before dawn and slipped out with Ma's necklace in my bag. No birdsong: their beaks iced shut. I wondered, wearing Ange's greatcoat, if the architects of Berlin ever imagined this. Their stalactites now a sooted picture rail for icicles.

I wasn't hanging on an overcrowded train to rural Germany with hefty and unsplittable jewels, just for dairy. Break up the asset. Kurfürstendamm gave good prices but in Reichsmarks (which devalued overnight) so I went to Potsdamer, watched traders set up and gripe about the Roma kids - the thieving starlings - through comma-steamed hands. A taciturn iron sky snowed.

When a jeweller was available I took the necklace laid on my hand: white gold split to tributary semi-precious stones ending in a discreet ruby. This stocky Teuton wore a monocular; years of glint-squinting had creased his face. (The finally-solved had left a gap.) I bore the necklace votively. Said nothing.

"Hand it over."

"Let's talk price before manhandling."

"I'll give you a valuation. You either accept it or take your late mother's opera-wear home."

My eyelashes gathered an unmelting crust. I looked at the Platz's roofless domes and de-glassed blocks, the trams rattling. I was trading my mother for cigarettes and dollars. If I smoked the cigarettes would that be a long, drawn-out cremation?

"It's a shame you're trading now. Nice piece. Can't you hold out?"

"For what?"

"Its real value."

"Am I missing something? Gems don't devalue."

"You think? What use is a ruby to someone right now?"

As if to prove it, all his wares had a snow coating. He absently brushed a duck-shaped soap dish.

What shall we do Ma? Trade you? Maybe survive another week. Or invest in the future, with an imploding cavity so painful it stops you sleeping, which makes you colder still, and hungrier. What, Mama?

I rumpled my hair feeling sour. "If you've no faith in the Reichsmark, which I can totally dig, then... surely this is a what-you-call-it, a gold standard. "

"Maybe in the long haul. Who's got time for that?"

I stared, willing him to regain market-confidence.

"Who would I sell it to?"

"Some west-end wife?"

He shook his head. "For the same reason you haven't."

"Just give me a price then."

He gave me a price and, from behind, you'd have seen my shoulders sink.

I traded some Virginians for a new pair of wool trousers - high-waisted, baggy and pleated - and some braces. Another grandpa shirt. (One day I supposed, I'd wear a tie.) A scarf poked out of the fabrics, midnight blue with golden parakeets. If it wasn't her taste she could wear it indoors in winter.

Next hop, the train's running-board crammed like sub-continentals; holding folding and my record bag full of American gaspers. You had to keep changing the hand you held on with before it froze. The bombed city fell back to green Ruralia. I love the countryside, I do, but the people. They'd eye a city toddler like it was corruption unmade, spawn of their undoing. The village laid tables, keeping an eye on each other's so us slickers didn't lift.

I only wanted butter and cream and fresh bread but I loosed more Virginians and added some wurst. Trains back were more comfortable and talkative, as a shabby sun broke the frost.

To get to the 'International Congress of German Writers' I had to tramp through Kreuzberg's wasteland in Adolfa's heels. I'd been told attendees at the Hebbel's reopening were paying coal.

Outside this Epoque theatre - miraculous by its presence alone - I'd glanced warily, wondering what a rebirth meant. I needn't have worried, inside was open hostility. All the colours of the rainbow (red, a tinge of blue) had arranged themselves accordingly under Hungarian swooping curves. Drink, though plentiful, failed to lubricate the ton of writers - some jangling with decorations.

One intellect's goat was already got. In the lobby I heard: "Europe and Asia are ours. You will sit there in North and South America and we will shoot rockets at each other...."

A specced Yank of letters then spluttered offence about claiming Europe for the hammer and sickle, to which the original speaker replied, "Stop being childish."

Excellent.

Jousting continued on-stage with Melvin Lasky - a New York sprat barely my senior - and Kremlin-stamped Vishnevsky; each bulls of their own stripe denouncing the other. To Vishnevksy's talk of 'iron curtains' born in Washington and London, Lasky lacerated the Kremlin's sinister 'fads'. How soon might the declasse author become worse than unfashionable: either a decadent counter-revolutionary with autocrats holding his pen, or toxic sludge dumped in the Moskva.

But it wasn't open mutual interest that concerned me. It was the closed interest on the streets, of homebound invitees.

I traipsed to a tramstop feeling eyes: the disinterest in his creased *Zeitung*; the same shirt I saw him in on Krausenstraße. To people-gaze, it's wiser to don warm goodwill than institutional chill, behind those October sunglasses.

And I'll vent now... retrospectively, that people were so awful. Sweeping our lives, there were thousands of others spotting vantage. It should have been a time of garden-fence rapprochement, but many were getting a footing. I say it, because I couldn't have dreamed such venality as we caught our breath.

I sat on a yellow sofa while he went to a bedroom and murmured, returning with food and vodka from his kitchen. "You're fleeing rats now, aren't you? Trustworthy as lice."

I was barely audible: "It was trust got us the lice."

"Oh, who could that refe--"

"Lice! You know, frostbite and lice... They get lively when you thaw, don't mind cold blood sausage. Lice, from the fucking basements. They speak Russian among themselves."

Vormelker took a while, let me swelter in my air. "We took you out of that." he held his tumbler but didn't drink it, turned to his book shelves. "And we're not remotely interested in whom *you* trust." His back didn't move. "You won't get home Günter."

"I have to," I was conscious how close I was, and also of my bloody collar; I didn't sit back. "My wife thinks I'm dead. I appreciate what you've done, Generál-leytenánt."

He turned back to a cabinet, saying nothing. A discourteous silence developed. "You heard what I said?"

He looked up to find me startled. I'd put too much bread and fisted pickles in my mouth and couldn't speak. I inclined my head with stretched cheeks.

"You'll never get home."

He watched me, blinking, while I governed the mouthful.

"They can't control food and housing because there is none. Turn away old people and babies. How welcome do you believe a strapping soldat is. But that's not what I'm talking about. I'm not talking about immediate crises." His eyes looked a bit fanatic. "I'm talking about investment."

I looked round his impressive rooms. Solid furniture, patterned wallpaper and a large radio. "Why the pursuit? The interest..."

"In you?"

I nodded.

"Plant 186." He raised his glass at me. "A survivor."

"I suppose."

"And your firm of course. Köhler & Bebel. You worked closely with Bielefeld university, and Aachen."

I was slack-jawed at his knowledge, his archive.

"The only way you stay is with my say so. If I place you west of Oder-Neisse, or over to Siberia, it's open-ended really..."

I said nothing.

"I have a proposal while the dust settles."

I nodded, and poured his vodka.

"A few weeks proper training. Certain techniques. Allowing you to move and transfer unhindered."

I shook my head in riddled confusion.

"Technical knowledge. We're rather buried in the nuclear question just now, but..." penny dropped, "...Your profile's satisfactory. Your history obviously isn't, but we'll remove that."

"What for?"

"State rebuilding. East Germany."

The vodka warmed my stomach and spread. "You mean eastern Germany."

"East Germany, though Koba expects to unify it."

I wondered his meaning, but probably just sat there, ogling. "Sleep on it Günter."

I was put in a comfortable room in a spartan corridor. Nice quilt. But I swirled, all I could do was ricochet thoughts: *does he know me?* ...then wonder about König, where he went after our beating. They must have left him in the street. A sleepless dawn grabbed me, broke Vormelker's spell. I'd eat breakfast and be gone.

In paisley gown that rippled sunshine he handed me coffee. I slurped through steam - wondering when pleasantries might kick off a required response.

And then I bust the silence. "I had a think..."

Vormelker nodded without interest.

"I appreciate all you've said but I have obligations."

He'd heard enough and turned for a copy of *Rzeczpospolita* on the table.

"That is, a family. I couldn't forgive myself if I abandoned them for personal gain."

"As you abandoned them for Hitler, and abandoned your division at Mamayev. I ought to say, I've not proposed you join security forces for personal gain."

"Yes, indeed. However--"

Vormelker's shoulders stifled a yawn.

"Well, where would I train?"

It must have already happened a while back, this Vormelker was just ornamental, my concierge. Any convictions I had were buried in Uralmash's snow and rust.

☆

A store opened on Kurfurstendamm with hosiery, and when RIAS coughed up I diverted to buy Ange stockings and a suspender belt. On presentation, she accepted with such awed gratitude she'd only wear them with socks, to stop her boots splitting them. And wouldn't let anyone, least me the benefactor, touch her legs.

"Falke's seen it?"

"Skim read."

"I haven't."

"You're not around."

"You're not here when I'm around. When do I see it?"

How could I explain? Otto must see it when it's right. I can show it to the pinko hedonists next door 'til the cows come home.

"It's about Uncle Joe and co., yes?"

"Not entirely. Yes."

"Don't you need a library?"

"I spend all day in libraries because as we know, books don't burn. Neither from bombs nor Nazis."

"Don't act the clown."

"I'm entitled." I huffed. "Anyway I used to read a lot, before Shouty Chaplin. I have a good memory."

"I h'yam eyxiled old Russian vooman, wriyting from h'memory. Thi harvest fayled thees year and Uncle Vladimir weel shur'ly starve. And h'yim with hees gout."

"That was abominable."

Otto snickered with a wheezy laugh, meaning he'd genuinely amused himself and his lungs weren't doing great.

"Can I read it?"

"It's a chapter and a half."

"If Falke can, I can."

"When it's ready."

"You don't hear my radio show, and I don't read your work."

"Darling," kid gloves required. "I've asked you three times to barter or rob a radio, and you'll see my efforts when they're polished."

"Hmmf."

"We're going out with them tonight. Be a sweetie-pops."

"Hmmf," he repeated, with a bright flick in his eyes.

I wanted to run a flying kick to his chest but sat on him instead. He was right: if I left him, which I wouldn't, what would I have? I shunted his murmuring face with mine and shut his stupid trap with my own.

"I'll join you later."

"What?"

"Hon, it's called Midnight Jazz Hour."

"Can't you pre-record it?"

"I'll ask. Join you when I'm done."

The silver Lisunov took off, climbing cloaks of Schönefeld rain. A suited fifty-something with a horseshoe pate smoked at the back as we bounced east. Until - in timeless compression and drifting with sweaty sleep - we were suddenly descending on Moscow.

Vnukovo passport control saw the NKVD stamp and syphoned me briskly. Outside the airport horseshoe followed on my heels and a driver so dense his seams complained ushered us to a Pobeda's door.

I didn't feel talkative. Horseshoe smoked. It was too late to get into the Lubyanka building, needing clearance at night.

This pristine city gleamed like terraced cake. Hitler never reached Moscow; Typhoon almost breached the north but got stuck in a spell so cold that grease froze. The driver handed us evening reading.

"It's general. I'm aware you're on different programs."

He threw us in the street where hotels poked. Adjutant Zetkin had supplied me a rouble roll.

Directive 00780: broaden the power of the Soviet authorities in SBZ to the full extent.

Comrade Bebel
Training in subsequent weeks will equip you to strengthen the influence and security of the Soviet Union in Germany through the Comintern / NKVD /GRU.

Your role
To liquidate new anti-Soviet organizations and groups that have emerged after Germany's capitulation. The following are the major tasks for which your basic training is intended:

1. Organization and administration of operative agent activity

2. Exposure and liquidation of spies, diversionists, terrorists, and enemy organizations and groups, including 'newly established' ones
3. Search of war criminals, political and war officials of the Third Reich
4. Exposure and demolition of illegal radio stations, stores of ammunition and such arsenal as illegal printing presses
5. Administration of work with the German prisoners of war in the SBZ.

I sat in my thin hotel in Kuznetsky Most: stained red walls and grimy sheets; the owner had left an icon of the Virgin Mary in a wall cabinet. Mary looked worn out.

I flipped pages, looking for an induction on architecture, technical dissemination, transfer of expertise, west German universities, anything but these instructions for pups with lolling tongues. A car picked me up in the dank and silent dawn; a time only for dustbins.

We study away from Lubyanka Square, far from the natives, at an old finishing school north of Bitsevski Forest.

I'm getting cold quakes about the Generál. At mess, pre-fabbed off from the beautiful cedar and beech, one of the cadets baldly stated: "He killed outside of wartime, you know, widowed a KriPo's wife."

I felt a slithering in my back, of time gone wonky. "He killed a polizei?"

The man nodded, assured over his moulded tray like the truest archive.

"Vormelker did."

Nodded again, soaking my interest.

"Why isn't he in jail?" I stopped my fork from scraping, so I missed no detail.

"Well," he finished a mouthful, savouring. "He was. Moabit Lehrter for trial, and got sprung. So the story goes."

The man beside him cut over, "That's wrong," and he too took a moment swallowing. I felt relief, it was wrong.

"You mean Moabit Remand, not Lehrter. That's where they await trial."

"Whichever, he got out. All over the papers. Vanished. Only he didn't quite, as you've gathered."

So I was about to launch a few facts that I knew, but kept my mouth shut. The story was badly skewed, and worse, it confirmed my fear: I wasn't going mad.

The Detlef I'd known was held in 1927 for killing the Chief of Neukölln, Kriminalinspector Gründgens. He was a minor (our paps refurbed his papa Albert's theatre). Albert Brüning was in trouble with gangsters over unpaid protection - you may've heard of the Hahn brothers? - and Gründgens' deputy gathered evidence for Detlef, with a view to prosecuting his senior. Detlef avoided the guillotine at majority on diminished responsibility. An orphan - his own ma and paps were slaughtered the prior year. Dets saw ugliness very early. I'd relate more but it's sliding out of view.

Chappie's maw continued anyway-- "Famous safebreaker." He was talking strong Swabian, his pale food rolling, finger joining his teeth to lever it. "Blowtorches."

My head spiralled. That safebreaker was Kapuze, a Robin Hood-style legend, cracking discount banks and distributing so well the Berlin Mayor made the KriPo drop everything to find him.

"How did Vormelker end up here?" I asked.

"Well that," --chewy Stuttgart kid reclined-- "is for your interpretation."

It was a bad time for anything to happen, let alone what arrived. I was peeling a sorry clementine with one hand, reading *Die Welt* - a rag the Yanks push from Hamburg. I thought it would cheer me but it doesn't: it's worse.

An article on repatriation and recompense, which according to the Bundestag was 'going OK'. At least, Jewish *Yekkes* were reporting thousands of decent awards from American loans with formal state apologies. And it mentioned the concerns - the clamour - from residual Roma in Berlin.

I felt carved out because this emptiness arrives, even if I've stuffed a day with rocks and baubles, gossip strained in soup, a sudden claw hits my stomach and it's not hunger - I get so unutterably sad. Like Time's on my shoulder, flashing her void. (I don't know what it was they took - some sense anything might be just, or... just again. They carved it from themselves and from us interns too. All I've kept is anger, not even fear as you can't have both together.)

That was when Gertrude's face poked in: "You left your letter this morning." --Waved it, as I was gazing like a bullfrog, and I opened the door-- "from Maria."

But its ink stamps weren't Maria's.

I tore it, read the official type and read it again, began to feel faint.

It was from the Federal Finance Ministry, stamped by the Society of Obstetricians. I'd an appointment at Fliedner. Don't laugh. Though we scarcely have a tin of peaches never mind a roof, Germany doggedly resumes service including gynaecology.

I was found from Maria's record, and told by pigeonhole to be at the klinik on 13th December. A state gynaecologist would be on premises.

I felt a cold, panicked wave wash over. In my head I saw slats, uniforms in frosted rubble and scarlet from windows - I looked round and gripped the chair. Like I'd been dreaming the war's end and woken in a Reich unchanged. I was terrified, really it was an hallucination. A thunderhead of despair outside the smeared window. But I read on with trembling hands. That the obstetrician would be on site, once and once only, for claims.

"Look at this," I shoved the letter under Otto's face walking straight into his stomach, as he hadn't actually stopped walking.

"Post? For you?" He'd had a few lunchtimers with Dwight. "I mean, for any of us."

"Hand-delivered you lunk."

He focused into the state stencils and wonky type. "Required examination..." He breathed heavily thinking, as I stood there still piercing his ribs.

We were in bad territory. Otto tended to heal to my wounds manually, not verbally. His palms said more at night than is mouth dared. Maybe denying, pushing out the intrusions on

Angela Schmidt kept the pair of us whole. I know he wanted that.

"Well, it's Fliedner," he finally said. "You trust Maria."

"Claims?" --I said to her when I breathlessly arrived in her lap, upending her spam croque monsieur.

"Sweetheart! Yes claims. Should we...?" Maria flicked her eyes back to a cubby hole with white stable doors and, feeding me actual tea, probed sheepishly about 'certain events' due to my 'previous status'.

"You don't need to be coy," I said. "Yes, I was. I have marks, and there was no other reason for me to be in that room. It was lead-lined. The desk I sat at had a hole in it."

"You must forgive me, for speculating on..."

"You're a darling," I said feeling numb, feeling the room retract.

"Why so glum?" she said. "I mean, it's a horrible thing to come to terms with, but you looked happy when you came in."

"What?"

"When you arrived. I explained the outlook, the recompense, and now you're a stormcloud."

I held her hand. "It's not what you think. I don't feel much for dropping kids, don't fret. It was a waste of Brack's time anyway, the damage was done in Hamburg. A kindly Jew got rid of my Lebensborn."

I left the klinik with little birds - a few thousand Deutsche Marks - flapping in mind. It was a foray really, a glimmer before the next decade, but I was to be there for 10am that Thursday. It wasn't that making me dizzy. I know what was.

There was a Romani relocation office squatting nearby, just two rooms in a building a block away. The only reason I knew was I'd seen a few unusual headscarves go in; bright above fabled eyes. I could ask, put in a verbal request, a paper docket, if they'd a pile for such things. It was a strange feeling, faint flames gusted by guilt...

I went to Klub Friedrich alone with Falke, Adolfa and Johann. A sedate underground cafe by day and come night, the front signage turned neon for a jazz sauna. Seemed Falke in his anchor-clanker's cap, peacoat and roll-up, ruled the roost. At least, Adolfa and Johann swooned in his Potemkin gas.

Otto said he'd join us after jazz hour, for the end of *The Holbein Players*' set.

Falke seemed to own dyed hair. Handsome with sparky eyes, he still believed revolution's endgame was no leaders or hierarchy; a cooperative sprawl. I mean we'd all hoped that but history pissed itself laughing.

He leant into himself, tobacco-tinged: "Nazism was a popular feeling Hitler tapped into as himself a failure. A way of blaming others."

"No it wasn't," I said, and got their hot pale faces back.

This club was a magnet for talkative politicos and of course... jazz, with Holbein on the piano and erect blonds on bass and drums. Falke was a Samizdat pamphleteer: rough-and-ready publishing and distribution. *Where the hell was Otto?*

"So what then, Angela?"

"Nazism was backed by tycoons terrified of socialism." I looked at my stolen wristwatch for the twentieth time and craned around. "If the Communists and SD had ignored Moscow, the left would've owned the Reichstag. And if they'd rallied a proper militia, not that ragtag RFB, we'd have a different story. The only popular Nazi feeling was with idiots who knew nothing and hoped for nothing."

"No popular feeling but won power? Miraculous."

"Hitler's installation was a sole gesture, by frail and clueless industrialists."

I was angry at Otto's no-show. I could hear my boots thumping, and the considered, hefty breathing of Falke beside me. He seemed to be forming something to say...

"Know your stuff, eh?" ...like an interrogative snow-plough.

"There's a lot of hours in the day."

"I have the demagoguery but my history's shaky."

Dema-fucking-goguerie?

"Facts fuel polemic." I could hear that my wig was flipping. "Without those, you're no more than a tramp shouting in the street."

I realised I now looked like a tramp shouting in the street. Berlin, slush white and black with cleared snow and shiny, baby-shit coloured cars. *Where are you, my lean and lanky lover?*

"You and I should collaborate."

"In the Vichy sense?"

"A history of socialism in Germany."

I shook my head. "Dull, more mileage in the USSR."

"Well... either way, we should collaborate."

I stopped, looked at Falke. His eyes were coal-black, his face rock-pooled. His brows and hair bounced thickly like Samuel Beckett: an indignant raptor peering at me. "I'll think about it."

A hand reached out to mine as I was turning. *Whoa!*

"Falke, I think you met Otto remember? He fixed your wall? Got you a typewriter. You want to redistribute flesh as well as wealth?"

"Come on, we have so much to offer."

"The trains run now. Try working."

I carried on walking and the buildings stayed put; no earthquake in East Berlin, the slush roads still shining.

We walk on coffee soil, our feet blue while a thick black sky creaks in the canopy. I've my dog-eared reading in hand, brow-buried, summer dress damp from my drying costume.

You listen from up ahead (always ahead, emptying your head) as my plain red Hamburg mouth reads to the Boizenburg trees. Rain begins, spattering high. I squint for text. Evening creeps between trunks but there's no fear yet; fear is being conceived in homes and Semite cartoons and concocted uniforms; for now there's just Germany, our amphitheatre.

"Ow!" I push you up against rough bark, drop Trotsky's Writings '36-37.

You're all humid and fresh from the swim; your mapped back restless snakes. I'm all bone and introspection. You pull my wet orange costume from my arse and snap it on my bum.

"Assault," I shout and mount. The rain takes a while to leak down, the heavier for it.

Maybe apprehension is the ghost of coming events. Hovering over ground we'll pass in dark times, the future taps us and says look out.

☆

I was taking a leak in Klub Friedrich. Ange was out on the sticky table with the Pinko Pack. I looked up and saw, two urinals along, the comrade of blown-apart Kostya. The serious one.

He'd long noticed me.

I put it away and went to wash. As he arrived I looked up and met his eye. "Sorry about your comrade."

It was insincere, I wasn't, but I sensed a chink in this man's armour: maybe in his immobile face a disapproval of everything.

He gave a shrug, as though blanking me out. But then said: "He was a good man..."

Couldn't agree with that.

"...once," --in epilogue.

Come on Otto, make the effort: "I suppose war changes friendships."

The dour Red looked at me in the mirror. He was certainly calm in his unknowable world. He turned. "We knew each other since three years old."

"But the other day..." I floundered a bit, vanquished at a latrine. "The day he... I mean--"

"You must understand, his wife and child were slaughtered. The battalion in his village in east Ukraine were ordered to take no prisoners, shoot all inhabitants and keep moving. What do you say to that?"

I shrugged, nervously.

"Don't be scared. I cannot justify our activities either."

I realised they wanted home. To see patchwork cloud in a huge sky. One so vast the cloud gets lost.

"You and I weren't built for politics, eh?"

"And not war. I am a painter."

"I'm a DJ."

He inclined his head.

"I play jazz records."

"Aahh," he nodded studiously. "Anton."

"Otto."

I'd a mauve, gashed forehead running down my right cheek. Ange still bore scratches and a scar from temple to hair. Seeing me leaving the toilet talking to the rape gang, you may understand she wasn't happy.

"The hell was that?" She must've been watching the toilet door, bored by a diatribe on Soviet literature now swiftly closing.

"Was what?"

"Him?"

"He's called Anton."

"First name terms? Jesus."

"Wait Hon."

My departing girlfriend was a whirlwind. I headed after her and only caught her arm on Friedrich and Mohren where street signs were comprehensive, signifying nothing in a wet wreck.

"Don't touch me."

"What do we actually know about Anton?"

She flashed like lightning. "That he would turn a blind eye."

"And you've never been on foreign soil, among the enemy, for years."

"Good thing you weren't conscripted."

"He didn't condone it."

"A blind eye is the same."

"It's not the same, Ange. It just isn't."

"That tells me a lot about you."

RIAS was housed in a stark, roast-beef building on Winterfeldtstraße; the old Reichspost telephone exchange. The big cheese under the US Information Control Division (all suited, smileless), was one Hans Rosenthaal.

This legendary Hebrew escaped as an orphan the last death trains and then pissed off the Reds at Berliner Rundfunk, moving over to RIAS.

> "Willkommen beim Rundfunk im Amerikanischen Sektor, Jazz Stunde! I'm your host Otto and we played in with the original French 'Autumn Leaves'. And now, guys and gals for your listening pleasure, it's 'On Green Dolphin Street'."

I sat in my tiny room, shellac and vinyl racked, the microphone in front of me, the metal-framed window closed against the cold. I'd sit back feet akimbo while the record played, or dance with an old jumper left in the room, pretending it was Ange, careful not to jog the needle.

Returning one evening to drop off borrowed records, join Ange and the pinko triage at Klub Friedrich, I swore I saw a familiar face opposite our tenement, but it pulled down a trilby quickly and walked the other way.

The trouble with lacunae'd adulthood is memory games. Everything's out of place and your life is measured in sections. Growing up happens behind your back, and any whiff of recognition may be deceit.

But if any authority found our tenement interesting they were wrong: it was all Bolshies except me.

I dropped the bag and looked at my watch. Ten-minute nap. I came around with a bleary blink and sigh two hours later. "Bugger."

The ensemble cast of this dusty tenement were walking home loud and drunk down the corridor.

I received aerospace secrets, you see? I met Schiller at Friedrichstraße, which became a customary exchange point, manually or via lockers, or the railworkers' entrance.

"Find somewhere quiet?"

"No need. Just take it." He was proferring a briefcase.

"And payment?"

"Specification of the Sea Fury with Bristol Centaurus reciprocating. Automated cooling system. A fast and agile plane just entered service. And there's a little something tucked in. Bounty. I was quoted a value-based fee."

"That's British."

"Problem? A lot of countries are buying them."

"Russia has a MIG jet."

"Wait until your Machine Building technos see the gift inside."

"Hmm." I wasn't convinced but what did I know? I wasn't the evaluator.

"My fee?"

"Three thousand Reichsma..."

"Dollars. I'm Yank-side."

"Three thousand Reichsmarks. If the information's... progressive... we can top it up."

"Sheesh. I risk it all for a couple of tubs of butter."

"Mmm." I had rolls in my pocket, a thousand a piece. I handed them one by one, conscious we were in the corner of a concourse but agent Schiller seemed cavalier.

I've had to stop nagging the Vormelker story; things got busy and I'm not clear the NKVD like you investigating your boss (though it may be encouraged.) I never saw the Bitsevski cadet again, and his source material stank anyway. What rattles me is: an old school tie, some kind of corner man, would be useful now. I'm unbalanced, my nethers in a post-Hiroshima easterly. But it's the wrong school tie! I fall asleep with fake memories.

We walked under trees south-east of Berlin in May, round inlets and leisure platforms, until dappled grass became the sand hugging Little Müggelsee.

Water always excited Ange. "I'm going to freshen up."

"Do. You stink old girl."

No boats and few people. A stalwart old swimmer with bronze back, nutty head and silver ear-curtains (and of course, gold swimming briefs), limped to the water's edge. She punched me and ran into the muddy shallows.

"Come on you yob, you Westerner," she shouted, "you silly townie..." she laughed as she lay in the water, "...pseudo Yank."

I took my trousers off. "Jazz doesn't make me a Yank."

"Come on. Are you scared of water? Who's afraid of water?"

Why so flippant with a dark place? Angie's once hard wiring had somehow been knocked I thought, rerouted, made fragile as voltages sparked new neurones. Her moods were so changeable, oddities from her mouth. I couldn't settle around her like you can't when kids run around a vase. I was finding my old self, she seemed eager to lose hers.

"Get in!"

"Yes," I trudged down the sand into mud, but she'd backstruck as far and fast as she could.

I finally caught her in the green depths with a manic expression on her face; I didn't want to just grab her so bobbed, looking.

"Are you a buoy?"

"You're being weird."

"Sometimes…" she dipped vertical. "I don't think I control my body. Other people want it, and I don't know what the thing is. I don't know who owns it. I'd give it away permanently if I could."

"How would you swim?" I asked. But she'd somehow made me redundant, no value in my hands.

The lake was calm under blue, but gusts occasionally whipped the surface. She sounded schizo. When she talked of having no consent with her own body it reminded me of Leo, saviour and water counsellor. She missed him, I missed him, and I missed her when she missed him.

"Everything was taken but we're OK. We're rubble and dust," I said. "One day we'll afford what we need, dapper duds and chintzy cocktails." I gave an encouraging smile. "You've given up on your body for a life of the mind anyway. Things will improve."

"People said it in 1933. Things will improve. How does anyone know?"

"Did anything… happen to you at Uckermark?"

She flung her head in a spraying negative.

"Ravensbrück? The hospital? I've seen Red vengeance."

"Almost. It was narrowly averted."

"Tell me."

"I am."

"Not really, you're throwing clues. We used to--"

"What?"

"I've trusted in us for years… from far away."

"Shall we swim?" She did anyway. Headed off to the distant bank. I watched her smash the lake in anger or athleticism; the ivory back and tar hair, and I followed. She came up gasping in the roots and mud of trees and I arrived, sitting beside.

I panted, exhausted. "We're not so nourished now."

"I'm too thin?"

I nodded back to the beach, three hundred yards away. Sun set, and as though the true companion of our lives, clouds heaped at our destination. "Come on."

She lay in shallow water and nodded. A few feet in, she said: "Remember when I lost my knickers in Außenalster?"

I laughed a mouth of water, went vertical to cough it away. "Of course... A most indelible memory. We'll dredge them out one day."

She caught me nervously as I tried to start swimming, put her arms round my neck. Schizo. Her wet manic mouth pushed my ear. "Don't you feel like nothing's the same?"

"We're making headway."

She wrapped her shoulders round. Only we started to sink in that arrangement; with all the munitions shavings our lungs no longer buoyant perhaps. "Come on."

We lay on sand, our costumes caked and sagging. Elbows stuck in the grain I muttered, "What's changed? Apart from a return to feudalism?"

The nutty brown man was swimming far and long.

"We've grown up, haven't we," Ange said quietly. "Who'd have thought adulthood would be.... wreckage. That summer of thirty-nine, though everything went dark, it was the happiest time of my life. It's all gone."

"We're dealing with the wreckage."

"I'll buy you a guitar."

"With what?"

She dropped her face in arms and sand. Wrong words. We got a tram back.

I looked through the Hawker Fury diagrams, but couldn't make head or tail so took it to the Ministry, and my official handler now, the Generál.

"…Günter, are you retarded? If it's in production and sale, it's no use."

"There's something special inside, which the techies will like. I couldn't make much of the diagrams."

He was incredulous. "You're an architect man! Don't you stare at this stuff all day?"

"That's largely static engineering, with large print."

"So how do you set a fee?" He started sliding the diagrams on his desk, peering closely. "I don't want hand-me-downs. Give me prototypes. Design and development. You paid three thousand Reichsmarks for a Hawker spec that's on the market…"

"And he wants payment in dollars."

"Well he's not getting it." Vormelker carried on examining the diagrams. "The engine is quite advanced. The electronics."

"I'm a handler not an evaluator," I said quietly.

"Oh hang on, what's this," he murmured. A diagram took his interest. "Armstrong Siddeley ASSn. Snarler?" He pulled a magnifying glass from a desk drawer, and peered at the tiny print. "Turbojet… liquid oxygen-fuelled…1,350–2,350 lbf thrust… For provisional testing in the P.1040 Seahawk. Jackpot! I take back retarded."

"Thank you sir."

"Actually I don't." He picked up the jet diagram, "How could this..." he then picked up a prop-engined Fury photo, "fit inside this?"

"Sir, the exchange was at a crowded station. I said there'd be an extra, took it blind. Also..." I added weakly, "are there any spare magnifying glasses around the building?"

"You need to know what you're buying."

"I'll train, with the eggheads."

"Günter the blind handler." He rubbed his forehead, standing up. "I was intrigued at your recruitment..." he turned away. "...given your background."

"Wehrmacht?"

He strolled to the window. "Interesting family."

The fading ghosts returned. I'd to remind myself all he knew came from folders-- "Three generations of architects. Yes I suppose."

"And dissidents, Otto and Angela. Active young dilettantes aren't they."

I went warm, then cold. "They're alive?"

"You didn't know? Are you a sociopath too?"

"I assumed my wife survived, our house was far from the bombing paths. And Otto... well I thought it possible."

"Well now you know." He continued scrutinising me like an agar plate.

I was badly conflicted. Of course I hoped Otto and Angela survived the camps, the bombs, the marches, but this sinister knowledge base, whatever he tapped, was shocking in such a dismantled Europe, this false shadow before me....

"Don't look like that Günter. Background checks... Ability to be compromised in the field..."

"I don't think a man's family..."

He squinted. "Yes? You don't think a man's family...?"

Don't go believing, Otto, my affections are frivolous. Don't go believing I willed some affair. Don't go thinking, and then overdrinking, I long for your tread on the stair.

I was as surprised as you were: laying on the collapsed sofa and hearing a soft tapping. Thought it the wind. Again, and I leant forward and saw two shadows under the door. I got up and opened to Adolfa.

She never spoke when we were out. Johann often punctuated Falke's paragraphs with dim, druggy agreement but she was a shrew (no that's unfair, still waters run deep. Adolfa was the stillest water).

"Hello," I said, not knowing what to employ.

"You OK?"

"Yeah, fine."

"I know Falke makes people's blood boil." She talked quietly, beautiful orange strands of hair brushed from her face like stray sunlight.

I smiled. "Come in. Can't offer much except Otto's vodka."

"That'll do," she said. "And you?"

"Sure. I'm fine."

There was a long silence. I considered Adolfa - which I'd not - and filled the silence with: "What are your plans in the new world?"

She shrugged. "I don't know what I'd be good at."

"Come on," I said, "We all have aptitudes." But I didn't like the alto in my voice; a bit menopausal at twenty four.

"I read your manuscript. Well, what's written anyway."

My heart plunges when someone says that. "Any good?"

"Oracular." I offered her neat vodka and the collapsed sofa.

"Oracles see the future. I watch the past."

"Then you're an historical oracle."

"It rhymes." We sat.

The silence was disconcerting, but then it all settled bar her blue eyes, darting and flicking my face.

Falke loaded his player next door with scratchy Robert Johnson. I rolled my eyes: nobody'd call that wailing pleasurable except Otto.

She looked like I imagined Vermont in watercolour. It dawned on me what was happening. Adolfa'd plucked some courage.

Strange that scenery comes alive - I spent three years in a camp of beauties and nothing Sapphic ever arose. Not quite true, I dreamt of Berta once - a flautist from Königsberg two buks away, her golden face tweaked with giggles. It roused me to a state; you know when you wake from a dream and nothing occurred, but it pulsed the prospect? Only for reality to crash back; rollcall, lice, the card-game of death. But it was a dream, I take no responsibility (just obeying orders).

Now I felt something, a tingling and no ordinance. She was terminally shy and I took the initiative.

"So Adolfa..." I reached out a hand for her thigh. "What can I do for you?"

She leapt like a burning vole. "Slow down," I yelped, laughing in spite of myself.

I buzzed in the alley, among the plaque of companies. Hartmann & Schwartz was 'incorporated' under Goldfarb Verlag.

"Yes?"

"I was hoping to speak to Herr Hartmann or Herr Schwartz," I said.

"I'm Michael Hartmann."

"It's about a book."

"Good. We don't sell fish."

I giggled, with my manuscript poking out of my bag. "Sir, I wondered if I may speak to you about my book. It's probably controversial, but accurate."

There was no reply. Heavy breath as though pondering ten things he should be doing rather than talking to me. "How controversial? Like, Hitler was misunderstood? I'm supposed to be at a meeting. I haven't long."

I gabbled. "The early, brutal and false lives of Stalin's expropriators. The Outfit."

Silence. Then, "Oh."

"It was all researched. But written from memory. I have no books at present, they were destroyed in Hamburg."

"Yes yes, of course. Right... I'll pop down."

After a while there was a clumping on the stairs. The door opened, and a fat tramp stared at me. At least, he must sleep there and ignore mirrors. He eyed me up and down. He had curly hair and a fat hooter, his messy shirt trying to escape him by all means.

116

"Come in then," he held the door which slammed shut behind me as if usually slicing people in half.

I followed his interminable tracks up the narrow stairs. We entered the untidiest shithole in all Berlin. It wasn't dirty, just a man living inside paper, unremoved brick and plaster... and foil handout trays from the queues.

"So, quick rundown, very quick." He pointed to a seat. Then removed a spiral sheaf of papers and pointed again.

"It's the origins of Soviet terror. Unlike Trotsky, I'm arguing Bolshevism and the stated belief in the worker and peasant were ego-driven mania from the start, a cloak of respectability for murder and power-grabbing."

"I see. Do you have it? You don't look like a radical." He looked again. "Actually you do."

"I study history."

"Where?"

"I did once," a sigh flapped out of me, "voraciously."

"Is your argument sustained? Coherent?" He caught the script sticking out of my bag, checked his watch. "I'll read three pages now and you leave it. I've got about five minutes until I'm irresponsibly late."

I handed it and he did as bid. For such a large man, he pirouetted precisely around the office, producing two glasses and a bottle of whisky from a cabinet, pouring each without looking up from the script. "Drink, please. What's your name?"

I didn't want to at this hour, it was neat whisky, but did. "Angela Schmidt."

He read fast, judging by his eyes. "Well it's not the usual disgruntled tosh. I like the anecdotes. Maybe you have something. Will you leave it?"

That thought made me nervous. "I suppose."

"I really have to go."

"OK."

He fully took in my attire. "Are those army boots?"

I couldn't traipse Berlin in reclaimed sandals, so I'd put on a dress and the same boots I stole from the dead Hitler Youth. (We were still due our coupons for one pair of shoes every fifteen years.) I flushed. "We're struggling a little."

"Like the city herself. So is it finished?"

"Nowhere near."

"I'll finish this tonight. I'm meeting a friend at Der Tagesspiegel Friday. If it's all high quality I could suggest serialising. The Americans can't bludgeon Uncle Joe, not with things so tense but... well, Germans can. You follow?"

I nodded, a bit fluttery. He ushered me out. We clumped down the stairs again, my boots as heavy as his belly.

"Thanks for this. I like propaganda when it's factually accurate. Where are you based?"

"Me and my boyfriend are in the Russian sector, behind Leipziger Straße. He works over at RIAS," I said, noticing a little pride in my voice.

"Yank?"

"German jazz nut."

"Good man. You're both from Hamburg?"

"Yes. We took a few years off, camping trips to Ravensbrück and Moringen."

He shook his head sadly. We were back in the alley. He had a sudden merry twinkle. "Were you... swing kids? All grown up now."

I nodded. "Not without trauma."

"You only?" He'd a slightly Jewish lilt. He turned left, me right. "A pleasure," he smiled and bustled speedily away. "How will I contact you?"

"Uhh, there's a phone in our tenement. I should have taken the number, I'll drop it by."

I awoke clutching Otto and sweating - gasping - my dream stuck to the inside of my head. Papa had the same pursed mouth as when I dropped out of Confirmation, only now those quiet, wry lips confronted a sturmführer demanding religious tomes from his library, for the pile and the petrol.

It was more an experience of the dead alive than a dream.

The ruins of Hamburg were as now but the sturmführer was a corpse, his face exploded, leaving mandrils of flesh on the white and crimson jaw like a decayed manta ray. Books burned behind his long coat. I stood behind, telling Papa I was an atheist, and the skull-flapping troop grinned and poked him with a gun muzzle.

"Just dreams, Hon," Otto stroked my soaked forehead. He did calm me but... we're alone behind our eyelids and the dream was a watermark on Ots' face.

I know you think me callous. I don't speak of my parents. But I can't; what love I have left for them is non-verbal.

☆

Getting Otto out of Hamburg was hell. And it may seem strange to return - assaulted by the European diaspora - and not confront anything.

Heading over bricks in Hamburg-Eppendorf, I think I knew Otto was alive; hallucinating, but the hospital felt like a terminus. I saw his back, very still by his mother, and he became as solid as I was wraithlike. He must've known too, turned on my noiseless approach and sank his forehead in my stomach as if in apology. When we embraced we were more flimsy than we'd been. It made Otto laugh in a bark. Outside, beyond the clip and hush our feet seemed headed for Stadtpark Bäderland.

He didn't know what to say, like we didn't know each other again, courteous. He lifted my hands, squeezed them and kept hold of my back as if steering me from menace. All the way here I rehearsed what to say, my laceration of all that'd been plus the joy, but it got stuck. "You look older," --my mouth stumbled at.

"You're tireder," --he said. "You know we've been apart longer than together?"

It was ridiculous, we were foxed. My letters seemed those of an adolescent seeing Otto, embarrassed in the world. No pencil stubs or scraps, no horror, just detritus and clear sky. No family - *we,* he and I, were family.

He stopped suddenly on Jungfernstieg, took my shoulders and turned me at the light - looked me over as if for a watermark, cried a little. We started speaking but didn't really finish.

"What would you say?" was my gambit, on Binnenalster's promenade, the shore buckled like Thor'd hammered the thing. Further up where it opened, the sun was trying to get us.

"We said we'd weather it. We did that." He was tamping a ropey woman's scarf he'd found and obviously liked, but saw my arms. "Oh honey, what was that about blood. Did they instruct you in auto-punishing?"

"There was good reason. Why I'm here in fact, so don't judge after three years absence. Please."

"This freedom's queer, of a sudden. Like cattle with the barn door open, half of them probably stay put."

"Probably, I've had no time to think. You were closer to home."

His brow fell. "It hits me when I see the filthy queues, the trails. I mean six years." He thumbed over his shoulder, at the world. "Them, everything got an armband and everything got burned. It was like a cartoon in Moringen, dreaming what was out here, you know? When I saw Hannover it properly whacked me like a truck. Someone lost their marbles on this scale."

"It's not so easy, I thought I'd flood with happiness," I took his fidgety hand. "We were shielded, v-violated but shielded." I cleared my throat to explain that stutter.

And it was buried - I don't know if *v-violated* was the end of a conversation or should've started it, but we're faulty triggers.

"What about the docks?"

"What about them?"

"Where your father died. We'll do a private ceremony under the brick piles and get out of Hamburg."

121

I knew why Otto was quiet: abandoning bodies. The nurse at Eppendorf had explained there weren't many undertakers and the graveyards bursting. Those still existent might be busy.

Hospital orderlies were taking corpses to marked but makeshift graves out of town, but Otto wouldn't accept it. The nurse suggested a proper burial might be done in years to come.

"We could go to Ohlsdorf cemetery. They're expanding it."

"It'd take weeks to ever find her."

"Well, we have weeks."

"We don't. We have what we have."

I felt for Otto, truly. He'd at least found his mother and maybe that's better: a physical goodbye.

"We'll just do what we can. Go to the docks. I'll say a prayer for mine, you can whistle Dixie for yours. We'll hang our heads, cross our breasts, and leave."

"And the land?"

"Yes?"

"We have the deeds."

"Where did your father keep the deeds?"

He sunk. My attitude baffled the great lunk, his brow vexed and face dark, but Germany felt like hot coals - we'd to move.

"Or maybe visit city hall and demand they retrieve your deeds from the wreckage, right now?"

"Just leave?"

I'd asked after Eugen and Dorle Schmidt at the hospital, briefly dismissing a Eugen namesake as not my Paps. I didn't want to revisit my street, given Otto'd scoured my house for life and found nothing. If he couldn't, I couldn't. And I wasn't hanging around months for sprouting bureaucrats to stamp 'presumed dead' on paper.

Facing my shortcomings as a daughter was the last thing in mind. The bulldozers were coming, trains were starting to function.

"What should we do?" I said. "We didn't ask for Adolf and firebombing... Treated like vermin in our own country. We survived for what it's worth, and we'll start again in this shithole."

"What happened to self-harming?"

"Oh." I glowered at him, quite ready to slap that stupid face. "That's low."

"I just mean your tune's changed."

Now we sat on shovelled brick in St Pauli. Autumn had lowered the temperature and the trees lost their leaves. He'd come to the destroyed cafe district on a futile homing instinct. To find previous haunts.

"So where? Where do we start?"

"I have paperwork."

"Meaning?"

"There's a record of my mental health in an East Berlin clinic."

"If that still exists," Otto became sullen.

"Nurse Wagner promised me a roof."

"If she still exists."

The time had come. I'd had days of this. I held Otto's chin in my hand, raised his head lovingly and slapped his face. He looked at me like I was a psychopath. Barely jolted. Just stared with an odd expression and said: "I'm no stranger to violence, Hon."

"Domestic or survival?"

Otto blinked slowly. He looked at those few embattled civilians who'd tried to get cars working, now negotiating messy streets. He sighed. I squeezed his long silly leg. "That was for fatalism... and dredging up self-harm."

"What will we do?"

"The usual. Get the plate spins up. Maybe open a shop. I'll write a book. We'll rob, steal and get a roof. We'll visit the lakes. Hunger hasn't killed us."

"Berlin you say... You'd need a typewriter."

"Somewhere eastside. Wherever I get accommodation, but near Müggelsee."

"OK," Otto had apparently agreed.

"Let's go to the docks."

We'd been slumming in Stadtdeich's warehouses. Otto didn't want to go to another displacement camp or be around orphans. Next morning he said 'I need to do something,' and was gone, returning with a ripped and bloody sleeve, a gash in his arm and an engraved silver box.

At Hamburg station my bleary eyes saw something truly monstrous - perhaps another orphan - his churned-cream face purposeful, his suitcases lugged by that barrel torso like it was no holiday. Reinhard Inquart. He had plans not involving stumpy Hamburg either.

I was about to point him out to Otto but now wasn't the time for clashing antlers and far worse.

You see I felt nothing. Surrender had reduced us - our petty Reich, ambitions and bombs - to naughty children; albeit

Titan ones of steel and black fumes and ruin. Children of gods run riot.

Unaware of our presence, Reinhard got on our train to Berlin. Hamburgers parentless all: the dead city. We were all sinking into the woodwork again but some - Reinhard, rising - had showed such miserably brutality I didn't see how they could.

Berlin didn't inspire on arrival: Lehrter station had become a refuge for the limbless and homeless; and you can imagine the oozing state of those.

Dreams usually leave within ten minutes, but my flap-jawed sturmführer stayed for days, overlaying the ghostly structures under harsh sunlight.

I walked on Krausenstraße a little afraid, joined Leipziger, and wondered if Reinhard Inquart had simply made a train connection to more fascist places - Franco's realm - or if he now slunk around this charred sink.

I woke late with Ange gone. Heard her saying hello to Adolfa across the way. She spoke for a while, but I never heard much response from Adolfa; she's so timid. She's also a dish, in a translucent way.

"What's that?" I asked, frowning, still not quite out of bed.

"A newspaper."

"Squandering our coupons?"

"I bartered bread for it, cut rate with a toothless woman. How she'd eat stale bread I've no idea."

"In soup. Give it here then, doll. You've no time to sit reading the news. The place needs a clean."

"Go find food, hunter-gatherer."

We reached a compromise. She tore the paper in half at the centre pages. She kept the back, I took the front. *Der Tagesspiegel*.

We sat silent for an hour. Engrossed in the Czechoslovakian coup I forgot where I was, spirited back to Sundays in Hamburg. Just a sense of Ange's quiet immersion in the room. When I'd finished I was disorientated looking up, expecting the big bay window and a whiff of Sunday roast.

"Stalin and Truman are getting frisky."

"Mmm?" she murmured.

"Stalin backed the KSČ and now the Bizone wants a West German state."

"Mm-hm," It was musical agreement, to shut me up or allow me to drone on, either was fine.

"West Germany... how the hell would that work? What about Berlin?"

She murmured, "How can that work, darling? Without a conflict..."

"What you reading?"

"The long-form piece. They serialise them. This one's about Tito's Yugoslavia."

"Oh," I couldn't stifle a yawn, but Ange held it up. Marshall Tito looked more like Göring than Göring did.

Clackity-clack..... Clack. Silence. Clack clack, clackity clack. No point trying to sleep and it was mid-morning anyway. I got up, padded to Ange, laid hands on her shoulders, but she turned as though to block my eyes from the page.

"How's it going?"

"Slow." Ange's eyes looked at me but were somewhere else.

"I'll get out of your hair."

"No. I like it when you're here."

Well that's all well and good but you're away in Georgia with gangsters with huge moustaches.

"Gonna head to Kleiner Tiergarten. It's a nice day and there's a market. Then RIAS. "

She sulked. "We need joint hobbies."

"If you let me see your damned script, that's a joint hobby. I'll probably go over to the Ballhaus Berlins after RIAS. It would be great if you came over. It's not exactly hard-bop and it's rammed with Yanks, but..."

"Beuugh!" she said. Meaning, I suppose, she'd no desire to hang out with off-duty GIs.

Otto'd be at the Berlin Ballroom till all hours; he'd become a Yank German, boozing heavy, wayward and male.

"Will you come here, beautiful, don't lunge." She was brattish and untalkative, gave off heat only. My god why was this so anonymous; we'd never exchanged a word, and weren't now. My hand in the warm dip of her fatigues, I wondered what I might be.

For the record she's strawberry blonde, taller than me but more transparent, more bowed, like a willow on a bank. Me I know I'm high-def, high contrast. She needs certain lights to make her real. Behind her copper hair her shy smile; under her garments, freckles. A little explosion was in me.

We lay in mine and Otto's nest; our badger warren of cushions and sheets. Thrills still coursed and Adolfa's hand rested. It was a risk.

Otto's recent form brought him home around two a.m. on average, and it was long after one.

"Hon," I said, not really wanting her to leave. "Do you think we should break up the party?"

She leant her face on a skinny shoulder with strawberry fronds. So strange. Having dismissed Adolfa as an accessory in Falke's triage, she was captivating. The darting eyes, the impossibly straight nose, the freckled brow, the ruby bracket lips.

"Otto'll be home."

"Men like this, don't they?"

"You tell me, you're in the menage."

She huffed.

"Actually, I don't think Otto would like this."

"What about tomorrow?"

"What about it?"

"I want to see you often. Oftener than often."

"You took me by surprise. Shall we see how the days pan out?"

She left not a moment too soon. I heard questioning voices next door and Otto's approach.

I didn't feel guilty - it was just free pleasure in the long, ruined day. I dreamed of her as drunk Otto snored. Can you desire several people at once? One the gangly pragmatist in your life, another a memory, the last a new idea?

As dawn slowed Otto's snoring to normal breath, I held him like a warm carcass; my stranger my intimate. I fell asleep again and woke up randy, sliding over.

Otto was going to meet me and the pinkos, but the wretched boy fell asleep again, awaking when I slammed the door at dawn, clutching the first edition of Der Tagesspiegel.

He rubbed his eyes. "I'm sorry."

I felt waspish. "In your absence someone might snap me up."

"Who?"

"Guess."

"Christ, are they some weird cult?"

"You'd know. If you were here."

"I want us to move west."

"Because of the competition?" I grinned. "A commie with dyed hair? Life's cheap here."

"Only because I'm earning."

"Oh. I'm not working, not working in this twilight half-world of brick dust."

"You can't have it both ways. You moved me remember, and I'm working. Hon, if we don't move soon everything'll be rebuilt and cost money. You dig that? You should see Charlottenburg. It's coming on."

"I like it here."

"And I like less hot air and more home furnishings. That cretin Trotsky next door..." --he must be raising his voice in case he was in-- "Ungrateful prick!"

"Stop it!"

"No."

I slapped down the newspaper, opened it towards the back where the leaders were, and pointed. "There. Stalin: Deconstructing The Myth."

Otto, in fairness, did properly shut up. He looked at the article, the base with a name that was nearly mine; advised to change it.

I padded to the clothes rack Otto'd erected from table splinters and bent nails for hooks. I undressed.

He lit an extra candle (itself a plaudit) and started reading. Pulled a Lucky Strike unconsciously from its carton. After a moment he whistled in his teeth. "Hon... this is alright."

"Just that?"

"You might want the world's review rather than mine. That's who saw it first."

Oh Otto. I stood there in a vest grubby as a mechanic's. I'd done wrong I knew. But I was his equal now, at pride's expense.

"Go get some of Falke's booze and we'll go to bed. I don't care about the article."

"If you don't care, why couldn't I read it?"

He stared at me like one of those Afghan hounds; long and sleek with melancholy eyes. He got up and went next door. I heard laughter and conversation for ten minutes. Thought I heard my name. And Otto returned with a clear spirit whose ingredients - once the heat poisoned our stomachs - we neither dared question.

"Lakes tomorrow?"

"Sure."

When we were done, I lay staring up in achievement: payment. I thought our silence was conjoined like sentience, but when I murmured, "Just wanted some respect with the love," I heard the flap of nostrils, the drunk throat snoring, and felt angry.

My armour, my custodian; my dopey man. I watched his eyelids twitch now, some livid dream basted in Falke's illegal brew. I touched his face. Loverbird; peregrine. Mainsail and dorsal.

I'd buy a guitar with next instalment's money; cheap and shit or not, it would be boxy like he liked it.

Sliding my hand over Ange's stomach she screamed and walloped my face.

"Fuck!" I yelled.

"Bastard." She scrambled from the bed.

"Eh?"

She pushed hair from her brow and scrubbed her face, silent for a moment. But the silence seemed to pupate, emerging more peaceably. "Don't do that when I'm asleep."

"What's got into you."

Ange was now aware of herself. "Nothing. Dreaming."

"One hell of a dream," I slid my painful jaw from side to side. "Hon?" I added, a bit plaintive.

"You're the only man touches me so be grateful. Don't ever do that when I'm sleeping. Please."

"Sure Hon, but..."

"What? What but? I have rights, no?"

Awake or not, some memory moved her face like electricity. The twitch of sleep-circuitry.

"This is new." It was my turn to rub my face, in bewildered ignorance. "I mean it's all new. You've never--"

"Stop it."

"Have I done something?"

She shook her head, a little childish and chin lowering.

"We'll discuss it in daylight," I turned over to brush it all away, but I stared in the darkness, my jawbone mildly ringing. "I'll stay well away."

"Don't," her hand invaded my rights by grasping my shoulder.

"Just when I'm asleep. Sleep's vulnerable, isn't it."

"Apparently."

And what would I say? That they burnt it out?

Otto wasn't asleep, I sensed it. Stewing in the dark, browned off and drifting irrevocably. After maybe an hour I said: "Hon?"

"Mm."

"Did you ever fill in any forms? In a room."

"Constant."

"At Moringen. A special room."

"They were all purpose-built."

"You were ineducable. What triangle did you get?"

"What is this Hon. You know I'm ineducable. I'm the last rebel." Though sleepless, Otto sounded sleepy.

"Glass booths. Maybe not glass, maybe tougher. Lead-lined."

There was a long silence. "Oh that. No. I think I was earmarked but it never happened. And it wasn't just men you know. You were lucky."

Lucky. I slipped out of bed and got some milk, sat at the desk looking at the black, wherein a stupid bird sang too early. My glass raised to my reflection. *Chin chin, old girl. Lucky girl.*

"I thought you were a Marxist."

"I'm increasingly an anarchist, bidding the left farewell. I don't believe any ideology can work now except none at all."

Oh how fascinating. How whimsical.

I should really head west when Otto's done at RIAS. He thinks I've formed a clique on Friedrichstraße; a cafe society where radical ideas curl in smoke. I haven't and they don't.

Falke, Johann and Adolfa sat with me at the table, Falke's dank rollup attached to his lip, his fishy cap askew, waxing about anarchy since socialism'd gone mainstream. Adolfa occasionally shot me a smile.

I said: "Of course it can. Capitalism, Fascism, Islam. It's down to the incumbents and the legal system to uphold them. But I'm sure you'll explain..."

He puffed in his straggly beard. "Ideology... hard and fast... can't achieve permanence due to ambiguities. It's why empires fall."

Adolfa: "Example."

"Dialectical materialism. Trying to impose atheism on the superstitious. They'll agree in principle, until a woman has a stillborn baby and pulls out her icons to pray."

"That's one example."

"Hitler."

"N--ooo," Johann demured slowly, his head shaking in a fug. "I wouldn't lay an ambiguity trip on Hitler. He liked a solution."

"Racial supremacy works until you get to half-breeds and quarter-breeds. Look at Zigeuner legislation. That's why Nuremberg got so complicated."

"Chrissake." I was getting hot. "Tell half-Jewish orphans they were a bureaucratic nightmare. Or Marianne, my Sintesa friend got her face savaged by a dog. You're talking arty-farty bollocks."

Saying her name my stomach dropped: it'd slipped out just to quiet a barroom mouth. Politics shouldn't be filling memory, shouldn't try, stuffing the national vacuum. Let the memories fade, the night jags recede.

"You asked why I was an anarchist."

"Have you seen anarchy? It's the Red army far from home fucking without consent. It's partisans unleashed on their own brothers. It's terror."

Falke'd avoided service due to pneumonia, and sat out the war in a little hamlet south-west of Berlin. In fairness, he'd narrowly avoided euthanasia.

"Democracy survived two and a half thousand years."

"Did it now."

"Cleisthenes."

"Sounds like a detergent."

"You're so facile. And you don't have adolescence as an excuse."

I slung my coat on which had the pleasing side-effect of upturning his coffee, left, and headed home.

It was a short walk. I wrapped Otto's scarf round my neck, up my nose - a lovely red find but it needed dyeing. Pushed my hair under my beret and looked at my face. Examined, for money. That was the nub: for a moment it seemed whorish. The more so as these eyes had thought largely about themselves for years - me and those I loved already, but they'd only been a handful, fewer now.

The streets receded and washed, like water on the ears and I arrived. The door sucked, feeling louder than it was.

"Fraulein, be quite relaxed please. Come."

I walked the floor to his hashed surgery, Ots' scarf in both hands.

"The state pen-pushers push their pens different ways but for us nothing has changed, eh? Tending the people."

I looked at the couch, the splayed calipers on a table like a jeweller or smithy; the room no less spartan than Ravensbrück *revier*. I'm not squeamish, or frigid of my body but there is no dignity in orifices - the lights and smock, the hands that seek.

"It'll be a little cold, that's all."

I looked at the ceiling as he began, felt the unwanted saliva pooling in my throat. Why always a man, these fotze-gurus, I mean statistically it would be, I thought, with the alternate warmth and nip of gloved hands; the cold pinch of tools, a sudden hard poke. But what doctor - including that SS-beast Schumann - wakes of a morning and thinks, *I'm going to pursue vaginas*!

"Pardon?" he squinted with his municipal eyes, pale blue.

I shook my head.

"You muttered something. Do you recall, did you count how many... intrusions you experienced at Uckermark?"

"Just one, not physical," I said, as if his glove wasn't up me-- "only the room." For some reason I aimed to be quite accurate about this.

"No intrauterine injection, before or after."

"Formaldehyde?"

"More likely *caladium seguinum*, a plant extract. Or talk of a 'Clauberg method'? Did you hear of that? "

I shook my head.

"Good," *a pan clattered*. "There is no evidence of anything physical after the radiation... Just those burns, commonplace now I'm afraid. We'll confirm in writing with results. You'll also receive some questions, for you to consider in your own time."

Confirm what, I wondered. I waited for him to continue, divulge my future, but he bottled my swabs, turned his back and placed what implements I'd touched in antiseptic. Swapped the old with new, including himself, and I was looking at a woman with a kindly smile. She'd a lunch crumb on the dent of her chin.

I didn't want to gas with Maria after, wafted a hand and smile as she bustled closer. She fell away again and I was sitting outside.

Yarrow poked up a neglected wall across the way, and my eyes followed the stream of workers, passers-by, a particular man with a droopy moustache. I knew where my gaze ended, and my feet. I got up and followed him, until we were under the window of the room I knew Roma were sequestering. Looked at the door.

Droopy went in and I followed. Heard voices in a corridor behind the stairs, daylight filtering by a smoky office. I looked up the stairs where his feet were vanishing. Went up, to another corridor.

A girl with a scarf over her face was walking toward the staircase at the rear, perhaps nine or ten, with caramel hair on her shoulders. I almost burst and ran towards her: "Marianne, Marianne. Good grief!"

The girl's eyes widened behind the scarf, backing away, but I must've been physically reaching at her face. A worker shouted at me, then softened her voice as I stared still... well, a bit crazed I suppose. The girl hastened down the corridor with little brown feet, browner than Marianne's.

"I'm sorry, I thought it was... a friend."

"Roma friend?"

"From the camp, I'm sorry I frightened her she, you see... well she has no nose, so I thought..." I twirled her fingers in a circular way round my face and head.

The woman was doubled, I was sure, in a photo behind her shoulder - playing a violin for Eisenhower. Both were smiling, Eisenhower with that same thuggish joy Bob Hope gives out. Perhaps the photo was a dear possession, lugged about. There was a stack of rags and toys - donations maybe - and beyond it I noticed suddenly, a man in tatty wools and dickie, gaunt-faced by design, seated wagging a shoe; in a fleeting thought I wondered if you could be both Roma and Jew - Hitler's favourites.

"No, little Hester is Xoraxane," said the woman into silence, as if reading my mind: "A Sunni Muslim, some wear burquas." She looked faintly embarrassed.

"Marianne wore a headscarf indoors, in secret. I think she called it a diklo."

"Hester is not Vlax. You are trying to find her, Marianne?"

"Germany's a big place I... know that..." --I had nothing sensical to say. Whatever was here, it wasn't for the public. And it was clear in how her eyes flicked the corridor, I was alien and trespassing their business, chaotically piled on green cabinets.

What a job, people of no fixed abode by choice scattered further; under fields, dust and smoke. Perhaps the gaunt man in wools was helping. I'd later know this was relatively high spirits for Sinti and Roma - with Nazi fumigation the Zigeuner became royalty, briefly. Only later as ordinariness returned, did their old status.

"Look, they'll give us three thousand," --I shoved it under Otto's nose. The gynaecology results had come in a staunch, very German letter. "Guess why, remuneration? Apology? No... More experiments, they want to patch things up by doing it again!"

"Hon slow down, we've never really... discussed this." I allowed him to steer me to the table with my rumpled letter. About to volley him again I felt queerly better in a pulsing silence.

"It's delicate," Otto said finally. "I've not felt... qualified to speak. What was it, formaldehyde?"

"Ha! Bunging up a toilet. No, it was x-rays and none of it was authorised, not by Satan, not by Himmler. They were freewheeling, you know, like Charlie Parker with lead and syringes."

"Can they undo it?" --He was looking at me with levels of complexity, eyes darting. Must've been thinking of Dr. Werner in Hamburg, behind the docks.

"That's what they'd like to know," I shook the offending letter. "*You* could, if you were snipped."

Otto shook his head. "There was talk of that."

And I realised I'd never asked - wondered, not asked. Not that it worried me, repercussions and such, but I was just as awful.

"Well if Marianne got out of *they-aa*. And you know the guard got out of *they-aa*," --Dwight drawled his Missouri. I watched his quite-still hands; he doesn't fidget. "And the Ruskies don't have her, we're worth a shot."

Otto'd gone for cigs so Dwight and I could acquaint at the Bathtub. So dingy by day, I don't know why they come here. Volpriehausen should've stopped any wish in Otto to be underground.

Dwight foxes me. It's like he and Ots are oddball cronies. I like him, I don't distrust him any less than I believe all Yank activity serves itself... but he must hide stuff, people do, and the bold attack of his demeanour is maybe defence. So spruce and energetic, even at close of day, perhaps he's only seen dirt from above, no traumas to plough.

Anyway I was still getting *Die Welt*, following Romani recompense pleas, and it was a hound scent in chaos in the end - a locking of eyes in newsprint.

After Nuremberg, Dwight retained his access to his files. The camp trials of '47 in Hamburg filled the press, and I saw a Ravensbrück face in my nightly cuttings, background fuzz. Just that, a nobody, the guard with the puppet face who carried her, now confused in a booth as grainy ink but... trials need acres of documents. Bulk death needs a signatory and each name an executioner. The evidence they massed for the Hamburg proceedings was, for many, their only trace. (We are gumshoes now, in our jetsam.) I met Dwight twice, once to tell him about Marianne, and then to see if he'd produce. It was a vast sift but he gave that buffed smile.

"Don't fret Angela, I have assistants now. We all do."

And we nodded as Otto returned, looking spare.

The second meeting wasn't as pleasant, though Dwight had done his homework, his very best homework.

I took a train to Ravensbrück but there was nothing to see, no memorial. The sky skulked and glowed from the compartment, and I walked in luminescent green towards the remains of Uckermark and its subsidiaries, from Fürstenberg.

To the last place I'd seen her. I held myself tight in my mac, leaves pattering overhead. *Jesus god*. Marianne Kolompár, that's what the certificate said. Cause of death unknown, only I knew. Or rather... I'd spend nights turning over exactly how it was solved, in the needless days of defeat. If *solved* isn't too grand a word. I grimaced, maybe it was concussion from a chance whack; valueless. Yes it was a needless death, but in the maths of the sky all *life* is needless. Kolompár was a Hungarian name, she'd never mentioned it and her ID said Marianne Z. From her I got only 'Marianne' and a pair of folded arms like a full stop.

So that was it, an inked name in a Hamburg vault. My sole consolation, as I wept along the path, was that the last thing she did was wriggle, face down the enemy, not go gentle into that good night. Perhaps with her arms held she had spat at him after all.

Back at Krausenstraße I took my Siemens blades from the chamois, my souvenirs. Turned them in my palm. I saw Mama's face for the first time since Gomorrah, its vision that is, and everything upended. Never faced my shortcomings.

I am not cruel but there's cruelty in neglect: I couldn't forgive her stupidity, her myopia and superstitions, though for flesh and blood one forgives all, yes? - as if her glass-eyed belief reflected on me. Even now, vanished, dead, I couldn't allow her simplicity a fond memory, whereas Paps' I could; Papa the acid-tongued bookworm, Papa's private humours. ...It was too much. The vacuum of the Roma office and Dwight's Hamburg files, Uckermark; decisions made, these wrung-out spaces we'd been left.

The thing about release, the harming, is... well it can always wait; it can be put off or succumbed to, as the junkie toys with a morning fix I imagine, but, I couldn't lift the blank mist. Folks got on now, with stuff, but it was renovating an abattoir to me, for the new owners with pinched, unsavoury faces. With closed eyes I could see boots getting a foothold, a heft in the shrapnel wilds - see what the blinding mushroom on the horizon had hidden. While we'd been blown to pieces the corridors of the mighty still existed - gold-plated rat runs.

One of the steel blades had a spot of rust; the chromium was somehow stained.

Perhaps you'll understand it's difficult: to see a decent road, personal pride after all - the motor turns, but under it is one's sump tray. I rolled the blades back into the shelf on the dresser. It would have to wait until the mist got too thick or... cleared. Nobody is spotless. *Push it away, Angela, push it away. Have a boiled egg.*

But I took the blades back out. Now was the time to shear.

It was eleven o'clock. The filmy green mirror shard from the sideboard I could see myself in; my ungainly black mop. The longer it got, the more like the ghost of a child in a bush my face was.

I hacked at it, an inch or so from my scalp. By the time I was done, I looked like the lunatic from Gropius. I cut it back to post-Uckermark length. The place where I stalled. The place where young Ange ceased. But I felt more real, could rewind and dream of what was next.

Never again. Never again. I bashed at the typewriter like a possessed gargoyle freed of stone. *No pamphlets. No Lebensraum no Lebensborn. No Germania. No non-aggression pacts no collaboration; no junk bonds or Junkers, lugers and Luftwaffe. No second front and no winter campaign. No sacrifice for old men. No appeasement by those with all to lose. No adults knowing better. The future is ours. The future is...*

I felt my belly; stomach flat and hard as iron. Once we'd had the pair of us growing there. We were so terrified for our mistake we mercy-killed. But it would have survived, as we had, to see venal Chaplin stubbed out.

And then what, this carousel of hope and despair, long pallid faces trying to smile, groaning stomachs...

T4'd our own child, the unknowing thing, over ideology. I looked at the blades and a piece of mirror. Both sharp. Maybe I'd release after all.

Feel a little faint, feel my eyes roll back. But what about Otto? He thinks me his forever. Perhaps I should treasure his certainty more in this bitter wind of unknowns.

The soft tap at the door. I looked around, disconcerted. Whoever it was would see a chop-haired scarecrow-- "Adolfa."

"Wow!"

"What, my hair."

"Drastic."

"What are you doing back?"

"They're full of themselves tonight." She brushed Johann and Falke aside. "Let's go to the Ballhaus. Have some fun for a change! I've got money," she added defensively.

I looked at my paltry wardrobe. "Sure. It's time."

We got a trolley bus that claimed it terminated a few streets from Nürnberger Straße.

Like buddleia in ruins luring red admirals and painted ladies, Berlin brings jazz to GIs. The Ballhaus Berlins is hot and attracts anyone with an instrument, wage or buzzcut, though the rear ballroom is bombed out.

Unannounced Ange swans with her arm round Adolfa's waist, several Bolshie moonshines the better, her hair shorn to stubs. I was with Dwight and a couple of drunk GI gum-chewers, and I gulped in anguish as she made a b-line, hips with a new swing but not with me, not with me.

"Here's Ange now."

Seeing the pair approach, a GI said: "Which one, the boy or the girl?"

Dwight saw the tension freezing over the conversation.

"The boy," I said. "Problem with that?"

"Not for me sailor."

I launched myself at him, figuring I was soberer. I wasn't and Dwight bumped me with his chest en route, shunting me yards onto the dancefloor. He immediately turned, made words I couldn't hear and signals I couldn't see. The two GIs raised their glasses smiling, and headed into the shadows. I turned to Ange who'd stopped aghast.

I was stooped, embarrassed like Frankenstein's monster. "I didn't expect you in this neck of the woods."

"Gummi-baiting?"

I looked at Adolfa on her arm. She said nothing. And in place of silence, Ange said: "Where do I place my bet. What are the odds on you?"

"He insulted you."

"I don't think you need me here to kick off."

Outside the BB, Nürnberger Straße was cold. Adolfa was happily ensnared on Dwight's charms and subsidised drinks.

"What did you want to talk about?" Ange not only looked like a boy, she looked like a hoodlum, a punk, some strange Valkyrie.

"Adolfa."

"Got a crush on her?"

"I see why people would."

"Meaning?"

"You tell me. You're the dark continent."

"And you're a ghost."

I pulled a smoke from a tin and groped for focus. "Hon, I'm trying not to get in your way. Then you waltz in with a butch haircut and your arm round a girl. I didn't know you were coming. I was gonna introduce you, but something stared me in the face."

"As you said, she's attractive."

"Is this punishment?"

Ange said nothing, waiting for our eyes to meet. And the glare and shine answered first. "Don't be ridiculous. She's a girl. If I'd slept with a man I'd feel guilty. Insurmountably."

"So you have."

She didn't answer.

"You've betrayed us," I said.

"It's not betrayal. It's a holding pattern. Come home!"

"If I did you'd stop?"

She smiled. "Probably."

"Don't do that. Don't bloody do that."

"What?"

"You're messing with her too. Maybe she's a real one, dig? Man or woman, you can't shift your affections like weather."

"Can't I? Not even in a vacuum? I told you I'd never sleep with another man. I've never wanted to."

"Unless Leo was back from the dead."

Ange went unintentionally quiet. My heart broke for the umpteenth time. I paced around, sobering the corners of my brain. "No betrayal. No bloody betrayal. You're fucked in the head, you know that?"

"Yes. A piece of paper reminds me of it."

Ange had included the stockings with her androgynous look. She was suddenly raw and tiny.

"Once you tried to save me from the other side of Germany, just like Leo did when I was young. And now I'm here, you've given me up for drink and music and that bloody studio. If I'm fucked in the head, why don't you help me?"

Kleiner Tiergarten unlike its lovely name was unloved.

If Tiergarten proper was your Times Square or St James' Park - quickly swept and cleansed for parades - Little Tiergarten was where they heaped the broken and famished; the uncaring hand-to-mouthers with no wish to rebuild.

The escarped, bruised buildings and thin lightless walls. As if each morning the settled dust was kicked back up again by the emerging dead. But... being so hand-to-mouth, they'd a market laid out on trestles along the park's rim.

After a while wandering, thinking no-one needed what it sold, my brow furrowed: a thing of beauty. I walked quickly and from its carelessly laid position on the trestle, maybe the owner didn't realise. A *Harmony Monterey* archtop with floating bridge, f-holes and a trapeze tailpiece.

My heart pounded. Stay cool, Otto.

"Can I play it?"

The shrewd-looking old man looked at me closely through wire spectacles and messy grey hair. "Sure kid."

If I play well, he'll think I know guitars and up the price. The rest of the junk on the table, lampshades, cardigans and coloured bottles, looked worthless. Although I might get that mustard cardy for Ange.

The nitro lacquer was rubbed away where your right arm rests on its hip; Monterays were only produced this decade so the owner must have played hell out of it. Maybe a dead GI. Uncherished looting.

I stuck my tongue out the corner of my mouth like a moron and played a bad G, then rearranged my hands slowly to play a better one and the thing resonated. My heart leapt. I picked out notes to hear how they sustained, but I'd longed to play and all I could think of was the first suite for unaccompanied cello.

I played it perfectly. Knew I'd shot myself in the foot and I'd now never afford it. People on other stalls were looking at me. I played some Lonnie Johnson, smiling blissfully, some Django.

The stallholder wasn't transfixed enough to allow a steal.

I put it back on the table. "It's alright," I said, clearing my throat. "Terrible warping in the neck, and the lacquer's badly rubbed away. Cheaply applied. I think it's an imitation Zephyr. What do you want for it?"

"Make an offer son."

"In what?"

"Cigarette cartons or dollars. No Reichsmarks."

"Five dollars."

"Come on. I just heard it sing like a choir."

"That's me, not the guitar."

"Twenty dollars."

"What! Think you'll sell it at that price here?"

"Well, I won't sell it *here* now, will I?"

"I'll do you twelve, but it'll have to be over three months."

He laughed.

"That's funny?"

"You take the guitar, give me four, and I'll see you again?"

"I'll bring security. Some vintage recordings until I've paid you off."

He considered, his mouth skewed. "Sixteen over four months."

So I'd got this hand-to-mouth Tiergarten thing wrong. He was a futuristic bastard who'd latched I had a wage.

"OK, if you throw in that cardigan. And that printer ribbon. Will it fit a Continental?"

"Should do. If not, spool it on the old reel."

"Chuck that in as well. And the gabardine raincoat."

"Easy son. That's an extra two."

"OK. Eighteen over four months. I'll be back in two hours. Don't let anyone near the guitar."

I borrowed recordings I never play, but before I collected the Monterey I decided to recce accommodation. I would, I was sure, convince Ange to move west.

I was a spider with compound eyes, hunting empty buildings. But anything uninhabited was smashed and derelict. After a few hours ready to give up, I looked at the collapsed rubble and floors of a building, behind which or part of which was an intact wall of sandstone, which couldn't be in the next street: wrong colour.

I walked to the mountain of rubble and climbed over someone's exploded living room or hall. Over the hump the rubble had jammed a doorway, so I removed bits until I saw daylight and a staircase: dusty and dark.

I got enough of a hole made to get through and went up the stairs. To the right, daylight and hanging timber, to the left and ahead were two intact doors. I pushed one. A tiny bathroom with a tiny bath. I peered at the toilet, pulled the flush chain and heard a gurgle. No water.

Need to fill a bucket. I opened the left one, couldn't believe what I saw: a spacious, clean bedroom unblemished by war with a small double bed, desk, wardrobe and... a vanity unit. Even the panes of glass remained in a window overlooking a courtyard. What about washing?

No matter, Ange swims every day. She's gotta see it!

I took the guitar but thought taking it home insensitive, Ange having promised one. I lodged it at RIAS for now. I folded up the cardigan and put the ribbon on top to take home.

Otto was drunk. He leant at the bar in a haze but saw me, my home-cut hair rough as a hedge, on the arm of coppery

Adolfa. Night light worked well on her, rendering that translucent skin sharp as a marble sculpture.

He blinked. "Oh, here's Ange now," he blurrily focused, surprised to see me.

"Which one, the boy or the girl?"

These were the words I heard, but Otto lunged from his stool towards the thickset Yank and got pinballed out of harm's way - presumably by Dwight in a civvie suit. Otto fumed, but also swayed. He murmured something about '...neck of the woods', stumbled again, and stared angrily at Adolfa.

Welcome Angie, welcome all, to Ballhaus Berlins, and all who sail in her. If he was this drunk five days in seven, what was he up to?

Adolfa'd had homebrews, so when Otto stormed out she talked to Dwight, who'd sent the charmless GIs packing. I left the club to find my paralytic babe in arms. He was steaming.

I knew that pacing intense off-focus interior monologue introspection argument accusation wobble. It always built up from inward nothingnesses to melee.

"So?" He looked me up and down. "Adolfa."

"Had your eye on her? I stole her?"

"I can see why people would."

"You left me idle." (I almost said barren.) "Idle hands."

"You're an unknown continent."

"And you're a ghost."

He paced about, smoking like he was fumigating his brain. And then he laid one down: "You've betrayed us."

"This is no betrayal. I wouldn't sleep with another man."

"Unless Leo returned from the dead."

I stared at Otto fiercely. He knew he'd done wrong, but kept looking at me as if wrong didn't mean not right.

"I'm sure he'd be pleased to discuss your points at length."

"Don't do that."

"What?"

"Shift what I'm saying. And you're messing with her too. Maybe she's a real one, dig?"

"Ha! You're so sure I'm not?"

"I'm sure of nothing."

"Come home!"

And then, as luck or sorrow had it, when we'd both gone stubbornly silent, Louise Tobin piped through the brick, soft, insistent, curling up around brass and strings, like some alarm call: *I didn't know what time it was.*

Otto held his hand out hesitantly. "Let's go back in."

"No," I took the hand and pulled him to a clasp. My Hitler Youth boots grazed the pavement. My mad punk hair probably a mess. Otto'd salvaged his brown pinstripe and brogues from Hamburg, and wore them to RIAS if he was heading here. He smelt of man in hot gusts.

I pushed my face into his neck, he guided me clockwise, and we slid along the pavement. He was less self-conscious than when young. He held me gracefully as I leant back, and then span me out of it in a twirl back into his arms.

People passed us, a bloke with his squeeze saying, "I'll loan you the cover charge mate," and they walked on sniggering.

Then a couple of grave-dodgers stared, mouths shrunk and gummy.

We broke and I swooped a graceful arm towards the pavement like a ballerina, tiptoeing back, and we finished the song in a clasp, until we reached a bank of rubble in the road.

☆

Life's weird now, thinner even in sunlight, more fundamental. You turn a corner half-expecting to see a friendly face - god knows why - and realise you won't, though in the times you could've done you never did, really.

I must be clinging to my Schmidt certainties; a simple thereness of her.

A fool to deny it. And today's young products, who saw the raids with baby-glass eyes, see something different; an awakening - I need to buck up.

I was walking east of the Gate, near home, in my hire-purchase raincoat with a fresh *Tagesspiegel* for Ange under my arm when I was stopped. From behind.

"With us." It was a a Volkspolizei, clamping my arm firmly.

"What for?"

"Contraband."

"Search me here."

"The newspaper."

I looked at the paper under my arm. A free press and the unchecked movement of people remained, bar holding up US vehicles as an irritant.

"You must be joking." I tried to wrestle free. He took a coat lapel alongside my iron-gripped arm. "Don't grab the Gab, man. I just bought it."

"Smuggling is one thing Bebel, resisting makes me think you've more to hide."

"Smuggling?!" I was taken by horrible surprise him knowing my name. But I rolled my eyes and got into his green BMW.

"Enjoy writing the paperwork. Man stopped with newspaper. It's the gallows for me."

"You live east but work for American Radio. So, you cocky shit, we can hold you on suspected espionage. Keep your mouth shut unless asked."

"While you drooled over Nazi orders I delivered articles to the pinko press. From prison. My guess is you kept your uniform, just traded the epaulettes."

"Marx was born in Germany," he said, weakly.

"I will shut my trap. Now. And at the station."

"No, you'll speak Otto." The assurance was back.

I sat in the cell, and the clang-door opened abruptly. A bullish uniformed man brought in a chair and sat down, the door clanging behind. I'd laid my raincoat carefully beside me, now just rolled shirtsleeves.

He eyed me on the bunk for a while. Quite a while. He was bulky with a German face, but those wrinkled, linear eyes that know snow-blind distances.

"Arkady Schlesinger."

"What a pleasure," I heard my mouth.

He said nothing. Just sat looking at me.

"Before you start, I want to ask you something."

153

Schlesinger inclined his head. "Is there a phrase in Russian foreign policy, goes something like: If you hit flesh advance, hit bone retreat?"

Schlesinger smiled and considered. "Imperial or Soviet?"

"Either."

He let a little laugh scoff out of his mouth, considering. Finally. "Before I start what?"

"Interrogating."

"I'm here to ensure you have everything you need. You'll be here forty-eight hours while we do some checks."

I stared disbelievingly.

"Got everything you need?"

"Man can't live on blankets and toilet alone."

"Excellent. You'll get slop later. The administration can be slow with checks. I wouldn't want you to be uncomfortable while detained by the Volkspolizei. We have a duty of care, even for trouble-makers."

He laughed, lifted the chair as he rose and the door opened and shut.

"Over at the Interior," --Vormelker thumbed some coffee cups and I shook my head-- "they're not sure if Otto's girlfriend is a dissident or provocateur. She's clearly a socialist, but she writes terribly rude things about Stalin."

My blood thinned. The more he talked about my family the more my comfort was a crucifix. Rather than make Otto and Ange's lives tranquil by disappearing, they were under scrutiny. No shortage of shame either. Disappearing is fine if you're devoid of affection (a sociopath to coin Vormelker) but I'm not, really.

I researched Vormelker, the public one in the Party biogs: gave a speech in 1932 about Determinism when it was in vogue, since forgotten - that capitalism must lead to fascism, overthrown inevitably, as the Nazis were (so nobody should feel bad killing fascists, it was foregone). The speech annoyed the Kremlin, detracting any merit from achieving a Soviet Union in the first place. Anyone could, and would. But... if you followed his line, nothing was your fault.

"You needn't mention my family," I said. "They're not collateral or... a risk. They believe I'm a pile of bones in Stalingrad."

The incredulous expression was back. "Günter, how have you made it this far? They compromise *you* because you know *they're alive!*"

I don't think I'm that stupid actually, I knew what he meant. It had nothing to do with double-agency or switched liability, easily achieved by blackmailing a family. He was threatening me direct: camouflaging his SED directives as Yankee hands on my marionette. It would be they, should anything befall a Bebel, that ordered it.

"You're the expert," I murmured.

"I suppose apathy towards your loved ones reduces the risk of compromise." But he didn't say it in a way reassuring.

I'd stopped my dalliance with Adolfa, with sensitivity. Her thin tears were just that; skin-deep, not mature. Though short it had all been rather hot and flushed.

I know Otto's burying his dead in absence. Otto is the Black Sea on a calm night, not used to washing up fear or sorrow on me, letting it sink instead to fight with the unknown.

He's been gone two days!

Implied in my not leaving him is he doesn't leave me. I've not been that mad lately. I've been madder and he scoured Germany to find me. I know Otto and I cling to his early work: Alster Otto; string-plucker Otto the shellac-flipper.

Had he left me on some malign insignificance there was no way to contact him in this overground dungeon. Disappearing was always easy in Berlin, easier now. But Otto never left without saying his piece...

"Fucking hell!" The door opened and he stood there. "Anything to drink?"

I sucked air like a landed fish, gasping, "Two day bender?"

"No Hon, two days in a polizei station. Longer. Fifty five hours."

"What?"

"I tell you what, there's interest in us."

"You've been at a polizei station for two days?"

"What's new?"

My present fears had melted away. "Got this only." I poured him Falke's home-distillation and he drank.

"Gaahh! That's so toxic."

I shrugged. I also nestled in so he couldn't really hold his glass. "I was worried."

"Come on Hon, we've had worse."

I heard him drink the toxin over my head.

"Yes but, who by?"

"Your lot. Slamming people up."

"What for?"

"Everything and nothing. A newspaper, working for the Yanks."

I lay looking through vinyl I'd been pilfering from RIAS. Some electricity had been wired in by a thickset old electrician and we had intermittent light, when eastern power stations functioned.

"Where the hell is it?" Ange was fiercely agitated. She'd been bashing about the room for five minutes.

"What?"

"My manuscript?"

"You gave it to Hartmann, or Der Tagesspiegel, or lovergirl next door." (Not the time, Otto.)

"I collected it from Hartmann two days ago!"

"Did you leave it in a cafe?"

"No," she paused. "It always comes home with me."

"Oh no Hon. How many pages now?"

"Eighty-odd."

I chose my words carefully. Five minutes was long enough to search every nook of the room. I knew what we were both thinking. "Don't shout but... would you remember it?"

She stood staring at the Continental, hands on hips, murmuring, "Most of it. That's not my real concern."

She walked up to the typewriter cagily like it was a squatting beast. The light was almost overhead. She didn't touch it, just peered very closely into, then around it. Intaken breath.

Slipped her hands under the photo of Yerevan Square and held it up horizontally to the light, peering with one eye along the top. She put it down again, and looked along the base of the typewriter. Put a finger in a dust line - we don't clean much. "Bloody hell."

She yanked open the door and strode next door. I followed in concern.

"Falke. Don't touch anything, but is all your work still here?"

He was lying on his matress. They'd made the place comfortable with billowy hareem muslins.

"I don't know." He floundered like an upturned beetle and went to rudimentary shelves of reclaimed lintels, pulled out a large book. Opened it. "Yes."

"Mine's gone."

"Why don't touch anything?"

"Disturbed dust. Finger marks."

Behind her I said, "Someone's been in?"

Ange made a gurgling sound of frustration and flung her arms in the air, pushing past me.

"Hon," I said, following like a dog. "Someone's been in?"

She headed down to the room with a double hatch-door where Gertrude lived. When she opened the top, Ange said: "Has anyone weird been here? Yesterday or today."

"No."

"Nobody you didn't recognise?"

"Lehmann the electrician, but I know him. A man came in asking for Falke. I said I wasn't sure he was in but he could try."

"We need locks on our doors." Ange was shouting at Gertrude now. "Something's gone missing!"

She didn't wait for an answer and went back up the stairs. I wandered over. "What did he look like?"

"Usual bullshit Commie worker outfit. Young. Dark hair. Barrel chest like he uses a chest-expander thingy."

"Thanks Gertrude. Ange's lost something important. She's right. We need to get keys for the doors." I started for the stairs, then thought, "D'you know what time? How long he was up there?"

"After eight and no, I didn't hear him leave. Heavy boots maybe a half-hour later and the door slam, but could've been anyone." She now looked sheepish, like she'd had a few at the time and been lax.

Days later I heard shuffling in my dreams, realised they weren't in dreams but at the door. I looked at it, looked down, and faint moonlight showed a white square. A card. I got up, fumbled with the light, picked it up.

> Angela is being watched. Interest in her leisure activities. Watch your backs.
> Your Best Interests.

In half-slumber I wondered what our best interests were, and should other people know those?

A threat? The sign-off belied it. I pondered waking Ange, but I can't when night holds her fast. I like watching her sleep and mend; nocturnal workers fixing my finch.

I slid the card in my trousers on the chair, then slid the trousers and a jumper on, and sat at her desk. I didn't want to disturb anything. I looked around the room, somewhere I'd Cognac: Dwight's gift on handing back his Jeep at Ravensbrück. I'd been saving it for my Gibson...

I poured, looked at Ange's calm face. It twitched once. *I'll watch your back*, I thought as the burning luxury went down my throat. *But how?* I was at RIAS, our room had no lock and I didn't know what to watch for. Trilby man, VoPo, what?

I rolled a cig and stared into the photo of dusty Yerevan Square, Georgia, 1907: peaceful, every hatted boulevardier believing in the future just before it was blown to bits.

Dawn broke and I'd drunk most of the bottle. There was one cold-water-only shower behind Gertrude's room for washing and I got up to sober up.

"Hon?"

"Present and correct."

"What you doing at my desk?"

"Drinking heavily."

She pushed her eyes, frowned and propped to elbow height. "Is that Cognac?"

I nodded.

"Selfish bastard."

"You were asleep."

"Only because you didn't wake me."

I frowned, felt blurry, reached into my pocket and retrieved the hand-delivered card. "Don't get alarmed Honey. Take this in the spirit I think it was intended."

"Why so mysterious?"

I handed the card. She read it. It was only a dozen words but her eyes kept darting to the beginning. "From whom?"

"Our Best Interests."

"Where's it from?"

"Under the door."

"Why didn't you wake me?"

"Because now it's morning, so now you can worry."

"Hmff," she fell back on the cushions. "Sat up drinking on my behalf. You're such a brooder," but she didn't say it unkindly.

"Someone's on our side," I said, getting up unsteadily.

"Who?" she groaned.

"Someone knows who's watching you. Maybe who took the script."

"Who? And who?" she sounded exasperated.

"I don't know. I'm gonna wash and get to RIAS. They want an extra show on the Hamburg scene. Will you take care, look about, keep your wits, all that?"

"You sound like Papa."

"And if you sit at that Continental all day, stick the work in the sofa stuffing when you're done, or find a loose floorboard or something."

"You're going to RIAS after a bottle of Cognac?"

"Only this morning. Then I'm meeting Dwight for a drink at the Ballhaus."

When he'd gone I looked onto Krausenstraße. Berlin's oblong sunshine hit fenders and bike rims. The cloth caps and drooping cigarettes of old men with a vague plan, trying to salvage innocence and move through this deafening peace. Women in headscarves. I wanted to scream at the white noise.

A man of indeterminate age looked at our tenement with a tweed cheesecutter shading his eyes. He walked to a news kiosk, as if conscious the watcher'd been watched, and paid his pfennigs.

3. RADICALS

Dwight finally arrived in a checked sportcoat and thin tie. The Ballhaus'd started a day jam called 'Lunch with Louis' in the gloom.

"Still not deported, reprobate?"

"I'm indispensable."

"Don't you have anything else to do?"

"Me, nah." He slapped my back.

I should explain Dwight if I can; he may prove instrumental.

See when I first bounded on his Jeep's running board with my one change of clothes and splintered life, he grinned the shiny grin of a ruling colony. (Unlike the Brits who, banter aside, remained worthy.) A confidence that may've existed all along but now flowered in victory, perhaps.

Broad and young and well-ironed, moustachio'd - somehow out of fashion - he'd a gaze I believed honest. Like you do with Americans overseas. Well that gaze - I now think - sought honesty in others, not itself.

The band fired up *Do you know what it means to miss New Orleans*.

"You never told me what you do now."

"I never did?"

"You never did."

"I did."

"Tell me again."

"Associated Press, UN secondments. The usual."

"There is no UN here. It's in Vienna."

"Yeah, well. I'm scouting premises."

"This club is so fake."

"Bullshit. If not for us you wouldn't have jazz."

I tilted my head. That was true. "So, who got you sniffing us?"

"Eh?"

"That we're being watched."

"Come again?"

"The card through the door. The cloak and dagger."

"You're talking in riddles, kid."

"Can we straighten something out? Clear the air. You were at Montecassino."

"Fuckin' A, bloodbath. Nobody believed you Hun weren't occupying the monastery, which you weren't because ...get this..." Dwight's drink had arrived and he pointed it at me. "Adolf wanted to preserve it."

"Like he preserved Warsaw."

"Serious. So we bombed it and you weren't there. Left a rabbit-warren of, er, like catacombs? Anyway you lot figured you could occupy it now as a vantage point. It took rock-climbing Polaks to break the deadlock."

"And it was also the first ALSOS mission. Manhattan Project. Enriched uranium. Heavy water."

Dwight pierced me. He'd a tendency of turning in an instant from your best buddy to something sealed and dangerous. "Go on."

"Just clearing the air, old pal," I slapped his shoulder theatrically. "Because at Ravensbrück you passed papers to the Red Commandant. Discreet, mind. He didn't return them. Either you spoke fluent Russian or he spoke fluent Yank. But you spoke each other's language."

Dwight's jaw had drawn tight. He didn't blink or break gaze. But neither did I.

"ALSOS failed. We shipped a bunch of boffins home, but you lot had no nuclear capability and no roadmap. So I was moved to camp inspections. Where as you'll recall, we met."

"Mmm," I said. That didn't answer the question.

"It was no false flag. It was a real job and I'm proud of it. I serviced Nuremberg."

"Moved by whom?"

"Who d'you think? But you're implying something else I think."

"Well I assumed you were tied to the OSS, or CIA or whatever it is. Then that exchange at Ravensbrück threw me."

"No Otto. You've got ahead of yourself. CIA only. Not beyond."

"And the commandant?"

"Misinformation. Bad coordinates. Dead facilities and migrated centrifuges."

"You see, pal? We've cleared the air!"

"So what was that crap about a card?"

"It wasn't you?"

He closed his eyes slowly. "No. I don't deliver cards. I'll probably never tell you what I do do, but not that."

"It told us to watch our backs, someone's watching us."

"Why, what are you up to?" He said it innocently enough, but it still sounded highly interrogative.

"I can only assume it's Ange's book. Doesn't cast Stalin in a good light. It's being serialised in a western newspaper."

"Was it a warning or a threat?"

"Sounded like a warning. Hence…" I nodded at Dwight, twirling my whisky and ice. "I thought of you. Can't think who else. Signed off Your Best Interests."

Otto slept. I traced 'INF' carved in his back, done with razors at Moringen; a mauve-pink shadow. I shoved my hand under his sticky arm. He shuffled and groaned. Poor Otto. He'd told me the penalty he paid for not informing. The water and choking. So's I understood what drowning felt like, feet clamped in a stock.

If he'd been less needful, he'd have remembered my own relationship with water. For a decade it had been good, but that didn't stop the Nienhagen dreams.

I lay back, ran my finger over the 'F', deep enough for life. If he hadn't informed, why did Moringen Commies think he had? I had a slightly unworthy thought. His half-brother had been turned. *You horrible bitch.*

"I know what you think about," I whispered.

But alarmingly he turned. "What do I think about?"

I was surprised and placated with my mitts. "I was talking to myself."

"What do I think about?"

"When does it end?"

"And you?"

"When does it begin?" He sighed heavily but shunted round.

"You wouldn't leave me over black dogs, would you?"

"No," I said, decisively. "They'll go."

But I was staring up at a ceiling of bullet-holes and nothingness; second-hand living, cuckoos in some old German house. He was too hot, his sweaty feet on mine.

I walked to our tenement. Looked up at the faint light within, reached a decision.

"Hey Hon," Ange looked up.

"We need to talk."

"We do? I thought we'd made up." She was sat there in hunched nail-bite, at the Continental, reading a sheaf she'd typed, chewing the skin around her nails.

"I'm going to head west. I've found somewhere to live. Not grand. Not as good as this."

"Am I invited?"

I scruffed my hair in pain and anguish. "No."

Once that word stopped reverberating, there was a horrible silence in the room. Ange gripped the sheaf of papers tighter. I could see a slight tremble. "Because of Adolfa?"

"No. Not really."

Her eyes brimmed. "I was happy as a loon last night. I slept like a baby. Believing my doll was back."

"Mmm."

"What then?"

"You know where to find me, RIAS if you need me. I'll be squatting in Kleiner Tiergarten. Got a bedroom with a toilet."

So quietly, it was barely audible, "I would move west."

My silence was unbearable.

"I screwed things up. You weren't here."

"You've done nothing. I'm slinging my hook, Ange. Like I say, if you need something, I'm always at RIAS in the evenings."

Ange accepted with a pale nod, then turned her face. As I picked up last possessions, Ange didn't watch me. "It's Easter in four days."

We had our backs to each other when she said it; I felt empty.

I sat at the Continental, bereft and befunked, fingering the keys for hours petulantly, in a blue haze. If he wanted me to understand his black dogs, he'd done it in the most horrible way.

It was the night before Easter, and my wristwatch said eleven twenty eight. I took my homebrew downstairs and asked Gertrude if I could borrow her Rogers *Majestic*, which she hoiked into my arms. I felt the knob, the soft click. The toxin spirit lay beside me on the chair.

> Guten Abend, all Berlin! A treat this evening: Lena Horne's *Lady is a Tramp*. The Yanks mastered irony many moons ago and I love the lyrics to this. The

brass stabs are just the way you like 'em, backed by the Metro-Goldwyn-Mayer Orchestra.

I sat in a reconditioned chair. Gertrude had recreated the Passion of Christ in painted papier mache on the unit top, and decorated the tree in the courtyard out back with coloured eggs.

> *I like the free fresh wind in my hair Life without care.*
> *I'm broke, it's oke.*
> *Hate California, it's cold and its damp, That's why the lady is a tramp.*

What happened in Europe didn't happen on Yank soil. That's why they're so humane and resplendent in their open-throttle economy. It was Easter I missed Hamburg most; Ma and Paps celebrated heartily. Abundant food.

> *I'm alone, when I lower my lamp*
> *That's why the lady is a traaa-aamp.*

Too much. I lifted the bottle and swigged. Gertrude popped her head out.

"No Otto this evening."

My head slung low before I answered. "Not tonight. Not again."

"Babe, what happened?"

"I don't know."

She was quiet a moment. "This his show?"

I nodded.

"Now listen honey. I'm no fortune-teller but I'm sure he'll be back."

I stared glazedly at her. "How do you know?"

☆

I knocked on Vormelker's door. Sunlight bathed his coiffured head buried in Der Tagesspiegel.

"Sir?"

"Memo from the Interior. They need spies in the west Berlin press."

"Yes?"

He held up an article. I squinted. It was entitled: *Tito and Yugoslavia's Communists*. He dropped that and held up another edition. *Why Beneš rolled over in Czechoslovakia*. A third. *Stalin: Deconstructing the Myth*.

"Come in man, don't stand gawping like a deep sea cretin."

I padded in.

"We have a range of candidates to approach, and their home addresses. All have something you can lean on for cooperation. A history of debts, a weakness for tail."

"I see sir. Only. I'm a handler, not an operative."

"So, go handle the candidates and get me a new bloody agent!" His eyes said: *start earning your keep*. "Two of them work at Der Tagesspiegel. That's the priority at the moment. We want the source of anti-Soviet articles. Some are so well-informed they may be living in our jurisdiction or deeper east. Written on our watch."

I frowned at this remit. I handled existing agents, not new. And furthermore, at no point had Vormelker shown any confidence in my abilities.

"There's the folio." He nodded at the corner of his desk. "One's a terrible gambler, the other a bigamist living on a dead man's identity. Oh, and get information on the chap in there, Dwight something…" he nodded at the manilla, "works for Associated Press. He's CIA so we could blow his cover, but go gentle. We've got a gap. Not sure where his interests lie."

I washed early in RIAS's restrooms or swam in Jungfernheide, so I didn't stink the place. And swimming in spring's cold water bent my brain a little to the light. Bi-weeklies became dailies as I felt the shock of the cold.

There was a hump to get over. Easter Sunday. I did my show the night before, and then hid while they locked up. Spent Sunday trapped in RIAS. I'd panicked at closedown, unable to think where to go for Jesus' Rising.

There was a little food in a refrigerator - corned beef and cheese - and toilets and water. And of course, the player. Behind my deck, a sofa sprawled and I gathered people's discarded clothing for blankets.

I knew the political correspondent was an alcoholic and searched his booth, finding vodka in a metal drawer. I wandered the dark building that retained its energy even empty, like a fortress or outpost.

As Easter night fell I swigged, put Helen Forrest's *Bewitched…* on the player. I danced with my empty jumper

172

while the piano tinkled April showers on her vocals. Stuck the record back on again and switched the broadcast button. The light went on, to my surprise. I was on.

If I'm alone at Easter someone else must be too: "Enjoy Helen Forrest, and may your gods be with you".

I wobbled down to the radio in the lounge area. Switched it on, and heard her faint strains, amplified through the air.

I'll sing to him
Each spring to him
And worship the trousers that cling to him
Bewitched, bothered and bewildered
Am I.

The hunger floors me quickly after booze. I lay on the couch and fell asleep and woke with a *rat-a-tat* mixed with the scratch of the needle at the end by the label.

I was confused and headached, no idea of time, but knowing I'd broken all RIAS protocols. The mere broadcasting of a scratching needle for hours would sack me. I sat in a confused funk, pushing hair out of my face.

The *rat-tat* repeated and made me jump. Stones against the window. I opened it and looked out. A beautiful woman with punk hair was looking up. She'd a hand full of gravel.

"You said I could find you at RIAS if I needed you. You left dead air for two hours. What are you doing?"

"Hon. I'm locked in."

"So I'm locked out."

"I can jump."

"Don't be stupid."

Too late; I missed her horribly. I clambered out and hung on my finger tips, then dropped.

"Aagh, shit," I said, in dust.

"Are you hurt?"

"No. Let's dance."

"You're drunk."

"Half. Half asleep."

She pushed a face into me. "Not doing Easter alone."

I sat on a bus struggling through central Berlin, passengers tipping hats, the odd tree dappling. My emptiness remained: our hollow world persisted but our Germany'd gone. We'd been a country less than eighty years; Ange calls it a bundle of misaligned feuds.

You can only watch so many folks willing their cars on, faux-jolly ads for Brylcreem pasted on anything standing. *You are now entering... You are now leaving...* Once-proud turrets of department stores staggering in unclothed gloom.

Was it Adolfa? That didn't feel like treason. More like when you pick up a mollusc quickly and stick it on another surface and it immediately clings. Does it know? Does it care?

...No my despair went back. I was trying to fill the tall, dead Mischling's shoes. Maybe I'd see Angie's psychiatric nurse. Mahler? Wagner?

I understand despair isn't attractive: it seeped out however I plugged it with radio or booze; I knew it to be both infectious and revulsive. Ange wasn't happy, but she did seem stronger than this wandering ghost.

I got off near her tenement, but didn't go up. Kept walking towards Fliedner Klinik. I looked at its bland facade. The thoroughfare was wide and the buildings unrestored.

"Does nurse Wagner still work here?" I asked the woman on reception.

"Who is asking?"

"My name's Otto. She treated my girlfriend... Angela Schmidt."

"I expect she's on rounds. Would you be able to wait? I can't really leave..." A man moved through an entranceway. "Heinrich! Heinrich?"

His face came back round the pillar.

"Is Nurse Wagner free?"

"As she'll ever be."

"Could you find her? I have an ex-patient request. This is..."

"Otto Bebel."

"Sure."

I sat in her office for a long time in silence. It was really a cupboard of files with a frosted window.

"Is she doing OK?" Wagner planted crossed arms on her thighs.

"I think so. I don't know."

"She was... quite traumatised."

I nodded. "You know about trauma. The expert in that field."

"Hardly an expert, er... Otto. Is she having problems?"

I shook my head. I couldn't speak here.

"I don't mean to be rude but, how can I help you?"

I stared between my shoes. "This was a bad idea. I'm sorry."

"You haven't said anything."

"I thought…" my fingernail lunged to my mouth, "as you'd helped her you might be able to help me."

"What's up?"

"There's a heavy black void in me and no matter how… optimistic I try to be, this blackness is pulling me down. Like I said, this was probably a bad idea."

"No darling. It wasn't. Have you spoken to Ange about it?"

"She sees it but I can't. I'm her wall, her protection. I can't break down in front of her. I can manage. I can function. But just this evening on the bus I felt total despair."

"Ah darling. You may not be alone."

"No?"

"All of us. Trying to find our pride, maybe German pride, maybe personal. You mustn't despair. Just think of it as a black fog the sun will break. Doesn't matter how long it takes."

"Is that your clinical diagnosis?"

She laughed. "Well I can't prescribe, you just walked in off the street."

"Sure, but… can I ask you something?"

"I expect so."

"Are you married?"

"Due to," she smiled.

"Does your partner ever disappear in front of your eyes. To a place you know you aren't. For longer and longer periods."

"Sure. He found a shed," she smiled.

"No, when you're together. Ange is kind of a tonic but she vanishes."

"You both lost your parents, yes?"

I nodded.

"So there'll be times you need each other, and times you look out the window and wonder what possibilities are out there. It's natural."

I nodded unconvinced.

"I don't know what traumas you've had Otto, but you'll be OK. You know she hitched through the downfall of Berlin for you. Firestorms and heavy artillery. Credit her a little."

I nodded. "I'm sorry to steal your time."

"Don't be daft. Both of you were lucky. You should build."

As I left the clinic I felt better. Ange was right, Wagner had the disposition of an angel.

By June Ange and I'd re-unionised, seeing each other from separate digs. Life was starting to feel possible. And then...

The Yanks brandished the Deutsche Mark in Stalin's face, making the Crimson Walrus ruddier than usual. He blocked all routes in and out of the city for western traffic. Two and a half million Berliners starving unless Truman withdrew it. But as the squeeze took hold the West scrambled all demobbed aircraft. The Walrus believed anyone trying to feed Berlin by air was gaga; nenormal'nyy.

Operation Vittles: every available plane pinned to the sky to feed us.

Tramming home with Ange, our hungry bellies joining the conversation, I pondered this political dickswing: the pilots weren't flying a thousand tons of food a day to Berlin for politics. One tied candy bars to handkerchief parachutes and hurled them out the cockpit for kids: 'Little Vittles' he called them.

We volunteered for unloading Skytrains in the mornings; I really dug those greasy sky cats. Seemed there was a brethren scene happening.

I approached him quickly in rain. "Herr Krüger."

He was certainly startled. But recomposed his face with a faint fixed smile.

"No sir. I'm Luciano Beck. Perhaps I look like your Herr Krüger from behind." He tipped his hat and continued walking.

"Elbert Krüger," I said, much louder, which made his shoulders tense. He stopped, walked back with that scaffolded smile.

"Sir, I think you have mistaken identity. And I would appreciate not being barked at in the street."

"Well if you're not Krüger, you're not being barked at," I said, pleased with that.

"No. So shall we cut this bizarre conversation short?"

I pulled a photo from a slim zip case. "OK, I'll check in with Frau Krüger in Frankfurt, show her this and see if she can help me. Or indeed Frau Beck here in Berlin."

I held up his photo and particulars. Krüger for a moment looked cornered. "What's the deal?"

"Shall we walk?"

He nodded, and we walked on. I phrased myself carefully, thinking of wiping the disdain off Vormelker's face.

"I expect like everyone, you're suffering from a devaluing Reichsmark. The shortages."

He said nothing.

"I can fix it. Just need the sources of some articles at Der Tagesspiegel. Along with their home addresses. You'll be paid in Deutsche Marks."

He paused. Seemed to weigh it up, and came out swinging.

"You fool. Look at your bargaining position. There's a blockade on, currency is worthless. And as for unveiling me as a bigamist..."

He smiled at me, and I found my own confident face in need of buttresses.

"What do you believe to be the consequences of that? I work for the press. Grub street. They like my copy. I go tell them I'm not Luciano Beck, they shrug, and on we go. And my ex-wife? Where would you find the paperwork for that?"

"Look here, Elbert," I stuttered. "Don't mess with the Interior. There's plenty they can do to make your life impossible, or worse."

"Worse than impossible?" he grinned.

"Perhaps lose the freedom of the city."

"Bullshit. Go lean on some other mug. You're not cut out for this."

July afternoon was hot under RIAS' steel-clad panes. One evening slumped in my chair, my show nearly done, I was flicking the news bulletin: *995 tons per day arriving in Berlin.*

Since my brief overnight stay at the VoPo's pleasure and Angie's vanished manuscript, I'd become a bit lax on this 'persons of interest' thing. Nothing'd happened. The final stabs of *Let's face the music* bellowed through the room. I got up wearily and was startled.

A white card had been slipped under the door.

> Angela will be accused of breaching exchange control regulations, pursuant to authoring or aiding publications of anti-Soviet materials in Western Berlin. Go to Kuhlake in Spandau Forest, north-east where the path splits five ways. Head east past a lightning-struck oak and you'll find me at the lake. 2pm tomorrow.

I walked through Spandau Forest until it opened out and thin birch untidied the sky. A back on a bench had a bald crown and wrapped dark hair. I pulled a bag of duck bread in case it wasn't Our Best Interests. (Twenty-somethings do that; visit remote woodland alone for ducks).

Once alongside the head turned. I dropped the bag, felt dizzy and bent to retrieve it. I walked towards him.

"Hail number two son, well met."

Günter looked so tired. Dumbfounded, in the end I just muttered, "Adelheid?"

He shook his head. "I don't exist."

Wow.

"I expect she remarried. She wouldn't survive without something to wipe her feet on."

He cracked a smile and I barked in hysteric joy like a seal. "Günter!" And I rushed him arms outstretched.

"Don't get excited, we're not resuming dinner parties."

"Five fucking years! What if you bump into her?"

He scoffed. "Adelheid's only left Hamburg twice."

"So Ange. Tell me."

"I can only tell you what I can tell you."

"Whose jurisdiction?"

Günter raised his eyebrows and his pinched face opened, "Volkspolizei."

"How much danger?"

"They'll arrest her."

"When?"

Günter shrugged. "When they're good and ready."

"By which," I looked at the weed-strewn ground, "I can assume you're on the payroll."

"Not VoPo. I'm a handler at the Interior, Ministry of Machine Building."

"You said currency violation."

"For the western press, if they're sniffing."

"I've a friend at Associated Press." I huffed and stared between my shoes. "What can you do? Can you intervene?"

"Usually... well," he became more bedraggled. "Usually, it's a deal. What can she do for them?"

"Who?"

"The Interior, SED. NKVD. Vormelker. A rose by a hundred names."

"What's a Vormelker?"

Günter looked pensive. "Who I answer to. We knew him in Berlin, of him, you were in a pram. Need to watch it beyond western jurisdiction."

I nodded.

"So?" Günts peered at me.

"What?"

"What can she do?"

"Chrissake. Teach German history from the eighteenth century onwards, any use? Or were you thinking honey trap?!"

Günter spoke quietly, "Which only leaves informing."

"How did you find me anyway?"

He laughed. "RIAS gave me your address, after I'd proved I was your long lost brother who'd heard your show."

"You survived bloody Stalingrad!"

"In some ways."

"But the army letter. They didn't know?"

"It was desertion, but that lands you a red rifle shooting Germans, which the Wehrmacht censor. So I surrendered, *we* surrendered, making us PoWs."

My aubergine-shaped brother, his pale skin and paunch and clamouring hair, were highlit in bright sun.

"Look," he said, unlaced his boot and whipped off a sock. His foot was a stub. He'd lost all his toes and the pink blood-pumped skin of the healthy faded to shiny white and angry pink. The hand that grasped the foot had a hooping scar on it, like a ruched carpet.

"Christ."

"Frostbite. Typhus. Skinning rabbits, hiding in basements. Shot at from the air. Poles breaking my ribs and teeth, then Russians. There was an attrition of the soul. I doubt you'd have survived it Otto. The journey back."

"I'd have deserted long before."

He redressed his foot awkwardly and I scanned the lake's unkempt banks. After long familial quiet I said, "So you move east-west."

"Yes."

"How's that?"

Günter smiled. "Sometimes I take the U-bahn. Sometimes I walk."

"I mean papers, identity."

"Employee at Machine Building when I'm east. IG Farben when I'm west."

I nodded south to Spandau prison. A thin, off-white factory plume drizzled up through the blue. "Albert Speer's in there. Moving when a claxon sounds. Dishing slop. We're out here rebuilding a meat-ground cake-sliced nation."

I flapped my shirt, the day warming up.

"Germany thought it could deal with its own conscience. It needed strapping down like a beast."

"Ha, you've changed! Eight years ago I stood outside Fuhlsbüttel watching the renovations, before I was thrown in myself. With Papa and Albert popping in to rethink... efficiencies."

"We all did our best. In our constraints."

"Don't know if I helped or hindered."

"Eh?"

"Nuremberg. I testified."

Günter looked at my face as though it were a new invention.

"Don't look like that. What do you believe in now?"

"You once said loyalty can be given once." His face squished a frown and shake of the head, but his eyes travelled me. If that proved a point, he'd waited a long time.

"I see how they got you, brother 'o mine," I said. "This er... Milkmonter--"

"Vormelker."

"Brainwashing, coercion, violence to you and yours. It's old hat, isn't it. Okhrana-style. Now they get the shit kicked out of you through other agency, right? Instil a hate of your fellow man. You'd gladly ship us all to the Gulag."

Günter laughed. "I like my fellow man. And it's a certain order keeps me liking them."

"So the VoPo took her manuscript." I finally asked.

"Left to themselves, they wouldn't be arresting her. It was some careering jobsworth that read Tagesspiegel and matched the two, asked who the manuscript belonged to. Inquart I think his name is."

I must've started flushing, between deadly pale and anger. "Reinhard... Inquart?"

"Yes," his brow queered. "That's him. Nasty piece of work I hear."

"I need to get back," I murmured.

"You have information?"

There he goes, my half-brother, you see? Toes intact unblacked by any steppe, his tall and craning looks. Lush hair and charmed life.

Even his birth date was charmed: never marching east or west. Never seeing comrades barked at in shattered urbanity, gunned by snipers in dead warehouses. To sit in juvenile correction, a bowl of soup and all god's hours to dream. Yet I can't hate him; still less since Papa's death. Cocky generation, bolshy and moral, but he's all there is. I've no idea what he thinks of me. Older, wiser, dumber? A brick in the establishment? Even that's changing and the corruptions aren't quite formed.

☆

I reconstruct in the mornings in the guts and piles of Berlin. Moving reclaimed brick in buckets. Or timber to scaffold buildings. We butch rubblewomen clear this endless carpet for extra coupons. Leaving my afternoons clear for the airports.

I'd gone to Tempelhof to unload with Otto, but he was put on runways - the heavy pierced steel planking carted back and forth, sixty-five thousand yards of landing strip.

"You don't look too..."

"What?"

"Well excuse me Ma'am. You're quite petite."

"I can move bricks, I can move food."

"Can you drive?"

"Yes," I lied.

"Fancy a nice uniform?"

I inclined my head. "Honcho's got the hump about pilots away from their planes. He's obsessed with turnaround."

"OK."

"He wants women to take canteen to the planes. Speed it up."

"Trolley dolly?"

"Well you're an attractive Frau... Fraulein?"

"Fraulein."

"Right. We can put any old beefcake on unloading. But the pilots like Berliner women making their coffee. You'll get a Jeep."

"Foxy Fraulein."

He grinned a big Atlantic smile. "You said it Ma'am."

So I got a Jeep-cum-cafe instead. A benefactor Tunner may be, but that honcho is also strictly logistics. And I saw his point. A pilot couldn't have an affair in the five minutes before departure, so my stocking'd dolly colleagues flirted like hell.

Otto has explained to his brainless dolly the significance of Superfortresses landing in Britain. They may, or may not, be silver-plate B29s. If they are the Yanks are signalling a willingness to A-bomb the Walrus. But nobody knows. Nuking bloody Stalin! That'll certainly give him sunburn.

I sat with Otto in the room as though we'd summoned ourselves for punishment.

"So I'm a counsellor now?"

"We wouldn't have come otherwise."

"Well maybe Otto's right," said Maria briskly; we'd not spoken since the examination.

"How?"

"Time apart is good."

"We had four years apart."

"Now living on top of each other, trying to find yourselves in this mess. You're young."

I wanted to say something, but preferred Wagner's voice to my own.

Otto said, "We remember before all this. We're not that young."

"So why can't you get on? ...There's not much food, there's blackouts and an international crisis. You've weathered worse."

Otto looked at me. I caught his eye with a twitchy mouth.

"You earn money! How many people can say that?"

And I felt like the spoiled, lost Hamburger's daughter needing validation somewhere beyond us. Like Leo needed his yacht, maybe, and some lounging spectators.

"Have time apart, but don't scour elsewhere. No stocking fillers." Wagner looked with mild remonstration at me. "You came to see me together, so you know how the play ends."

We nodded in unison, almost.

"You're a pair of dopes. You need your heads knocking together."

I had a dressing down from director Rosenthaal, for running amok over the Easter closure. "Trespassing, stealing, drunk on the premises, vagrancy and worst of all, dead air!"

"How do you know I was drunk on the premises?"

"Schäffer's vodka."

"He's open about that?"

Rosenthaal shrugged.

"Sir, I've had some problems. I split with my girlfriend and I'm living hand-to-mouth in a bombed-out shambles."

"You only! There's just two reasons you're not getting fired. One, nobody was listening..."

One person was.

"Two, you're quite good."

"Thanks." I looked at my shoes.

"But, Otto, it's a two strikes and out policy."

"Understood."

"We all have our lunacies. Keep them out of the building."

Otto came in breathless. "It's kicked off in the French sector. There's German workers heading for Tegel, fucking... thousands... where the Berliner Rundfunk mast is. And angry Soviets."

"What, like protests?"

"Not protests. The blockade ...scene. Workers. Heavy trucks taking bricks. It's all gone a bit Victor Hugo."

He dropped his bag with today's vinyl haul. It occurred to me he was robbing his own livelihood unless they were duplicates.

"American or Russian trucks? Christ. We need a radio."

With a mystery expression Otto held up a finger, leant outside the door, and produced a brown bakelite *Philco Transitone*. I clapped my hands in glee.

"French trucks. And that plug now works."

"Napoleonic Wars round two."

"The Yanks will save the day."

"You always side with Yanks. Should we head and see?"

"The S and U Bahns are closed."

"And the trolley bus?"

"Let's try."

We arrived near Tegel and walked to the French airfield. The streets were full of people; a worry and a gauntness back on faces. Except the French, who laughed and braggadocio'd and puffed smoke.

Once we'd got to the edge of the airstrip it was pandemonium. French and British troops were trying to keep people back as German volunteers laid a new runway with reclaimed bricks. Several Soviet officers were in a state of scarlet rage. They hadn't the presence to overthrow this kick in the teeth, but they were staying put like the cavalry were due, or to imply it.

Trucks drove as fast as they safely could through the chaos. Lighter aircraft needing only grass or the short runway were milling and landing and leaving. Children watched with joy - every tadpole loves a shiny plane! - while parents had a different expression; a weary trepidation.

Nobody believed conflict - war again - was impossible, and nobody had enough food or heating.

"The electricity went off in Winterfeldtstraße last night," I said to Ange.

She was chewing her unvarnished writer's nails, curious as a child, anxious as a parent.

"There's only one power station in west Berlin, out near the stadium."

A man leaning on a walking stick looked like he'd been here a while. "Excuse me," I touched his arm. "What's the scene?"

"Russian and French standoff."

"Red sabre-rattling?"

"French sappers didn't help. They blew up Uncle Joe's radio mast."

I laughed.

"This city's gone nuts. Railways shut. Electric from the east turned off. The bridge over the Elbe's closed as 'unsafe'. No boats, no cars, no trains."

"Over the Deutsche Mark still."

He nodded. "That's his excuse."

"Harsh."

"The only thing the Reds can't close is the sky. Hence..." he waved a hand at the rapidly building runway. "But they still buzz 'em."

Thousands of German volunteers, specks, broke bricks into rubble from any destroyed building in the vicinity (clearing room for the runway itself) - while stacked Skytrains circled avoiding the Fairchild deep-bellies bringing steamroller parts to level the land, all bumping onto the old runway. Some of the kids cheered. I cheered too, in sudden overwhelming love of Yanks.

"You got Sunderlands landing on the Havel river too. They mean business."

"Tempelhof's stacked like a beehive."

"This is where you and me part ways you western capitalist," Ange murmured in my other ear. "We are a love divided."

I looked quickly at Ange, but she was smiling through her nails.

"This is getting serious, Hon."

"No heat, no food? What's new?"

Fair point. Technically, our adult lives had only known scavenging and freezing. The screw was tightening again, only it looked like people with epaulettes in far-flung offices cared this time, perhaps.

RIAS' money and coupons became useless. You can't buy nothing. Proving Stalin's contradiction: Red Plenty should bring equality and it does, that of being worthless.

Do you ever get an inkling of alternative fates? Nobody in their right mind wants ghosts, dead ones, reminding them of horrible epochs, but how much worse is a live one? Corpsing the street with lifeblood.

I was in shock he was here, but almost dead.

I was in sunny Boxi Market - a half-day off to fondle antiques - when I saw, and ducked to avoid, König. *Yes.* Klanger König. Shell-loader Woźniak.

He still looked typhoidal, light-averse, but that could have been his shrunk stoop - the edges of his face green like Soviet striplight; a coppery, quaking hand using a wall for grip. His bald crown was matted, his concave cheeks... well, I dare say you know what a tramp looks like.

But he looked twenty years his own senior, certainly closer to the angels than Otto. Good grief.

I crouch-hurried the length of a loaded trestle; at the end I ran headlong into a girl's stomach, a grubby girl being chased.

"Stop that brat! Hold her. Grab her wrist, her hair."

A wave-armed old codger, limping like a polio bracket, had alerted other stallholders who converged round me and the magpie, probably a Zigeuner.

For a moment my eyes locked with hers: "Run like the wind," I whispered.

Once in open space with my back to my former friend (focused on his undead goals) I walked briskly over the verdant garten to the street.

Sat at home I looked at my sock. The right one, where the end contains no toes. I thought of the savage playfulness of the fates. I mean truly. Like those flippered pinball machines: you're the ball, shooting up the arc, awaiting the buffets and pins that bounce you unceremoniously to ground.

How you fall is out of your hands. One wrong buffet, you are unforgiven.

Otto continued to live in his Kleiner Tiergarten bolt-hole, but came over three or four times a week. The hunger leavened as Avro Yorks and C54s brought in more voluminous bounty. When Otto wasn't here, I was there, or we were both at Tempelhof airstrip, sweating.

July was deepening and the room hot. Three greenhousing panes remained, the fourth re-boarded. I put my swimming costume on under a light dress, happy to return squishy on a bus, packed my bag with chapter three of *Socialism Betrayed* and a towel, grabbed some coins from a bowl and left.

Off the tram, I took my sandals off and walked under the trees to sand beneath white cloud tails in the blue. Wondered whether to leave my stuff, figuring nobody'd steal it, not here, and padded to the bank where the lake slowly glittered.

Out here as driftwood, water like gelatin, it seemed bad faith was impossible; bad men irrelevant. Out here it seemed the male species tried hard with their silly ambitions.

A cloud hid the sun and my heart started beating fast and irregular, lungs not responding to instructions to breathe. The water pushed at my chest and I started to panic. I flipped upright and saw I was far from shore, wondering what was below.

My hand shook in front of my face and I ducked under, came back up spluttering and breathed deep. I started to moan and it rose to a shriek. I splashed to try and get above the water. To get out of it. I must have been hyperventilating and my brain was exploding colour. All I could do was splash and try to rise. I felt a pair of hands grip my upper arms.

"Don't struggle, I've got you."

I turned my head to the nut-brown old swimmer.

"Just put your arms round my neck and we'll swim to shore."

I did as I was told, silently. Halfway back, "I'm sorry, I had a panic attack."

"Don't worry girl, you'll be fine." His strong arms pulled the shore nearer. But lying on this man-raft, I could see something on the shore, two dark, bleary shapes.

"Fraulein Schmidt." Two Volkspolizei stood stupidly in the sunshine, their beetle-crushers incongruous with day, black sun reflected in them like little universes. "Please come with us."

The old man righted us in mud and sand, propped me up.

"Why?" I spat Müggelsee and pushed my hair clear; covered my chest, thigh deep. I looked around the long beach with

193

recliners and relaxers, all basting and elbow-propped in Stalin's sun.

The old man barked, "She's had a shock. Leave her be."

"Get about your business now, old man."

"What do you want?"

"We'll talk at the station."

"Talk here. It's a damned silly place to arrest someone."

My raised voice made nearby heads turn and go quiet; which had a domino effect, ripping sound from down the beach. But of course they would. When I'm vulnerable. Less fuss, more compliance.

The old man stood stock still beside me in the water, staring angrily at the officers. I looked down at the VoPo's hand, clutching my bag with the manuscript. What a bloody fool I am.

"Put down my things! Has a woman no privacy?" Downwind, the beach shut up.

"That depends, Fraulein, on how she uses it."

In shaded trees to the south a man stood in a grey suit. I squinted past the officers. The shape of his head. The barrel torso. The hair that wouldn't lie flat. It couldn't be. I couldn't stay in the lake forever, and slowly sploshed out for my public arrest.

I stumble up at one a.m. with the Monterey to play, but her room is empty and wrong.

The clothes rack holds her night-out selection. Neither of two outfits are missing so she's not socialising. The HY boots

194

sit beneath, toes convergent. The apricot summer dress is missing.

Nothing in the typewriter. I look around. She said she'd swim this afternoon. No sandals. I peer at the drawers in the diner-dresser. Open one, meagre underwear ranged on the base. I ransack gently. Her swimming costume is gone, that most important apparel. After midnight, alone?

I stayed there. Sixteen hours later, no sign. The VoPo'd made their move. Some decision or connection in their annals. I clutched my head. What now. Günter? Dwight? Or storm the bastille...

"You. How on earth did you get in? You're ex-Nazi. Except there's no such thing is there, just the changing of the guard."

"I impressed the Commissioner with the skills I possess."

"And you love a uniform don't you. Being told what to do. A shiny badge and running with the pack. Rodent."

"Ahh, you haven't changed Schmidt. But that's fine. Without you they wouldn't need me."

"What happened to your pal Scholtz?"

"I've no idea. One cannot tie one's horizons to Hamburg. That western cesspool."

"Poor Reinhard. Little boy lost in freedom."

"Right. We'll make a start."

Inquart picked up my script from the table and started reading:

"In 1907 Josef Stalın stood on a roof in Tiflis, Georgia watching a bank robbery he'd organised, smiling at the carnage of dead workers and Gendarmes below through smoke and dust. It would net the Bolsheviks 341,000 roubles." Reinhard smiled. "Well, that's rather damning isn't it. That's on page, let's see.... one."

"Yes Reinhard. Damning is the point."

His stupid wide head started leafing through to where he'd presumably drooled some notes. "Page thirty five. 'Though Lenin did ost.... Osten--"

"Ostensibly."

"...believe Communism would save and elevate Russia, he was an elusive figurehead who cared as little for the lowly as Stalin, never getting his hands dirty, and forcing the people to swap Imperial slavery for chains to the state. He finally balked at violence carried out in Bolshevism's name when his former golden child, Kamo, tricked new recruits training in the Finnish woods with a faked White Guard attack. When one of the trainees broke silence under questioning, Kamo had the man held and ripped his heart from his chest. Only then was Lenin revulsed, and turned his back, ejecting him from the party."

"It's alright isn't it, when you read it back."

"Stalin's one thing, Angela. But despoiling Lenin too?... That's heresy as you know."

"And you only know because you learned to read last week, and read my book."

"I should have cut your tongue out at Neuewall, and got a pat on the back for it."

"Here it is, Rutthand, luscious and pink." I opened my mouth and waggled it at him, then laughed loudly.

4. THE PEOPLE MARKET

We'll shine one day Ange, parasolled on the Ku-damm, stopping for lemonade, perhaps. Swim unmolested leaves turning gold. We'll retire to Marienwerder and tend veg with April on our backs. I see you with body stooped and belly crumpling but your eyes unchanged as we leap from a boardwalk, laughing geriatrics, blind to the future.

What's wrong with people. Bastards - don't they have hobbies?

I trammed to Adlershof VoPo. The buildings were nineteenth century, one with large ornate windows, the other's pissholes in the snow. A bored guard at the barrier.

"Yes?"

"Is Angela Schmidt in custody here?"

"This isn't a police station. We're not open to the public."

"If she is here she's allowed a visitor? Or to contact loved ones and let them know."

"You know for a fact she's aiding enquiries?"

"I can't guarantee she's *aiding* them."

"Detained."

"I've been swiped off the street without warning before."

"What were you up to?"

"Ahh," I waved it away. "American radio. Not political."

He looked on with doubt and menace. As though if he was bothered he might delve my secrets, but he wasn't. He was distracted by the dirty chain of Douglases in the sky. "Everything's political. Try your luck. Cause any fuss you'll be out with a gun at your head. ...Or in."

He waved me between the barrier and booth. Inside I looked for someone useful. After a while becalmed in the vestibule as officers drifted from door to door ignoring me, one came over snapping a file closed and said, "There's no unauthorised access here."

"I need to speak with the... case handler for Angela Schmidt. I have information useful to him. The guard let me in."

"Did he. And which enquiries is Fraulein Schmidt aiding?"

"Political probably."

"You're sure she's here?"

"Pretty sure. It's my best guess."

"What is your information?" Something in his eye said he did know she was here. I ignored his question.

"Would it be Reinhard Inquart running that investigation?"

The officer looked surprised.

"I really think it's in his interests to speak to me."

"Inquart is having lunch. If you'll wait twenty minutes, I'll ask if he'll see you. You are?"

"Otto Bebel."

He opened a door a few yards away, switched a light on and ushered me in. Windowless, claustrophobic; table and two chairs.

I felt a chill, realising I'd hand-delivered myself to the shadows behind Berlin. I should have told Dwight and Günter I was coming.

"Still the deviant," Inquart strode in, "But grown up."

"Well, one of us is."

He bared teeth, far from a smile. He'd a smart green-grey Oberleutnant uniform and - I should have expected - a gun pouch on his belt. "Good way to bring you out of the woodwork."

"I've already been arrested and detained," I sighed. "I've been sucked from the woodwork, or sucked back where the worms are thriving."

"Survived labour camp. Wonder what you traded?"

I didn't answer, scraped back my chair and lifted the back of my shirt, so he could see the scarred 'INF' on my back. I sat back down.

"So you have grown up."

"I'll get straight to it."

"No hurry, I've eaten."

"You're holding Angela without access to counsel, for a charge unrecognised by international law."

Reinhard frowned disagreement. "That you don't recognise Soviet law doesn't make her detention a crime. We don't need recognition."

"Well, that may be true behind closed doors."

"Which is where you are now," Reinhard said.

"Don't threaten me, I've got friends. CIA. Agents and hacks know I'm here."

He smiled in a way unfazed. "Come on, spit out your deal or threat or whatever."

"The Associated Press feeds stories to hundreds of newspapers. I know you're holding Angela for subversive publications."

"Are we? I thought we were holding her for currency violation. Which incidentally, I could throw you in a cell for."

"Why haven't you?"

"Because your tart is a bigger fish."

"Then there's RIAS, where I work, which broadcasts all over the Soviet zone."

"Beaming your little show tunes?"

"Release Angela or the western media get a scoop, and the world's gaze falls on the Soviet response."

"You're deluded. One scribbler, a woman at that. I doubt it. Besides it's not my problem. Uncle Joe's brigade take care of those matters. I just interrogate trouble-makers."

"The article goes to print in two days." I got up forcefully, though this place scared me, and opened the door.

"You're wasting your time," he said. "She stays put. And she is fun to question," he grinned.

I walked for the exit with a prickle up my back. Something untoward was rising in me. Something unknown. I breathed easier in the courtyard, and easier still beyond the barrier.

What stupid bluffs. It was only staring Rutthand in the face I realised I should have spoken to Dwight first. And I now dashed across town to the Ballhaus. If he wasn't there a phone was.

I called and he was with me an hour later.

"Ange's been arrested."

"For publications?"

"Yes. And I went into the VoPo station and threatened them. Well, more an ultimatum. That I'd blow the story via Associated Press. An article in two days to all members."

Dwight looked alarmed, the whites of his eyes large. "Aah, not sure you should have said that."

"I didn't have a plan, just went in guns blazing."

"Yeah but Otto, for one it's not going to happen and two, well suppose it did."

"Yes?"

"This imagined media spotlight falls on the Soviet authorities, what do you think they'd do?"

"Well they'd be... er... forced to--"

"You can't force Russians to do anything. They dig in. They'd pick up more dissidents just to point out it's none of our business. The AP feeds American newspapers, primarily, so we're in the middle of a standoff, an unjustifiable blockade, and you think running a story about secret police holding subversives will help her? Or the crisis?"

"Public outcry."

Dwight clutched his forehead. "Nothing they do is justifiable. So they don't justify it. They just do what they do and see how near conflict they can steer. No apologies. No explanations."

"Fuck," I said, in summary.

"Which gives you two days."

"And do what? Now I've screwed it up."

Dwight rubbed his head, sipped his drink. "Do you know their intent?"

"I presume just hold her so she can't publish."

"Indefinitely then. So she'll be moved to an intern camp. Probably Sachsenhausen. And in two days you'll be proved a fake with no strings to pull."

We were silent a moment, Dwight probably more lucidly than me.

"Different approach."

"What?"

"Transaction. That's how Russians like it, not bloody ultimatums."

"They're German. It's the VoPo."

"Yeah, and you've made giant leaps there, haven't you. You said Günter knew she was being watched."

I nodded.

"How high up is he?"

"Not very. A handler, but his boss knows everything at the Interior. It started with background checks."

"OK. We go over the VoPos' heads."

"What with?" I looked a bit pleading, having bollocks'd it. Any sense of adulthood I'd cobbled together now seemed woeful with Dwight in deep thought.

"We had a good coup two weeks ago. An SBZ operative brought the biggest list of industrial spies in the Bizone. Everywhere, BMW, IG Farben, Siemens..."

"Valuable."

"He's too valuable for trade, I'm afraid. No disrespect to Angela."

"Then what?"

"The people on the list. There's hundreds."

"What use are uncovered operatives?"

"We haven't cut their tongues out."

"And to you, one political writer?"

"They haven't cut her hands off."

"Chrissake," I muttered. "Don't talk like that."

"Well it's a fact."

"Do you turn them? Before they go back?"

"Turn them?" Dwight looked amused. "They won't be seen again. And if they were, what great Soviet advances would they dispatch?"

Do you remember? Spring '47 we lay in Tiergarten by a white bandstand where the paths converged. The absence of men couldn't be ignored - girls danced with girls; stooped septuagenarians in smocks scuttled trays over a dancefloor to tables.

Fed up with ruin we'd treated ourselves, scouring Charlottenberg for Riesling or Sancerre. Found a Chenin Blanc which cost the earth, and lay on the glistering green, smelling soil and grapes.

I touched your arm and believed I'd the essentials and the rest was history; that prolonged human thunderstorm. Swifts from North Africa. The band played *Willow weep for me* with their fussy beards and blazers.

I watched your face, freckled and murmuring.

"In Stadtpark you asked if it was forever?"

"Yes old girl. You were non-committal."

You inched a finger amongst mine. "I can do that."

"That's wine and sunshine talking."

"Yes." You were downy silk.

So I brokered a meeting with Günter and Dwight - calling a number in a bar under Günter's tenement, asking for 'Wilhelm' and the bartender Kyrgios relaying his messages in the evenings.

We met at Spandau Forest lake. To the south white Sunderlands - giant gift-bearing pelicans - came in to land beside Gatow. To the east the crusty little Skytrains went stubbornly into French Tegel.

Günter looked a bit derelict with his rectangular limp and socketed eyes; like disillusion, like failure. But he nodded a lot and said he'd take it all back to Vormelker. The starting bid was ten industry agents.

I sat in a booth in Die Samtwurst under a fringed lamp, awaiting Eberhart Deutsch the gambling journo. Said I'd evidence regarding IG Farben's trial over Zyklon B at Nuremberg.

I didn't, and had other plans anyway. "Ah, Herr Deutsch."

"Call me Eberhart."

"I did some checks, hope you don't mind. A lot of western journalists work for the Soviets now. Spies inside spies as it were."

"Nothing untoward I trust. My skeletons are well buried." He laughed; boisterous and worldly.

"Nothing from my point of view."

He looked at me from his bowed posture, thinking I'd only paused. He'd the face of a resigned masochist, as though he secretly desired his misdemeanours read back. Prison for debt and robbery, unlicensed bookmaking, hospitalised a couple of times.

"They pay handsomely. It wouldn't surprise me. Money for nothing."

"Press plants? What ballpark?"

"Why do you ask?"

"Maybe there's a story."

"Well. Enough that if I were a reporter I'd be tempted."

"Mm. So this scoop on IG Farben?"

I'd invented some baloney I'd never get pulled for, there being no record of me as employee at Farben.

"Yes," I scratched my nose absently. "Heinrich Hörlein, Chemical Research. Looks like he'll be acquitted. They're missing evidence on him courting Goebbels with AGFA film products. He approached the Reichminister personally with huge discounts if Joseph used their film at the Culture Ministry."

"Interesting."

"Hörlein was very ambitious for Hitler's new world. A big fan." I warmed to my baloney, and raised my hands as if unfurling a slogan: *AGFA, filming the Thousand Year Reich as it was made.* That sort of thing."

He wasn't taking notes, or attempting to find a notebook.

"I suppose... you wonder why I'm telling you."

Eberhart nodded slackly.

"Well, I'm no lover of capitalism," I narrowed my nose. "If you find yourself feeling the same way, I may be able to help. Times are tough."

"The money for nothing you mentioned."

I nodded.

He'd been fiddling with a faux-leather menu, closed it, and put it down. "How long does it take a man, in and out of prison, fleeing card sharps and enforcers, trying to finance incredible loans, before he can smell bullshit, before he can smell a rat from half-a-mile?"

"I don't follow."

"Well, you can figure it out when you get back to your NKVD apartment. This capitalist's not for turning, you bloody idiot. You're as subtle as a hippo."

He got up and left.

I sat, my head a question-mark. I looked furtively around the restaurant and caught my red-faced reflection. *Dumpy Günter, Buddha with constipation*. The menu had cheesy Käsespätzle. And dumplings. I caught a waiter's eye.

"Your friend couldn't stay."

"No. However, I'll have..." I tapped my bottom lip, felt saliva pooling.

I took off my months-creased suit for a nap, smelling it tentatively. The sun dropped its westerly frame on my bed. I closed the curtains and stood in vest and pants, side-on to the mirror.

Once my belly, though large, had stopped at my waistband out of biological decency; now it didn't, ending at the place noone went. Black hair sprouted from my back in tufts: misplaced reparations for my scalp. One of my feet was shorter than the other. More a fin, a sea-dwelling mammal.

What would Adelheid make of me? ...If I shocked her by appearing, it wouldn't just be the appearance that shocked her, my appearance would too. All joining the Red Interior had done was make me rounder, softer and less talented.

I went to the loo and echoed. I finished and flushed but the water kept rising, met the rim and stayed there. I had to go and get a spoon from the drawer.

☆

I went to Hartmann & Schwartz to see if Michael knew his agitator was banged-up. After some intercom niceties I went up.

"DJ Otto. A pleasure."

I nodded.

"Ange's being detained by the Volkspolizei. Probably for transit to a camp."

Michael scratched his beleaguered belly. "Good god. I wondered why she'd been so quiet."

"Well she is quiet. Now she's very quiet."

"She used an alias. It was discreet."

"Sure. Until some dimwit Trotskyite next door got both our rooms searched."

His eyes became busy. "OK." He started to pace. "OK…"

"So you've heard nothing. Had no hassle personally?"

"Nothing."

"There's a VoPo officer. I know him, ex-Hitler Youth, matched her script to Der Tagesspiegel."

"Christ," he scruffed his curly head. "You can't legislate for that."

There was silence among us for a while. *Well you can, it's like driving drunk with a headlight out.*

"OK, there's things I can do."

"What?"

"I won't go into them now, but I'll do all in my power, OK? Can I contact you on Angie's hostel phone?"

I nodded.

He grabbed a thick leather bag and a stained jacket flung over his arm.

"This blockade. I respect the Yanks for not deserting us. Every pilot must expect to go down in flames." He saw me out down the steep stairs. "War again."

I couldn't think usefully so called RIAS to run a prerecorded filler. Headed for Tempelhof, figuring an evening's unloading would occupy me.

I tried not to think about Inquart - his private glees - with Ange locked up. I feared he'd do as much damage from below as he could before superiors stopped him, if they stopped him. Maybe he had warped sexual designs.

Salt water dripped in the cargo door and my hands got sack-raw. With the last canvas truck departing, I sat on my arse on the strip, awaiting the next Douglas halting to open. When the pilots walked our way, we got up to get started.

The head Yank in his boiler suit and peaked cap asked: "Say, sir, where's my Berlin dreamboat?"

"Pardon me?"

"The broad with the jeep. Angela. She's the only reason I fly these rusty whales."

He beamed his friendly enamel and I flushed. "I'm sure she'll be back in circulation soon."

☆

So Dwight Westwood and my brother go back, a spook and a jazz lush... Probably Dwight's real job has nothing to do with prison barter.

I picked up the folio. Flipped to Dwight, not wishing to bring Vormelker what he already knew. I walked to the light of my window overlooking Große Frankfurter Straße.

Princeton educated. *Joined Assoc. Press 1938, posted London 1940 with Scripps-Howard. Accompanied 141st Infantry in North Africa / Italy 1942-43. Moved ALSOS 1943, (sub-Manhattan Project), headhunted by OSS. Moved ALSOS to Death Camp photojournalism, British and Russian sectors 1945. Reason unknown. Current role: Unknown.*

The camps, where he met Otto. Moringen and Uckermark were north. I looked up. Outside, below all was demolition. When they'd said 'luxury apartment' I didn't think it would be in a wasteland of falling masonry.

Manhattan was the A-bomb. ALSOS was linked to it but it was in theatre, in Germany, so must be nuclear. And 'the nuclear question' was still open in '46, Vormelker said. A line of enquiry?

In my island wasteland at least Der Braumeister was open underneath the block for when Mr. Tummy rumbled. (I am missing Adelheid). Rouladen and potato salad swam into my head...

I left the folder on the table and took the clanging lift. Nice Mr. Kyrgios and his sauerkraut.

I've a way about me now. Sometimes I see myself in a shopfront - hangdog, expecting the worst - and I peer to be sure it's Günter, not some thousand-yard amnesiac. I'm dressed well but my face...

"You've done what?"

"Negotiated."

"You were getting press agents."

"That's proving tricky."

"Ok, tell me again."

"They're moving heaven and earth to get Angela Schmidt released."

"Your brother's girlfriend."

I nodded.

"So... when I said your family would make you a liability and you strenuously denied it, that was horseshit."

"I'm getting a deal."

"Which is."

"The return of as many operatives as we like."

"What use is a returned operative? They're... non-operative."

"They bring information."

"They do that anyway."

"Not since Dragunov fled, they're held now. Hadn't you noticed a drought?"

"From some people yes," Vormelker eyed me with scorn.

"So," I took a deep inhale. "Name your price. Their opening bid is ten, but you could stretch it."

"Why do they care?"

"The CIA?"

He nodded.

"I expect they'll place her in intelligence, given her knowledge of Germany and the Soviet Union. Or maybe they care at a humane level, she's a German citizen."

Vormelker guffawed into his hand, shaking his head. Then wandered around, fidgeted with a blind cord. "Well, let's make that thirty operatives, and I'll speak to Lehmann at the Interior. It just so happens..." Vormelker turned round and leant back on his desk, "I don't much care for this Inquart squirt. And also happens I've read Schmidt's work. I'd hate to see talent crushed in the Soviet's name under a Hitler Youth jackboot."

Inside, I heaved relief. Thirty industrial spies was a lot, but the wheels, I could feel them grinding.

I was swimming early in the morning in Lake Tegel. I waded ashore to see Dwight in Sinatra attire, concerned his shoes might ruin in the muddy sand. "Thirty agents?"

"That's what Günter said."

"Is he a negotiator or a lapdog?"

"That you can decide. Maybe they started at sixty. What are you doing here, it's six in the morning."

"Maybe I don't sleep either. I'll run it by my bosses, but they'll balk. And halve it."

"We're running out of time. My press bluff will blow."

"Agreed. Are they as good as their word?"

"No idea."

"You owe me Buster."

"Agreed."

I knew about Lorenz, 'Dragunov', the defector. A most heart-warming tale: he'd not come over ideologically; nor was he a double retiring. He was one of the initial recruiters of homebound Krauts for Red purposes, operating from Poland during the '45-46 reverse diaspora.

He'd gone west because an affair with a seventeen-year-old dancer made his life impossible in the SBZ. Knowledge of it reduced his salary and threatened his married life (in which he'd no plans to stand around claiming innocence). As a trapped rat he took what he knew to the Bizone: the names of all he'd delayed from reuniting with their families to become Soviet tics in west German hide.

It served him well: he was in demand both sides of the blockade. And western protection allowed him to remain horizontal with his dancing foal. It also won him trips to an alpine sanitorium for TB (where he was almost recaptured and only CIA goons curtailed it). A most generous and community-minded man.

Still, his list might set Angela free. And when she was, she was moving west.

Always voices, like it's a common room outside, snippets. Maybe not designed for my ears, maybe deliberate.

"Any guidance?"... *"Keep questioning"*... *"Camp no. 7?"*.... *"We need names before they go"*... *"We'll lose her after Sachenhausen"*.

You'd expect chivalry in modern times. A sanitary towel at least; even Uckermark had those. I asked why the claxon sounds in my cell every hour at night. Inquart's deputy said sleep doesn't benefit their enquiries. Even the sink was loose from the wall.

Almost hanging off and cracked, like the loose stained toilet.

I was passing a news kiosk next day and clocked like afterburn the words *...viet history held in Berlin prison*.

I backstepped. There was Der Tagesspiegel laid out on the racks: 'Author of revisionist Soviet history held in Berlin prison'. I bought a copy. Shit. Hartmann. Totally against Dwight's advice.

...Soviet authorities going a step too far in suppression of dissent... Not content with starving the people of western Berlin... Unwillingness to deal with historical truths... ...Brutal NKVD tactics employed in Soviet-run Berlin...

Maybe I should call Dwight.

At seven I was brought mince-mash slop on a plastic plate on a plastic tray with a plastic cup of water and spoon. I wolfed it quickly, left the empties near the door.

The cell was yellow with an iron framed bed, chair, small cupboard, toilet and... that loose sink. The window'd wire mesh, the door a sliding observation panel.

Brief thoughts of self-harm gave me an idea and I sat, pondering. I needed something to smash the sink, looked under the bed. If I could get the sink off the wall I could break it against the floor a few times.

I gave a few tugs to test. Not rigid. Being dinner time, the guards would react slower. I ripped the sheet into ligatures and twined a knotted rope. Upended the bed and yanked the cupboard off the wall. I tied the sheet rope to the high end of the bed frame. Stood on the chair and jumped onto the sink. It loosened but I clattered back and fell on the floor. Up again, another jump. Landed more securely and heard screws grind in masonry. I started yanking it up and down manually.

I'd interested my neighbours. "Girly? You smash your cell you'll get transferred."

I needed time. Jumped again and it came off the walls onto the floor. I landed badly and felt an awful pain through my ankle. But it was off. And had cracked in half.

I picked up the smaller, unplumbed portion, raised it, and brought it down on the other half. There it was, gleaming white, a five inch dagger. I snapped it under the swimsuit and dress I'd been arrested in, pulled the sheets tight, looped them round my neck and waited for the sound of hurrying boots. My hidden hand I used to keep the noose taught, then sat leaning against the bed, other hand palm upwards, loose on the floor, fixing a middle-distant stare.

The observation panel opened and the guard took it in quickly. He shouted to another, and the door was unlocked when he arrived. The man rushed in to grab me and I yanked him unbalanced, pulled the porcelain and put it against his throat. The second froze.

"Can you put your gun on the floor. Er... near me."

He vacillated, and I nicked my hostage's neck to let blood flow.

"He'll need your best behaviour."

Nothing was happening. Except Guard Two kept darting his eyes at Guard One whose eyes I couldn't see. I dug the shard deeper, oozed a bit more surface blood. "I'm between his windpipe and vitals."

The second guard could see the predicament of a far stronger man lying akimbo between the legs of a skinny girl.

"Second time asking. Gun on the floor." I pushed the shard a little harder. The hand I held his windpipe with I crushed causing a gurgling gasp. I heard boots in the corridor.

"Tell him to stay away."

I hadn't thought this through. To get out I'd need to manhandle this giant two feet taller and thicker than me. Unless I had Guard Two's gun.

"Actually close the door and lock it."

He didn't move. I pulled Guard One's adams apple left, exacting another gasp and cough. Guard Two pulled the lid of his gun pouch, removed the gun, put it on the ground and moved to the door, but the door swung back almost in his face and Inquart strode in.

"Dear me. What havoc are you creating now Schmidt?"

"I want safe passage out."

He appraised the room. "Mm. Except I know you rather well."

"Not well enough." And I flicked my eyes at the shard on the neck. Reinhard popped open his gun holster and was pulling the gun.

"Don't do that! I'm warning you."

He continued until the gun was level with my face. Then he had second thoughts, aimed it at my foot and fired, and I jolted harshly with a burning agony. I gasped. Then whimpered.

"You don't seem to have killed Fleischer?"

My hand fell away and clasped my foot arch, pulsing blood.

"You idiots," Inquart spat disdainfully at the guards. "She's a dilettante. A fucking socialite. You thought she would kill him?"

My shard tinkled on the floor.

I'd a beer for Tempelhof thirst, and another. The lights winked north and banked in purple dusk. Those grim pilots had a hangover from the flaming years. I raised a glass to my heroes in the oil-shiny sky.

We are the stark photo negative of Roosevelt's polio dream; a Disunited Nations in one country. Everyone knows what's best. Aren't they exhausted? ...The brink and the land grab and stand-off. The sheer logistics. It's like influenza, the battle rages within and as suddenly departs, leaving the energy to come out fighting again. And come out fighting they do.

Perhaps this was the last decade of the honourable Yank: beyond that decent southerner Truman lay McCarthy and Nixon, rearing their heads one day to demolish America from within.

And why bring back Reinhard for uniformed service; for adult life in a malformed regime. He's no use to anyone but a... oh... yeah.

As I may have said, Ange cannot lie. She is honest alabaster. And as her life is set on a course of authorship, she will fail to lie in print.

"Leave us alone," I murmured into my glass.

"This is bullshit," I heard round the corner and recognised the voice. But it was echoey here: interrupted audio bouncing off brick and iron.

"Come on Schneider. It's not bullshit, you've been busy..."

A common surname but also Falke's; and the voice fit.

I was walked out to the main receiving area at the front in cuffs, to sit under guard and await transport to Sachsenhausen.

"I'll use the rear exit. Am I safe here?" I heard another familiar voice, female this time, leaving an interview room.

"As houses. He's banged up in the back, and she's gone to Special Camp Seven, Sachsenhausen... actually it's the main camp now, One." the officer said.

I looked over and saw the copper fronds from behind, the waifish waist. The corridor swallowed them like fishtails in murk. Only weeks ago I'd seen a stack of old Tagesspiegels on Falke's floor, with Friday 9 July '48 on the top; my first issue. I was flattered.

Inhuman bitch.

Now the tin transporter has red stars, and it's boiling in August. Special Camp No. 1. The grey facade and bleak iron gate, Arbeit macht frei (felt no need to redecorate?), all symmetrical and orderly. Skinny birches jingle by the watchtowers.

The door opened and a Red German looked on as we stepped into summer dust.

I was sweating in my dress, pooled in the hollow of my neck; my shock of curly hair damp from the tin, with my old (insignia-relieved) greatcoat gathered over my arm, my HY boots in the dust.

Dominion, is that it? You remember we gave you Kant and Einstein and Ernst? The Bachs, remember them?

The newly-built brick barracks, womens' section, were worse than Uckermark. Just a giant wine rack of bunks; a cellar to lay down uncherished Krauts and see if their blood matured.

Here we go again, only now I don't understand the guards' language and that which I do - inmates' - is ex-Nazi. One thinks of denazification as something remote from oneself, a word bandied at Potsdam, and far more strenuously enacted by the Soviets. But there are other Germans, variously anti-Commies, agitators, SED-detractors, imprisoned over a bedrock of thirty thousand staunch Blitzkreigers.

I put my empty bag on the wine-rack berth, sat on my skinny arse and looked out the window where the crows carped.

The length and dynamic of my imprisonment is unclear: I'm an enemy of Nazis and a lapsed Commie. Not quite my enemy's enemy. The commandant is Roman Rudenko - a clean, officious prosecutor from Nuremberg.

Everything was far from everything. Always a chimney in the distance as reminder. If they want the German economy beating again - the heart of Europe - then stop treating us like a dead spleen.

I watch Rudenko scuff between offices, his fat rolling at the collar; Ukrainian flesh as secret and blank as an envelope. How does he see us? ...Alpine cattle with clunking bells, or ichneumon flies waiting to inject again?

I gardened in the evening (two square yards) after workshop and the claxoned dinner-flow. I planted cabbages, courgettes and shard. I'd crouch at the soil with my green shoots; my white hands moist with black crumbles. I like dirt.

And then? Night laughs, the winking stars saying we got it all wrong. But its almost a playful verdict, like the horror was childsplay. I find them comforting, or maybe they're Dakota lights; either way they wink like British cockneys: 'don't worry love, sort it in a jiff'.

We stood in Freidrichstraße Station, in the sad green light that would one day separate. Thirteen men and two women stood forlornly in railworkers' brown overalls with the new Reichsbahn logo. To pass these traitors through the workers' building to Interior custody without scrutiny.

Not that scrutiny much mattered.

Expecting a welcoming party containing Ange, Reinhard and whoever else signed dotted lines, there was only one slim man in a cream raincoat and banded trilby, in a far vestibule that opened to the station proper. Back here were only changing rooms, toilets, and a lounge canteen.

He walked towards us. "My name is Vormelker," he said with a courteous nod but no handshake.

He looked between me and Dwight a couple of times. "I'm guessing you're Günter's brother and you're the Yankee doodle dandy?"

He'd picked right, I must resemble him.

A faint smile, and he pulled out a Tagesspiegel from behind his back, flapped it on a beige table. The main piece was about increased volumes in the airlift. But lower down was the headline, third from the top, *Author of revisionist Soviet history held in Berlin prison*. "Oh dear," said Vormelker.

"Nothing to do with us, sir, that's a German newspaper." --Dwight's *sir*s were the distancing Yank kind.

"But Angela Schmidt was held for reasons of national security. The only person who knew this," he looked directly at me, "is Günter. I'm aware you visited Adlershof, Otto."

I gave a mini-shrug indicating so what.

"So I can only assume, the propaganda story was fed from your little consortium to the publishers."

"Well that's quite possible," Dwight said with a sideways annoyance at me. "But what has this to do with today? Are we ready?"

"Seeking goodwill with one face, and badmouthing with the other."

"Even if that were true, we wouldn't be the first, would we? That's a German newspaper. While I'm happy to keep US diplomatic channels open with Russia--"

"The Soviet Union."

"...We can't gag the German press."

"You can't?" Vormelker tilted his face, puzzled. "We can."

"Well, there you go Vormelker. One side trying to rebuild the German economy, the other enslaving it."

"Let's not sink to that."

"Is Angela Schmidt with you?"

"No."

"Why?"

He sighed. "There is a bigger problem."

"I hope it's bigger than that," and Dwight flapped dismissively at the newspaper.

Vormelker's watery eyes looked direct at Dwight; his grey hair shaggy at the collar. "Angela assaulted her guards with intent to murder. She's now on criminal charges as well as a political."

I looked away. Dwight held his forehead in his hands. I didn't believe it. My bright sparrow?

"Meaning?" said Dwight.

"The price is up, murderously high."

"How much?"

"To placate all would require the traitor himself."

"Dragunov? No way, it won't happen."

☆

The women in my barrack were OK. The girl in the next bunk, Gretchen, was the very young wife of an NKVD agent who'd stupidly had an affair with a GI and therefore... was a spy rather than, say, a randy girl.

Luckily, anti-Soviet agitators (or their wives and mistresses) were hived off from the central pool of mid-ranking Nazi women (predominantly guards, killers and experimenters). Stalin's son had died here, which might account for the savagery and renaming it Camp One.

The canteen was the problem. Herded as one, you can imagine there were some tough bastardesses in here with polar ideas.

I was with Gretchen moving with my tray absorbed by what the food actually was, and bumped a woman who might have been mid-thirties but you couldn't tell: she'd been burned on one side of her face. The dessert slopped onto her.

"Ever do that again, you'll feel steel."

I stared at her. She had a Polish accent, and Gretchen tugged the dress I came in with discreetly from behind.

I glanced at Gretchen's ill-advising face, but: "I lived with people like you for four years. So why don't you go fuck yourself."

She slowly broke a smile and walked away. And that was scary. That she didn't reply.

Once sitting, far away, Gretchen explained Marika was a Polish collaborator who'd named Jew-hoarders, got found out and been set on fire by partisans. When liberation came she was shopped and had no trial, just prison. And... she'd a habit of slashing people.

I looked at her retinue. All equally tight and bitch-faced. Smaller, larger, but self-contained; isolationist.

"I'm a fucking idiot," I tried a forkful of brown and yellow substance. Gretchen said nothing.

In Uckermark your enemy was obvious. They'd starched uniforms, strict targets and Alpine faces. Here, your inmates were not like-minded. Not clear. Here, crones who'd guarded us in the Ravensbrück complex mingled with SED critics. Eating wobbly blancmange.

And Red German guards couldn't give a shit. They'd got their brains round a system which will never free anyone, so when a fight breaks in canteen or yard, women clawing chunks or men lamping and slicing, the guards watch: one smokes, the comrade points, the pair smile.

I've a heart and soul, a use, an intellect. A womb. I'm not just words on the breeze, I'm a body of potential: a thing. I'm the full span of my feelings and vivid memory. All you hear is articulation, prattle, but I'm a woman. For god's sake let us out.

I sat with Günter and Dwight in Friedrich's, all cloak and dagger binned. The streets of Friedreichswerde were a bit aggro and demented this afternoon.

SED-fuelled protests clashed in confusion with pro-City Hall and pro-Deutsche Mark Berliners. The VoPo didn't know who was who, and claret flew from shopfront to gutter. Being dressed smart - my grandpa suit, Dwight the shady

Sinatra and Günter a portly banker - we were left alone bar people flying into us.

Dwight was uncomfortable and spoke into his glass. "Bad news. I mean, everything we'd agreed's gone to shit."

"How?" Günter asked.

"The Tagesspiegel didn't help. Who tipped them?"

"Probably a publisher, Michael Hartmann. I went to see him and he mentioned certain actions he'd look into." I said.

"But it's a regional paper."

"Turns a glaring spotlight on the SBZ."

Falke, Johann and Adolfa were in a far booth in fuggy smoke and bent hats. Falke'd a graze on his brow and it struck me protesting isn't working; I mean it's not an occupation. He seemed more interested in grumbling than a job. But then he turned and his eyes were hollow and traumatised; something broad and purple was on his other cheek. Adolfa fussed over him, but her face was blank.

Günter sat quiet in shadow. "You said didn't help."

"Eh?" Dwight echoed.

"You said didn't help. So the newspaper didn't help. What else?"

"Well," I took a breath. "He said Ange tried to murder a guard. Some... spike."

"Christ. Angela? What was the outcome?"

"Sachsenhausen. Probably already there."

Dwight reached into his case. "Seen this?" It was yesterday's *Neues Deutschland*, the SED's and Stalin's mouthpiece. 'Violent dissident spy attacks guards while in protective custody.'

Dwight looked at me. "I'd guess eighty percent of that article was ready to go, if your threat materialised."

Günter looked curious like a thoughtful fish. "Where do you get a spike in a police cell?"

"I don't know. Don't even know it's true. They're Reds we're dealing with. Anyway the price is now Dragunov. To quote Vormelker, only Dragunov will grind the wheels of civic justice to a halt."

We both looked at Dwight hopefully. But Dwight didn't look hopeful.

"Don't look like that." Dwight eyed me. "I can't do it. I mean, they just won't do that. They were already haggling on pawns."

I murmured: "But that's the downpayment on Angela."

What were you thinking, my clear-eyed doe? Your hands being the gentlest. Did you shiv Rutthand? I hope you drew blood. Spiked him with a bed-spring? Strangled with a toilet chain. I failed, my dove my falcon. They moved you further down the archipelago.

I'll get you and we'll resolve for greener days, abiding. Even in your angers I've a hotline - a presidential hotline - to the standards you expect. We'll swim, murky candle, among the flurried mud and weeds, a vanishing wraith of the river, water queen.

Just a waiting game, waiting on Dwight, but I couldn't sit stewing so went to Tempelhof.

Now I know you Brit creations have a thing about Friday Thirteenth and luck. Friday 13th August, the thick cloud and deluge of rain was so dense over Berlin the pilots couldn't see their own wings.

I was straining with flour. The damp children lined the airfield, expectant and miserable in clouds almost hugging the ground. A big Skymaster came through the mesh of water, shining, wobbling, trying a descent too fast having appeared late for the runway. It landed at an angle with the wing scraping the ground and the left landing gear buckled and snapped away, the plane went into a spin, this tin hydroplaning and shrieking on the runway. A few seconds of this and it burst into flames.

I stared, gobsmacked. The terrified children were still as statues; silhouettes now lit orange. But no sooner was this fireball halted than a second burst through the cloud, even later for the runway - no lights to be seen up there, it skidded to touchdown and must have realised with horror how little time they had to avoid the burning aircraft ahead.

From the fireball, the door finally smashed open and two crewmen jumped under the burning wings and ran, singed and coughing but otherwise alive. They almost ran into the path of the second plane taking evasive action, but one pulled the other back. The second plane's tires burst losing control of the landing gear, but it was slowing and out of harm's way. Then a third burst from the cloud, way off target for the runway, veered towards it but saw the flaming carnage and veered back, emergency landing on the sodden meadow, bumping back up into the air and then getting sucked to a stop by soft ground, buckling its nose gear.

Three Skymasters crashed before the remaining aircraft aborted.

Rumour was Captain-General Tunner was up there, the hero of the Himalayan airlift, now doing *Vittles*. We could hear the faint drone in the black fug but see nothing, stacked to 10,000 feet, radio comms in disarray.

I imagined moustachio'd Joe on a long distance call, just waiting for the right moment to shout 'fire!'

A call came and Gertrude shouted up. I grabbed the bakelite.

"We're on."

"With Vormelker?"

"Yup."

"How'd you swing it?"

"Dragunov's been sucked dry. A punctured tyre."

"So what do they want him back for?"

A silence on the line.

The grease-hulks move over the city as inverted sea fluorescence. Belligerent night pilots in unknown history.

There is no work here, no labour. Days are eeked in barrack or yard. I was in the vegetable garden after evening slop, watering the rows. The courgettes died, but Swiss shard struggled on.

I could hear footsteps on the gravel. Far away and irregular, but after a while it almost sounded like a march. I turned, low and warm sun in my eyes.

I shielded them. Down the centre path Marika strode in headscarf and canvas dungarees. Half clear-faced blonde, half burnt plastic. But on the paths by the side walls four more women walked. I looked beyond Marika for guards. The two who'd been on duty had vanished.

I rose from my crouch.

"So, who's going to fuck themself." She'd pulled a folding shaving razor and it glinted dully in her shadow.

The automated crew of Polish girls were standing around me, terrifying in their blankness.

"Will we never get past this."

She shook her head. "You'll know who rules the roost."

"Five women?"

"Well darling, as a…" she spluttered, "a gardening socialist there's a chance you'll get out eventually. I just need to make sure your face is ruined."

The girls stood still, and Marika advanced, blade winking. "They're witnesses. It's good for them."

Vormelker clipped down the Adlershof corridor. I hurried in his wake with manilla. Inquart was leaving his office in brawny uniform, with unspeakable eyes.

"Hold your horses," Vormelker pressed Inquart's chest, stopping him in the corridor.

"For?"

"I'm the signatory of your actions."

"What? Nonsense."

"Orders from above. Above being me. We're stopping the games."

"I take orders from the Commissioner."

Vormelker was a slender man and Inquart a bull barrel, but my superior's light hand on Inquart's uniform front seemed to retract his confidence.

"You'll take orders from me for the foreseeable, if you're of use. If you're of no use, you'll get no orders."

"What rot. And what exactly are my orders?"

"In point of fact, to get out of the way. Happy with that?"

"Over what?"

"I'll be managing the Schmidt situation."

"No way. That's my scalp."

"Your scalp?" Vormelker tilted his head, bent in, and smiled into Inquart's eyes. "You're locker-room scum, aren't you."

"I carry out my duties in line with policy."

"Yes but... I said, you're locker-room scum. Which you're not denying."

"Schmidt."

I looked up in the quadrangled garden. Saw Commandant Rudenko standing with a guard, Ilse Koch. She'd the young, drawn face of someone who might never have known anything, just permanent anxiety.

"Her?"

"If that's Schmidt then that's her."

"It's a common name, Herr Commandant."

"The typist. The rebel."

"Marika. Step away."

Marika looked at me with eyes of death. Rudenko and Koch gazed from afar, two imperious question-marks. The air was swollen, thrumming. *It must be commonplace this*, I thought, *a casual halting of violence without knowing it.*

"Marika! Step away!"

You are leaving the American sector... Berlin was counterpained in rain and the cream Merc smelled of upholstery.

Dragunov was dapper with a gold pin in his emerald tie. His face didn't move but the cogs must be spinning: figuring how to stay out of the gulag. Sold to secrets and violence, and undermining the modern world.

People like Dragunov I wanted to shout at, but what? All I knew - bar labour camps and the droning torpex sky - was that Ange and I'd tried to steer through the shit and thunder; like normal people with normal desires. We had dignity in rubble removal and cargo-bays, broadcasting and typewriters, crusted bread and a change of clothes - but Stalin wouldn't allow it. Like an orca who, having battered a seal to death, still keeps nudging it.

The engine idled, blatting in dusk, and the rear door un-chunked. Dragunov got out and stretched. A heap of shadows coalesced the far end. Great-coats and guns, fresh uniforms. Between us, Checkpoint Charlie sat luminescent green in the gloom.

That cockerel hair on his head; the barrel-torso. The arm that pleaded for a band. The collar that clamoured for insignia. You rat. You terrible rat. Reinhard stood with

Günter - my Stalingradder, my Barberossarer, toeless hero of the gunmetal steppe.

A white light shone between Ange's legs, rendering them thinner, the curly black hair a mad halo. Stood apart, mac-coated, was a man I might believe was a reasonable man, Vormelker.

And my end. The cream Merc. Just me, Dwight, two nameless bodyguards and Dragunov holding his camel-coloured coat, stooped and advancing on his fate.

"Get yourself back to dissolution, your only talent."

"That's a long word, Reinhard."

"Walk."

"You never liked the sound of laughter, did you."

"Nor you. Back to the western dance." He was shuffling strangely.

"Borderless fascist, east-west arsehole. The same boy."

But his eyes had gone glinty; baby-moons in the adult slab. "Go push someone else's tractor."

"What?"

"I said push someone else's tractor." He'd started squeezing the cloth of his trouser-hip, not that far from his crotch. "You heard me. Yes, you remember."

"I don't Reinhard... I don't remember a tra--"

"Blue tractor!"

"I don't remember a tractor."

"You do, so kindergarten when I pushed into the kegel pins and you stopped me, yes you remember! Yes you do."

"Reinhard I don't. Were you at kindergarten?"

"You'll remember."

"I won't Reinhard. I don't know what you're talking about."

But I suddenly did. Christ I'm Freud's dream, all buried. Kindergarten is the first call. How could I forget barging Reinhard, headed for the girl setting up the pins, scattering him unceremoniously to the concrete, veering wild and gouging his knee. Blood everywhere.

The teacher hadn't seen his intent, just me clattering him, and gave me a stinging slap on the thigh. Never forgot the slap, blotted him.

"So walk west."

I looked at him not trusting his eyes, his face or hands. If you see nothing wrong with buggering people's kegels aged three, what's to trust?

Goodbye Dragunov. Dwight gripped his arm along the road and I couldn't hear what he said, but it wasn't encouraging.

Ange left her brigade and walked, precarious, careful. At first I thought she was unbalanced by nerves, then realised she was limping, quite badly. My heart crumpled: how would my nymph dance?

She could see Dragunov moving in her direction. But as I felt sorrow and hatred rise, a shot rang in the wet, hot evening and I couldn't see what happened the other end.

Just Ange, dropped. Blood from her.

I ran up Freidrichstraße. Maybe later Dwight would explain how Inquart was manhandled to the floor. How the NKVD would explain it, and maybe later in life the world would explain it.

The street was hard as nails and Ange was soft. "Don't worry Hon. We have this."

"He shot me again."

"You'll be OK. Press the wound." I looked up the road. The Ruskies had piled Inquart to the floor and cuffed him. Why'd he fire; put lead in my finch?

"Kindergarten tractors..." Ange was gasping. "God, what's his problem?"

I'd been pushing her curls away from her face but her eyes were rolling up, as if fainting. She murmured, "This can't go on forever."

"No. I'll make a tourniquet."

I took my jacket off and yanked and ripped shirtsleeves down my arms. Once she was bound, I lifted Ange with an arm around.

...Always with impunity.

5. REPRISALS

It seems certain you'll understand, perhaps, these were provocative times: Berlin a simmering pot, its handle pointing down the autobahn to Marienborn.

"Ain't gonna happen." Dwight said. "I won't help."

"You saw what happened, no justification. Pure malice."

"How d'you think it works? I go to the quartermaster and ask?"

"What about yours?"

"Chrissake Otto, I don't carry."

Now *that* wasn't true. Once, confiding over too many Bay Breezes that the Red Interior knew who he was, his jacket flapped back showing a leather strap round his shoulder.

"Even if I did, what makes you think I'd hand it to you? My bosses frown at accessory to murder."

"I probably won't kill him. Kneecaps. A fingernail." I held up the finger where my own had grown back warped and angry. "Cosh him with his own baton. When he comes round he can do three years' labour in my garden."

Dwight said without mirth, "You don't have a garden."

The Ballhaus was half-full and the band was running a Hampton & Montgomery set. As prelude to my psychosis it wasn't bad; sliding octave themes.

"You want to see me go empty-handed?"

"I don't wanna see you go, kid. You ain't gonna."

"These are chaotic times. Who'd care."

I supped my drink in the sunless basement. I supposed I could cosh or duster Rutthand, but that was risky on an armed man and seemed a bit savage, a bit Raskolnikov. I wanted a clean kill you know, like revenge served cold and disappear.

I recuperated in hospital with several intense consultants around. I had complications to nerves and tendons.

"What do you do Fraulein Schmidt?"

"I'm a writer. Historian."

Dr. Popper nodded.

"But..." I said with faint hope. "My other love is dancing."

"Mmm." His face frowned. "We're doing our best. I don't think you'll be at the ballet."

Two operations, busy hairy arms holding metal, endless blue, sharp striplight going fuggy and motion sickness on the trolleys. The pain took nearly two weeks to subside to an ache. I was thankful he'd shot the same leg twice, or I'd forever lurch like polio-rickets girl.

With Ange in hospital I found us digs, paying rent but not much. A reconditioned two-bed on Friedenau-Schöneberg borders facing the S-bahn, above a loan-shark and a grubby restaurant. A plan was forming in the mist.

It was my twenty-fourth birthday in four days and Dwight promised to get blotto with me. Razors were a luxury so I only shaved twice a week. I decided not to bother and see what beard I had by Monday: the day of city-wide protests.

I went to find Johann. When I caught up with him he was asleep and took a while to wake. I made him coffee and once sat up I asked: "What kind of drugs are there in liquid form? Heavy downers. Sedatives..."

"Er... I'm more a pills man. But you can get opioids, morphine, that shit."

"You can?"

"Yes."

"No, I mean *you* can?"

"Probably."

"How soon. I'll pay top dollar for your troubles."

"Maybe like... day after tomorrow?"

"Enough to knock me out. A week's worth?"

"Sure. I thought you were more cocktails and blue notes."

"Can't sleep."

"Pop by, Thursday after five. I'll need the money up front."

As I was leaving, I saw Falke's bullshit dockworker or mariner's cap sitting neglected on his radical bookshelf. I tried it on: it fit. "Can I borrow this? Just a few days? Tell Falke... tell him... I'm supporting a canal workers' strike."

Johann shrugged. He'd be asleep again in five minutes.

I called Dwight from a payphone on the lower tenement landing.

"Otto. My preferred jazz Kraut."

"Listen, we'll just have a few beers indoors on Saturday. I don't fancy hitting the town with Ange in hospital."

"I'll come see your new place."

"God no, it's barren. I've just moved our stuff and our stuff consists of diddly. You've got the radiogram. I'll bring records."

"If that's your wish, it's my command kiddo. I'll serve cocktails."

One thing this homicidal kiddo ascertained was Reinhard would be at Monday's protests, either at Brandenburg Gate or Red Hall, or in between depending on the tide. Friedrichschain was his district and he'd be among the activists like a pig in shit, batoning faces too near his pristine cap and firing rounds if it got hectic.

I lay mulling. Dwight advised we kick up no stink, get no press, no diplomats nor his shady bosses involved. To Dwight it was an aberration; he'd seen Reinhard wrestled and cuffed, which in his mind meant a personal grudge that could be distanced from the organs of power.

"And besides kiddo, we got Ange back safe didn't we?"

With a leg she might never walk on properly let alone tango. Inquart's time had come, that venal dogsbody. Or maybe he'd got more than a reprimand, posted somewhere remote: Schwerin... Siberia. He'd shot Ange in plain sight of border patrol. Not that the NKVD cared about condemnation.

But what if...

I mean, they may not care about western opinion, but they do have strong opinions on the west and people shooting VoPos. My fate. Penury, labour and chains, a special camp or further back: the Gulag.

Ladies and gentlemen, it is my considered opinion I cannot get caught. Crowds. Protest day.

"Welcome birthday buddy! You'll be a man soon."

I patted my record bag. "I brought your sort of thing. Unfashionable, strictly Dixie."

"My taste is timeless. It's beyond taste."

His lounge had decent furniture, a small bar, several bottles, mixers and a shaker. *Good, a heavy one.*

But how much? Johann said a mouthful gave a woozy, unbroken night's sleep. A mouthful was about a fifth of the bottle. Two fifths plus the booze? I didn't want to kill my buddy. Have to play this by ear. Give myself enough time to find the bloody thing. And cartridges.

He pointed to the player. "Get stuck in. Let's get this romantic evening for two underway."

"You understand, right? My girlfriend's in hospital, I'm not slamming shots uptown."

"Sure. I understand."

"Yeah but... I'm just saying sorry. In advance."

Dwight looked at me oddly. He had a little table beside the sofa with a pot plant. I sat myself there. The chinking glass arrived and Dwight raised his.

"Here's mud in your eye. What's this?"

"Cottontail. Ellington."

"Yeah it's OK. No downbeat numbers when you get maudlin, I ain't cutting slow rug with you."

"Don't flatter yourself. Cards?"

"Backgammon. How much you willing to lose?"

"I plan to gain. Cost of living's gone up."

"Dollars? Cigs? Coupons?"

"Gaspers I'd smoke. Dollars."

"You planning something?"

"What?" I said, looking startled.

"Relax, I don't care. Only I tried unloading DMs at Tiergarten, they don't like 'em."

"Stock versus paper. Us Germans have a gloomy history with banknotes."

"So? Why you hoarding my greenbacks?"

"Savings account," I said.

"Set up the backgammon then. I need the latrine."

He left his sipped drink, headed out, and I poured my gin rickey into the pot plant, keeping the ice.

On return: "You downed that already?"

"It's my birthday."

He grinned and sunk his own. Got up to refill and handed the second. We started playing. I sipped, and next time he needed the lav the rest went in the potplant.

"Fucking bladder, too many beers before you arrived."

"How many did you have?"

"You were late."

The drinks got larger as evening wore on. He was up six games to four. My turn. I picked up my drink and headed for the toilet. "No sleight of hand. You've already won next month's rent."

"Taking that with you?"

I looked down, feigning slow reactions, stared at my drink for a while. "I only need one hand to piss."

Dwight laughed. "You Krauts are as stiff as poles when you're sober, but once you hit that first drink…"

By ten I figured I could now drink and stay *compos*. Dwight was getting tipsy because his fast game was getting careless and I'd won back plus some. He got up. "I'll fix more on my return."

"I'll fix 'em. What you having?"

"How about a whisky sour?"

"That's what, bourbon, lemon, angostura and something weird..."

"Egg white and syrup. There's eggs on the side and the bitters and syrup are in the unit."

I tipped two fingers and went to the bar. When he'd gone I dashed to my coat and got the opiate. Started the mix. When the angostura was in I judged a reasonable glug. Got the egg white and halved it between us. As he came out I was in his freezer getting ice. Put cubes in and handed Dwight his.

He wasn't exactly swaying but his line wasn't straight. All through the last game my mind had been interrogating places of concealment. I'd poked my head in his bedroom on my last bathroom visit.

"OK. Now I'm gonna send you into receivership."

"No way buddy."

An internal clock ticked through the game. I was about to win when Dwight said, as though having a stroke: "Jeesh man. I think you ratios got the wrong sours whisky kid."

"What?"

He was growing woozy. "The ratios in the whisky."

"Well I'm not a barman. Might be a bit strong."

"It'sh a fine evening. Got sh'ome celebrations in the uptown for indoor bar town."

He lifted the glass again and downed it. I couldn't win the game. It was his move and his eyes had rolled back, then his head rolled back, then his body rolled back into the chair. I was suddenly terrified I'd done too much. No time for remorse. He'd come round.

I headed for the bedroom first, his dresser. Each drawer, rummaging under clothes and underwear. Nothing; no wait. A box. I pulled it out. Plain white rattling heavy. I opened and I had the bullets.

I spent time checking the wardrobe. He'd a bunch of suits which I patted down. Tapped the base for compartments, felt underneath. There wasn't much else in the bedroom so I started in the open kitchen in the lounge. Units and cutlery drawers. Then a glass-fronted bureau. I drew down the desk top, looked in the drawers inside and below.

The bathroom. Nowhere big enough. Would I have to peel back carpets and check floorboards. I hadn't checked under the main bed. Went back to the bedroom. Under the duvet there was a drawer in the bed. Got to be here. I opened the drawer: sheets. Carefully took them all out and felt around. Tried the other side. No drawer.

I stood in the living room with Dwight's stertorous breath like an old man on Christmas Day or a death rattle. Compartment in the walls? Floorboards? I tried each carpet corner, all tacked firm. He must keep it at the office wherever that was. About to admit defeat and force Dwight awake I found myself staring at his coat stand. There were a few coats on it, two of which I'd seen him wear, the other two never.

I was patting down the coats when my hand knocked something heavy. I pulled an unused coat back and there it was, hiding in plain sight, hanging loose on the curled hook, only just concealed by the coats. The gun and holster. I took it, put it my record bag with the bullets and went to Dwight to shake him.

No response. I shook harder, his breathing intook sharply but his eyes didn't open. I got a jug of water, filled it with ice, gave it a minute or two to chill, and then threw iced water in his face. He groaned and his eyes slowly opened. "Wha' fuck?"

"You were making weird noises. I thought you Yanks could hold your drink."

"Somming knocked me. Getting old. God feeling fucking strange I am feeling strange."

"Do you want coffee? I was gonna head, but you were breathing weirdly. I can make a pot. I don't want to leave you in this state."

"Uh... yeah. Coffee. Make that. The coffee. You never my drinks again."

"Eh?"

"Making my drinks."

I got him a strong pot together, put it on the table where the backgammon was. Filled a mug and stuck it under his nose, made his hand clasp it, and got a new jug of iced water and a glass. When I returned the mug was about to tip out of his drooping hand.

"Dwight!" I shouted. "Do me a favour. Don't sleep again until you've drunk the coffee. In fact I'm not going until you've had a mug."

I topped up the boiling black coffee with a bit of iced water. "Drink."

"Not bad, just damn strange." He drank, and after draining the dregs, waved me away. "Get outta. I wanna sleep."

I topped up the coffee again. "Promise you'll drink one more cup before you crash."

"Outta here."

I left and hurried along Martin-Luther-Straße in the dank August evening, heading for RIAS to squat overnight. Had to hurry, they locked up at half-midnight: say I'd left something inside. I'd emerge in the morning and head to Barssee and Pechsee, on the quiet heath to get to grip with firearms; target practice. Dwight might try Spandau Forest. All I knew about modern guns was cliche: arm straight and let your shoulder take the recoil.

Waking up I studied the heavy piece with its wood-panelled handle. I turned it over squinting at the engravings: SIG P210, Made in Switzerland, a neutral country.

I got out to the heath to a deserted spot and practised on tree trunks. As each shot cracked, like God's fingers snapping trees, I looked around in terror for people; citizens. I was missing every trunk, by how much I'd no idea. Tried two-handed, one handed. Bloody awful. Just as I finally skimmed and splintered the bark of a beech (the width of a human), I heard the boom of a dog. Some rustling and cracking and a huge, very black Alsation bounded towards me, its bright orange irises verging on red.

I threw the gun in a bush, but the Alsation ran past and came back out the bush with the trigger guard between its teeth. It bounded back and dropped it at my feet.

"Fuck off" I hoarsely whispered. It kept looking at me. I'd never seen such an inky giant before. I waved it back the way it came. It didn't move. I pretended to throw the gun in that direction and it was briefly foxed so I threw the gun in the bush again.

"Helmut!".... "Heeeeeeeelmut!" came the owner's voice.

The Alsation looked back, having none of it, and loped back to the bush, retrieved the gun and dropped it at my feet. Three times would make it Judas so I put it down the back of my trousers, and folded my arms.

"Helmuuuuut!" The voice was closer. The dog cocked its head but still eyed me.

"Fuck off" I whispered, waving it to the owners voice like I was swishing water. Finally it loped away again.

I sat down cross-legged on the forest floor, breathing heavily. The dog's luminous eyes stayed when I blinked.

I got back to RIAS satisfied I could hit a man. There was a skeleton staff around the shiny corridors doing live shows, the rest pre-recorded. I wanted to call Dwight, just check he answered and hang up, but he was in bloody Intelligence so he'd trace the call.

I'd tried the opiate the night before and it worked, but I didn't take it Sunday in case it affected Monday's focus. Slept barely a wink with oily dreams of hellhounds bringing guns in their teeth.

You see... whether I fail or succeed or bottle or bodge; whether Reinhard continues to walk this earth or lies beneath, none of it alters the judgement, does it? ...Intent. Intent has burrowed down like a tick in my soul, and I will not sleep properly until the deed's done. This is what time's ugly contingencies have done. Uniforms and barbed fences, water torture and artillery blasts and barracks and police cells;

munitions filings and mines and mad girlfriends; torment and rape. It all accrues, and there's just no accounting.

Homesick Hamburger. Orphan of the adult world. A good kid or so I thought, well-aligned to my own conscience. But the question I've been asking all these years - perhaps hidden from my own mind - is how long do you turn the other cheek? Even Jesus went a bit V2 on the money-lenders in the temple. I mean, set yourself up as a paragon, some worthy beacon, you gotta practise what you preach, right?

Goodnight Reinhard. Take a bow. This is what you've done. See you in hell blind boy.

Grandiose Friedrichstraße Station is now a zone of tension; a huge transit hub of east and west. As such security is tight.

In fact all of Friedrichschain is tight. Commies mill until their numbers swell enough to hit Red City Hall. They slump on corners hands in pockets or cracking tobacco-fuelled jokes, in overalls or waistcoats, all SED-goaded. Nervous shopkeepers and restauranteurs peer through shop-fronts like aquarium fish.

It's not far from Große Frankfurter Straße, which was being mostly demolished to make way for Stalinallee, Joe's showcase boulevard. Right now, the VoPo and Soviet soldiers are active in checking papers.

I went to see Michael Hartmann on Friday with a photo of myself. See if he could forge something in his printworks. I knew he felt guilty about the ill-judged news piece, and I didn't want to get arrested before I'd located my Hitler Youth corpse.

"Best bet," Hartmann said, "is I photostat your mugshot over my courier's SED membership. What's the gig?"

"Ah I'm just joining the protests, swell the ranks."

He was flummoxed. "Which side?"

"The money-mad capitalist side."

So he did, and I have papers now. I was too young to be a paid-up SED member but... papers are papers.

Unlike the bellowy Chaplin-years where power was kind of myopic, Berlin now's locked in a childlike, arms-folded stare. In fact, I might as well explain in relative calm, before things get sweaty and sun-bleached.

The SED froze the Assembly's purse so the grease doesn't get paid. The grease throngs for Mayor Reuter's speech today and heads east to harang Grotewohl and Pieck, pinko bigwigs. Red shots get fired, people injured, a boy bleeds to death, and thousands of Commie greasers surround Red Town Hall. Rail-, hall-, canal- workers, anyone paid out of Berlin ducats, chooses sides and storms the bastille, gets shot at and batoned, but they hold. (Even the Filth've split politically: three-quarters diaspora'd with Deputy Stumm). A cordon of Pinks will break into Town Hall and demand acting Mayor Friedensberg - pushed in post as Reuter is too radical - unlock his office and stop hiding. But everyone's hiding. So the Commies barricade them in.

That's how the craziness unfolds. But my mist is on Reinhard who tortured, banged us to juve, switched sides and finished by shooting Ange twice.

Not acts with impunity. Not acts without consequence.

I walked the platforms of Friedrichstraße, light streaming tall windows and a glass roof on trilbies and shirt-sleeves. I kept my two-tone jacket on in September's midday heat. The strap slapped my back (Dwight's quite brawny) and the incriminating steel reassured.

A hand gripped my shoulder. "Business?"

I fumbled for papers, ensuring my lapels didn't stray from my body. Pulled the SED membership, handed it.

The VoPo eyed my papers. "Business?" he repeated.

"Work," I said. "House of Unity on Torstraße."

His eyes kept flicking the membership, and up to me. I probably should have got a haircut. Details details.

"Take the U-bahn to Alexanderplatz," he said.

"It's a nice day. I fancy a walk."

"Maybe not so nice today."

I was passed over, took my papers and kept walking. I'd head for Red Hall, then double back Unter-den-Linden to the Gate. These day-long protests: as afternoon sun heats the crowds they thicken to aggrieved tides, rendering Inquart trickier, but vanishing easier.

I was reclining in the Der Braumeister beneath my tenement, with Tagesspiegel inside Zeitung, and a coffee and beer brat roll. Food calms me, you see?

I was desperately thinking how to turn my last candidate. Failure with Beck the bigamist and Deutsch the gambler left only Egbert Weiß, a smackhead who filed decent press copy.

In fairness, the return of Dragunov for the safe passage of Angela Schmidt had levelled my credit while helping my remaindered family.

Kyrgios the bartender shouted, holding the phone up. Wary, it being Sunday, I approached the bar and Kyrgios clattered the bakelite on the bar. I took the receiver.

"Wilhelm."

"Günter I need your help." It was bedraggled and pained-sounding; it was Dwight Westwood.

"If I can, Dwight, if I can. And that would be... today?" I heard my note of complaint.

"I'm afraid so. Can you meet me at Spandau lake?"

My thoughts grumbled and belly slumped. "OK."

"Two hours. Let's say 3pm."

I took the S-bahn: Yanks needing East German help; perhaps Churchill's iron curtain was jammed.

I like Dwight, he's forthright and I suspect honourable in the masquerade. But my loyalties are casting around for blood-ties lately, and I've no loyalties to overreaching Yanks. I miss Hamburg. So what can you do for me, Dwight?

On the bench by the lake Dwight's pasty face had pink-rimmed eyes: not the man I'd met. A bit ruined.

"Your brother's taken my gun. He's gone cuckoo."

"What for?" But I knew. Dwight's face squished and an eyebrow raised. "Inquart."

He nodded.

"Do you know where he is now?"

"In hiding. I tried RIAS, his new flat, their old tenement, the hospital. He's away with the fairies."

"He knows you'll be after him." I nodded.

"He's not stupid, just crazy."

"How can I help? If he's laying low he's out of my sight."

"I need Inquart's movements. His schedule over the next week. If I can't find Otto I'll have to tail Inquart."

"I can't get that. His department are nothing to do with us."

"Nonsense. You're way senior to VoPos. They dance to your tune."

"Under what pretext?"

"Yeah, I turned that one over."

"And?"

"He's a spy."

"What, Inquart? Simple Reinhard Inquart?"

"Sure, think about it. Why else would he shoot a prisoner heading west?"

I did think, it took a while. Yes that was credible. Angela had dirt on Inquart and he'd meant to kill her but screwed up. "OK, it holds water."

"So can you do it? Like today? Gotta be mercury on this."

My restful Sunday in pieces I'd now annoy Vormelker during his roast. Otto the crazy boy, why didn't he just go relax with some jazz? I tapped my foot, tried to feel like a professional equal.

"What's your line, Dwight?"

"Eh?"

"Lot of work out here for the CIA. Your line of interest?"

"Now's not the time Günter..."

"Nuclear?"

"...Not the time, because there are protests tomorrow. Two protests. Commies at Town Hall and public workers in the west. It's bound to turn ugly and the VoPo will be drafted. Otto's day."

I nodded, battered down again. "You don't look well." After a while staring at the lake. "How did he get your gun?"

"Morphine or heroin or some such. Was out of my mind."

"I suppose the CIA doesn't do morphine training," I said.

"Maybe I'll suggest it."

If I'd bided my time, by now I might be ensconced with Adelheid in a re-built Hamburg house, working for Köhler & Bebel, sitting at my draughtsman's desk. Maybe a wailing baby in the house. But if I'd chosen a domestic path would that have affected all this?

...Johann Fichte said: you could not remove a single grain of sand from its place without changing something throughout all parts of the immeasurable whole. Said it in 1800. (What if he hadn't said it?)

I took calming breaths.

"Vormelker," an angry voice answered.

"I'm sorry sir, very sorry to disrupt your weekend. It's Günter."

"Make sure it's good."

"A matter of security sir. Quite urgent."

"Yes."

"I need a schedule of movements for Reinhard Inquart."

"That vengeful oik? Why?"

"He's a spy, and it's my belief tomorrow he may use the distraction of protests to pass files to a western contact. I need to tail him."

"How do you know this?"

"Well if you recall sir, it was my family or near enough, involved in the exchange. I've spoken to Angela Schmidt and it most certainly wasn't a personal matter made Inquart shoot her. He just happens to be a terrible marksman. Meant to shut her up."

"Well thank you for the information Günter. I'll get our best man on the job. Now if you'll excuse me..."

"No! Sir."

An incredulous silence on the phone. "What, Günter?"

"I'm best placed for this."

"You are?" He scoffed. "How is Günter Bebel best placed?"

I was trying to think. "Sir, I have some film I'm having developed as we speak. It's Inquart's contact, and given the short notice I really think I can pin the pair, if I know where they'll be."

"You don't have a firearm."

"Er... no. Neither does the contact."

"And Inquart will keep his powder dry while you break up his party?"

"I won't break it up sir. I'll tail the contact once the folios are passed. We can pick up Inquart any time."

There was a hefty silence on the line. I could hear cutlery and laughter, female voices speaking Russian in the background. Another, Germanic and male.

"No, not good enough. I'll give you a special operations agent, you can locate the pair and then you stay well back."

Scuppering Otto. This was becoming a shooting party.

"I'm not sure that's wise sir. It will blow the..."

"I've no interest in what you think is wise. The agent will meet you at Brandenburg Gate tomorrow at 8am, with a schedule and a brain and a firearm. Goodbye."

The receiver went dead.

That went well. Still, Otto might get consolation. Once we'd rugby-tackled him to the ground before bullets left chambers - safeguarding everyone's future - Otto could be happy knowing Inquart was deemed a spy, evidence notwithstanding. (And evidence doesn't need withstanding in the Interior.) But fail and Otto gets his potshot, he either goes down or escapes giving rise to questions - difficult and dangerous questions - for me.

I sighed, handing back the phone to Kyrgios in the shadows, ordered a beer and another brat baguette with mustard and onions.

The grey people on Große Frankfurter were summer-tanned, sundialling 6pm. The brass taps and gleaming windows and moving metallic paint promised leisure. A poster opposite gave us beaming Stalin in his white Nehru-collared dress coat. That winged moustache hid the decaying teeth. But the sun seemed to make his smile more benevolent; if that's possible.

I put almost half of the brat roll in my mouth and realised it was too much and I'd no leeway to chew. It was just stuck filling my palate, too large for my tongue to lever between my teeth. I looked around the bar furtively and spat it back out.

If my homecoming had been more boldly conservative, rejecting Vormelker, tomorrow may not be happening at all.

Captain Günter. Deserter Günter. Pobble with no toes.

If my communiques on Angela's surveillance didn't exist, or Inquart didn't pick up Der Tagesspiegel, would Angela be detained; continuing to write and provoke?

Fat epicure. Look at you, spitting food out.

At least my ignorance of these intrigues may have been bliss, but that's not Fichte is it. Dragunov was a disloyal defector, yet if he wasn't there'd be no exchange for Angela. Or not the same one.

Stupid Günter. Case-handling cretin. Agent-turning failure.

The squished regurgitation lay on the plate, wet with saliva. Kyrgios had been looking at me strangely as I stared at my plate.

Half-past midday, cold breeze hot sun. I walked with the archipelagos of pinkos also heading my way to Red Hall. Less showy back streets of tired signs and formica interiors still had restauranteurs and owners at the windows like nervous eels.

Overheard conversations were fanatic or artificial.

"...Arrogance is what it is..."

"...We'll shove those pot-bellied westerners in a shooting pit. Fill the assembly with right-thinkers."

"Right thinkers?"

"Left thinkers. You know what I mean!"

"Steady on. You sound like you mean it, brother."

"Don't brother me..."

"...I just live here and I don't like fat cats..."

Red Town Hall had escaped bombs and remained impressive, its vast clocktower and throwback facades ornate: you'd've thought Stalin would demolish it.

The throng was large, a cordon fifteen-twenty deep. All those people behind me'd fill up back to the far side of the street. Rutthand, where are you?

In the square I was zoning out from the unwashed, trying to think like a uniform goon: Red Hall or Brandenburg Gate. I needed an accomplice really, combing back from central Berlin.

"I'm with you today. I'm Brüning."

I turned hearing the voice, a call reaching past the decades, but gruffer now. He was unsmiling, his choice of worker attire incongruous against that slender neck; trousers skinny and short under an elfin body in braces. We were in morning shadow of the gate, leaning over West Berlin like it would mean business again one day.

"Good god. Detlef!"

He peered at me, a brain motoring through the mist. "I'm Jophiel Brüning."

"Detlef, it's Günts!"

My voice had risen and Detlef looked around, stroking his jacket wherein whatever hid was hid.

"You're the special? Say you remember... Gründgens and Lange, the Rotbart. Forensics Quarterly?.... It's *Günter Bebel*."

"Saints preserve us. Yes," --he didn't stop looking sharkish but leant with an ember of warmth, grabbing my hand.

"Ernst Bebel's son. Man it's good to see you, alive and well. Did you get his schedule?"

"He'll be up this end but the meeting's east, late afternoon. He'll be bashing heads up at Brandenburg for a while. But slow down, forget that a moment..."

"What time's his rendezvous, by your reckoning?"

"I've no idea. And Vormelker, that's..." my brow loaded-- "...that's *your* Ray?"

He was about to protest, presumably about decades been and gone, but nodded. "Didn't know you met Ray, in the day I mean. So. His movements?"

Seemingly unflappable, he was persisting with the job in the face of this.

"Who, the target's? I thought the service would root that, from what I told Vormelker."

My dearest special, my murdering childhood pal, rolled his eyes-- "He didn't tell his superiors when he'd be handing secrets to the west."

"Well OK, what's the rendezvous *point*?"

"Classified."

"But you do know. Detlef... you'll have to explain this, all of it, and give me some slack."

"Yes yes."

"So the rendezvous?"

"Don't *you* know it? This is ridiculous. We have people there, you needn't worry."

"And you have no idea what the contact looks like."

"You do."

I nodded.

"Show me the photographs."

"While you don't tell me where we're going or when."

No reply, bar a slow folding of the arms and a grin from elsewhere.

"Look say where, and what we're doing until then. Or let's fuck this sky high. I have preservation instincts, a vested interest in Inquart."

Detlef's eyes returned, orienting himself and smoothing his clothes. Eventually, "He'll be here with the Soviet army until two-thirty. Then heading east to a rendezvous at City Hall at four. Between two-thirty and four, we believe the exchange happens, somewhere on Unter-den-Linden."

"So when you said you have people there, what did you mean?"

"That we have people there."

"But you don't know where the exchange is."

"Your voice... It hasn't changed."

I circuited the fat boulevard and side streets round Red Hall twice, searching VoPo faces, tucked and shaded in uniform, darting eyes their only movement, arriving back at Spandauer Straße.

I deflated. Either I was the wrong end or he was biding time in a building. I gazed at the magnetic Commie cordon attracting its filings - with City Assembly workers mustering to break the line holding official bags, folders and pursed lips. I headed north on Spandauer against the tide with the Swiss Arms AG bumping my ribs like a pendulum.

On Unter-den-Linden I listened to passers-by. If I couldn't find Rutthand myself I'd glean where things might kick off; where he might get drawn.

It made sense he'd be at Brandenburg, that's where Westerners met Soviets, and where he could crack most capitalist collarbones. I felt more confident except... Soviet soldiers. Chances of success: middling. Chances of getting away?

The nearer I got the more barely-concealed T34s were in side streets. And maybe that was the point. Hide the tanks, but not so well they can't be seen.

I reached Brandenburg Gate, still damaged from ricocheting artillery and bullets. Still a mess. The esplanade had few troops, just a line under the gate, but that didn't mean much. Beyond, westerners in drab workwear - peppered with the colours of homespun fashion - headed north to the Reichstag for Ernst Reuter, shepherded by Stumm's new police.

Further back on Unter-den-Linden, civilian cars had puttered carefully between pinko gaggles. Here, military and police vehicles sped more purposefully to relay. There were more VoPos lining the scaffolded eastern boulevard, along the sides so Americans couldn't see them through the gaps.

My heart was beating fast. I looked down at my hand; trembling like a terrier. My damp forehead prickled. All this for Angie's knee, which was healing. Get myself killed. Or breaking rock with a chain and pick, knee deep in northern snow. What use would I be? No dance partner to support the leg. To warm the bony flesh. Noone to toy her hair like a grooming chimp. No Otto. Horizontal Otto. Earth-frozen Otto.

Unless after suitable grieving she found another.

Fool Otto; hot-blooded Otto.

My heart slowed slightly and I almost laughed aloud: I'd never find him.

"Got a light buddy?"

"What here?"

"Sure."

I reached and felt my own Lucky Strikes. I'd forgotten I smoked, and pulled myself one with the lighter. I lit him, then me. He was staring at me oddly; kind of scared.

"What?"

Idiot Otto. He'd seen the bloody gun.

"Nothing. Er, thanks bud."

"Pleasure comrade." I just sat trembling, the cigarette wobbling.

And there would be other days, without crowds, without tanks; without unsmiling troops. Quiet days where he'd leave Adlershof HQ eating a sandwich and laughing at a colleague's joke and my arm would rise from a shadow. ...Don't be ridiculous. Dwight will have traced his gun in a few days. But there was the rest of my life for this. Anything can be a weapon on the unsuspecting. A car. A swung brick.

And my heart sped up and my veins itched, while my brain went overcast; a numb veil, eyes hooded and reconciled. Looking glazedly round the esplanade, a ruined grey jigsaw with pieces missing: the inevitability that my arm would point the heavy Swiss barrel.

I sat on a bollard, having combed alleys and surrounding streets. Lengthening afternoon had brought jostling at the gate: anger, fuelled by rhetoric and beer. Barked Russian and bad German quelled the American sector tide but more kept joining from the back, the north and Tiergarten, pressing, pushing. It was a matter of time before the cork burst or the bottle was shot. I was pouring sweat, but couldn't remove my jacket. My chest hurt, fear in the sinews. My periphery was blurred pink. Each VoPo car arriving, I watched intensely as the doors opened. And then something happened.

The Yank sector broke in, via bodyweight rather than bravery. The troops shot in the air at first, then the batons swung. But as the pressure mounted Yank-Berliners were running in joyous release in the eastern boulevard. More shots in the air. Then someone went down, and those behind who saw shrunk to the south side still running but crouched. The VoPo came out of the concrete-work and started laying in with pent up violence. Some went down in pain, baton-cracked, the soldiers paused firing to see what success the VoPo'd have, and those up ahead must have felt briefly victorious but trapped.

I moved back east down the street, away from the fracas.

My favourite, Krankenschwester Wolf - a name at odds with her devotion to the ailing - was walking in the ward. Everyone, if not awaiting dinner, a cup of tea, or release from a drip, hoped the nurses were coming to see them. And nurse Wolf was looking directly at me as she walked, smiling.

"Angela, how are you feeling?"

"Better I think. It's a dull ache, but that's maybe painkillers?"

"The plan was to keep you in for another week, around the 13th."

I nodded.

"I have some good news."

My smile faintly mirrored hers.

"Everything's looking much better since that second operation. Inflammation down. Tissue knitting fast. The ligaments have healed. Your temperature is normal, your bloods are normal. You're quite a curiosity to the consultants."

"Oh..." I didn't know what to say.

"So," she beamed, "you can go home tomorrow."

"What day is it?"

"Sunday. But it's conditional on rest. Nothing strenuous. Get that boyfriend of yours on hard labour. And they want you back in periodically."

"That's wonderful Nurse Wolf. He'll be scouring dishes," I beamed.

A tired Horsch taxi pulled up in the sweep. I'd laid my crutches against a wooden flowerbed retainer which I sat on. I acknowledged I was his ride, and he got out to assist. I couldn't wait to surprise Otto. He'd left me the address and phone number of our new digs, but I decided I'd just either hobble in on him, or be there when he got back.

☆

263

"There."

He stepped from a BMW, green jacket unbuttoned in the heat, putting his peaked bucket cap on rust-coloured hair not quite flattenable, like a cockatoo. He shared a joke with the man the other side.

"That's him."

Reinhard reached back in his auto and retrieved a StG44 selective-fire, which he slung over his shoulder casually. It was 1:45pm.

"Where are the documents?"

"I expect he's dropped them near the exchange."

"Let me see your photos."

"I memorised the contact's face."

His nose flared in frustration; I tapped my head. "The old grey matter doesn't forget."

Waiting in the new and sweatless crowds, we leant a kiosk and I pressed, as one presses a hitman... with lemon lollies... for the gone years. He filled some. The murder of Berlin Chief Gründgens, clipped to Vormelker in the Soviet Union as trophy antlers - was truer and more warped than any Chinese whisper.

Sat as a minor in Moabit remand, Dets' lover Ray met with safebreaker Kapuze, the man who baptised Detlef in blood in the first place. A spectacular blowtorch heist sprang him, and the pair - opting first to finish the Hahns (one left), botched Gerhard's killing and ran. On a train to Moscow, a Comintern agent suggested the fugitives join the OGPU - which they agreed was a jolly good idea - Detlef being fanatic - but the agent was promptly shot on arrival, it being Purge Hour, and the pair fled again, along the concourse dropping their papers.

The Kremlin agents collared them within the hour, and presenting their IDs back - both dark, both with flouncy hair - asked which was Detlef Brüning. "I am," said Raymund, with quite selfless bravery.

And so it stayed, even as their identities returned. Nobody at Comintern believed cherub Detlef a cold killer, but the older taciturn Vormelker.... Knocking off a proto-fascist German polizei, and the rumoured killing of a Goebbels' hireling before that, stood Raymund in good stead at Comintern. Soon the Generál-leytenánt had 'Brüning' as an alias returning to Germany. Once here, he kept Detlef manageable by threatening to reveal him unless he did what Ray decreed, mainly liquidations. And as it turned out, speech-writing.

Detlef must be thirty-six or seven, I guessed, far along. He looked stooped and a little misdealt in life.

"It's fine," --he said, after the relayed years. "I'm OK with it."

"It's awful Detlef, obscene, living your life. And you're his rottweiler, a paid-up... kill hound."

"Kill hound. Is that new?"

"Knocking off politicos."

"Well they sell secrets. You sell secrets what do you expect, a snow shaker?"

"All of them? Or did a few annoy bureaucrats?"

I didn't mean to be lancing like a conscience but... I liked Detlef, all that business in youthful old Berlin, there was street law, a little karma in it. Gründgens was bad and the times had tilted, not Detlef. If anything he corrected the tilt a bit.

"Well there was *one*, I was told he was a spy. Turned out he'd just cheated on Ray with a Balinese girl-boy. You can't make an omelette..."

"Jesus, Detlef."

"That's what I tell them anyway."

"Who, Comintern?"

He laughed through his nose, tapped his forehead. "These."

As we spoke he was hitting his *Glock* handle against his hand, swerving his face at the nozzle as if profoundly studying. The stock under his thumb was smudged orange, as if he'd personally and inexpertly applied a decal, like a flame. I'd noticed a peppering of scars on his fingers - thought them gunpowder related, a misfire - but rapt by them, I realised they were teeth marks.

Poor Dets, the dreamer. Maybe a life, a path, isn't your choice. Nothing I knew of Detlef went to plan; though he seemed impervious in it; doomed to purgatory but never harmed.

"A photo would be useful, don't you think?" Detlef seemed strained by the noises I was making. "So I had some idea who I was shooting at?"

"Yes well as I say, you'll be needing me. I have a vested interest."

He smiled. "Like that is it? Maybe when this is done we'll have a good drink. We've both changed. You architect stuff, right? Public structures and so forth."

I raised a brow. "Sure, between espionage gigs."

The Soviet zone ended a little west of the gate, but it was quite arrogant of Inquart to actually park west.

He walked confidently back to Soviet troops under the arches in tall shining boots. General Kotikov called Stumm's new west police Black Guards, implying Nazis, but it was as clear as sun that the VoPo were the natural successor; if not willing brutalists, fearful recruits. A way back, smoking and making no attempt to look occupied, Dwight stood in shirt-sleeves, a trilby and unslung tie.

It was easy to look suspicious today - loitering with intent - because everyone did. Dwight just watched us openly. And seeing me nod toward the car to Detlef, it must have diverted his attention to the target. We'd be forgotten now.

And on cue Dwight was moving in that direction, slanting his trilby a little to the left, and passing him by another arch, into the east. He paused the other side, hands in baggy-trousers; Cagney surveying Mars.

Huge crowds - a drab worker's sea with a luminescence of fashionistas among it - were heading south, towards us. They didn't look happy on arrival and I overheard: "...cancelled for lunch with the fucking Kommandatura..."

Unofficial mayor Reuter had fired up the people only three days ago, with a speech insisting they'd beat the blockade. He must be a good speaker if they voted for him; shuttle diplomacy in the pipes?

What Reinhard Inquart had to say to the Soviets under the arches I've no idea, but he pointed west a lot and the soldiers laughed.

As afternoon wore on it seemed people were melting away but... they started coming back worse for wear. They'd expected a full day of sloganeering the east and weren't going home, just finding fuel. As they melted back, some laughing, some angry, all were fixated on the guards under the gate, and most were now male.

"It's four, I thought you said he was headed for the Rathaus at two?"

"That was my intel."

"Good stuff."

Detlef glared like he had a mouthful of wasps. We passed through the gate ourselves as Reinhard was now east, looking back at the angry mob Tiergarten-side. I discreetly flipped my Interior pass at the soldiers and we passed quietly, to stand in the shade of scaffolding on the ruined north side. I'd lost Dwight, but still could see Reinhard, so Dwight wasn't far.

I'm caressing the gun subconsciously; I haven't eaten in three days. Haven't eaten properly since I moved our stuff to Friedenau.

The esplanade, the square swinging in and out of focus, noise and jostling now louder in the west, pushing and pressuring the gate.

What was this, lunacy, bravery or nebulous karma? A shaking hand pushed sweat from my brow. We aren't brave if our actions aren't ours. Schizophrenics aren't, and neither are criminals of passion. Quivering wreck.

The hot sun was low and blinding over the gate. The people, the vari-hued uniforms of rank and structure, it all started to blur. It was the mess of man: a pretence in chaos;

little humans fighting entropy; dust to dust. All looking assured and knowing shit.

Integrity. I'm sure I had that.

When for the hundredth time the peopled plaza refocused, I saw him. I had to get up and walk west a little to be sure, get the profile.

He was dolled up in green and sheen, proud, the conformist poseur, his face leaning to his comrade who looked like a swarthier version of himself: same height, same arrogance and certainty, a little younger.

Except... the pair had semi-automatics over their white shirts. StGs. Made in the war. The curved cartridge and sight on the nozzle. To kill a man carrying an automatic gun I should probably shoot him in the back...

Can't happen. Tanks no longer scared me, slow-moving cowards in tin. Generic VoPos didn't scare me: Buster Keaton force. Red troops did scare me. They knew their shit and didn't think twice. How could I not shoot him in the back and evade Soviet guns?

That got answered without my bidding. The tigers broke free. The soldiers under the gate were firing warning shots in the air, which the crowd took to mean the guns weren't pointing at them and the rear pushed the loud, now-worried front line through and over the Red guard, breaking for shadow and alley as quickly as they could.

That's when more VoPo came out of the alleys; when tanks could be spotted as specks coming up Unter-den-Linden. I kept my eyes on Reinhard. This was the moment. Bullets would fly, batons would break, but not necessarily for me.

I walked towards Rutthand. When an excitable westerner bumped me, I stuck an elbow in his neck.

☆

Now I could see Dwight, but not Reinhard. So we had to stick to Dwight, follow his gaze, which remained intent. I followed it, but still couldn't see the quarry. That is, the secondary quarry, the victim.

Detlef was agitated. "The fuck's going on?"

"It's kicked off."

"Why's Inquart here. The exchange. The dossiers."

"Yes? I asked you that."

"He's still here."

"Well. It's kicked off."

"You said that. What's your game Bebel? I don't believe one word from your mouth."

"I thought you had intel."

"Yes... Yes I do."

"So? Your intel's wrong or he's changed plans."

"No," Detlef shook his head. "I'm sorry Günts, I didn't know it would be you today, but this is bullshit. You're not telling me something."

"What?"

"You shouldn't speak again, I suggest."

"Very well..." I took the opportunity to walk away, holding my nerve.

"Don't piss around," Detlef shouted.

"You'll have to figure it all out."

☆

I paid the pulled-up taxi, crutched out the door to the pavement. Flat 7b, 12 Bundesplatz. Perhaps now without interruption, institutional torture or bullets, life was starting again. But through this sun-glanced rock of optimism a vein of sorrow ran. The dance. *There's the limping socialite, trying to East Coast; trying to tango. Don't stare.*

Don't play the victim Ange, it doesn't suit you. Things could be worse. So much worse you'd have no consciousness of them.

About to ring the buzzer, another resident slowed and pulled his key.

"I've just moved in. Don't have a hall key yet."

He nodded amiably and held the door not saying anything; perhaps not German. I hobbled up three flights, now in pain at the top. Not doing that again for a while. 7b. I tried the handle, open. He was home.

Two boxes sat in an empty room. "Guess who!" I shouted.

No reply. RIAS? Asleep in the afternoon?

I went to the bedroom, where the luxury of a sprung bed stood. But the sheets were tangled and no Otto.

Must be shopping. He'd have locked up for RIAS. I'd passed a grocer on Friedenau side of the S-bahn. Though I'd spent weeks in bed I wanted to try this one and await my lanky lover. I leant the crutches in the corner and got in.

Could it really be life would be normal? Out of hospital early; surprising doctors with my regenerative superpowers. I smiled at the ceiling. I felt a new book in me. My original book. The influence of Feudal Prussia and Bismarck on the rise of Nazism.

Being neither dawn nor dusk, nor after-rain, the birds were quiet. Apart from the shunt and squeal of trains the area was silent. An anonymous place where nobody knows your business. If the police came enquiring, a murder say, the neighbourhood would just shrug in meatball-stained vests, or young migrant women would shake their heads. In summer, I'd hear pots and pans clatter through open windows, people practising instruments, lovers' arguing in foreign languages.

I'd passed a second, smaller room on the way to this - a studio? Re-fertilisation trials had failed, I read, but 'other promising avenues were opening'. Maybe I'd give Otto another surprise.

More sweat, now blearing and salting my eyes; the gritty town bleached. The sun is white with black specks, Douglases and Avros banking in glare to head south with their Berliner payloads; butter and coffee and potatoes, cooked by the sun.

Now sure it was Reinhard I circled behind, though it was hard because the flow and push of protesters was a river. The Soviets and VoPo were getting organised in three ranks each side of the street, six clusters. Once synchronised they moved out in a line guns raised, splitting the river of men into three pools. They still shot overhead but not by much: a couple of feet.

I couldn't lose Reinhard; I was in the middle cluster. He was in the thickest cordon near the gate so I was looking at his back.

Madness. Who's pulling my strings? You're no killer Otto, or if you are you'd better take some horse tranquilizers.

I might *have* to shoot him in the back. Judicially it was fair; he shot Ange from behind. Had he meant to kill or maim? No matter. Who was he to slug us like antelope?

I pushed west through a crowd facing east until I was in the back end, with clear concrete between me and the west-facing line. I could do it from here. But if I melted into the crowd they'd pay the penalty, like Heydrich in Prague. I was in range though; clear aim...

I craned to catch Dwight's movements. Pushed heavily through Berliners - I have ballast - no longer caring about Detlef, you see? If Dwight had locked on Reinhard, I was locking him till I'd relocated that damned VoPo, and I'd just have to scan for my brother's face.

If he was even here. What a fiasco Günter. What could Dwight do, unarmed combat? And Detlef, vanished with his flimsy instructions and a handgun.

It was impossible to identify anyone clea... wait. There was one man, tall, facing the wrong way in a shiphand's cap, right at the back. A new surge under the gate now pushed the cordon. Shots rang in the air except one wasn't in the air, because a body went down clutching its stomach. The surging crowd tried to clear a space round him but the pressure from the back quickly engulfed him with boots overhead. Underfoot. More shots.

A VoPo directly in front of tall shiphand-cap turned to his comrade. Reinhard! I started to push towards the tall man facing the wrong way. "Excuse me, get out of the way, move!" I was shouting at people; enacting the dream of heavy limbs in glue. "Move!" I pushed and made slow progress.

Turn round will you. Show me you're Otto. He was intent, whoever he was, head magnetised by Reinhard's back.

Dwight must have been distracted by my fracas through the crowd, spotted me, and followed my line of movement with his eyes.

But I could only see my tall brother's head and hat. Dwight must have seen something lower down, because with sudden surprise he started running towards my mark.

I'll call his name and he'll turn... His automatic in his hands he'll scan the crowd but I'll have shot him. If I miss, the crowd gets sprayed with German bullets. If I hit him, the crowd gets sprayed with German and Soviet bullets. Jesus Christ.

There was scuffling noise behind me.

"Hail, number two son," I heard a voice shout, "well met!"

I turned, looked between the backs of the crowd, just a sea of backs, alternately refocusing as drab, smoke-puffing humans, then flattening to a bas relief.

"Don't do it number two son."

It was Günter's voice I could hear and he deliberately wasn't using my name. I couldn't see him. Then I saw him, struggling to get through.

I stepped out onto clear concrete, and walked towards the line reaching into the sweaty holster. Took the gun out but kept it inside the jacket. A Soviet saw me.

"Halt! Don't come any closer."

I hesitated with his rifle pointing at me, then carried on walking. The barking Soviet had distracted Reinhard, who also turned.

"My dear Otto!" He said, grinning, holding his StG in line with my chest. My hand shook inside my jacket.

I could hear protestations behind me, and the soldier's eyes flicked.

"He's with me," it was Günter's voice, close.

"You don't move either," The soldier paused. Then faltered. "Ah, OK."

What was that? I turned my head. Günter was repocketing something. As I was turning back to Reinhard, I saw Dwight moving quickly towards me. It was now or never.

"Angela would never forgive you," Günter said, simply. "Whichever way it worked out. Is that what you want? The hatred of your beloved?"

My hand shook.

"What are you up to Otto," Reinhard was smirking. "What have you got inside that ridiculous suit?"

His gun was still aimed at me, but the Soviet had lowered his.

Dwight edged forward. "Come on Otto, man. Don't lose your mind."

Günter now: "We'll go somewhere quiet. Go visit Ange in hospital, plan your lives."

This pressure in my head. *Do it Otto. Do it now. Noone else will pay a price. How many times will you turn the other cheek?*

My shaking hand stopped shaking. My vision became clear. Now was the moment. I steeled myself. But Reinhard's head shunted to the right violently, and he slumped to the ground.

"Otto!" shouted Günter, in despair. A pool of blood quickly gathered under Reinhard's head on the concrete.

The Soviets looked north, where a svelte man in too-short clothes was repocketing his silenced pistol and holding up an Interior card, appearing to dance. There were many guns pointing at him now.

I was staring between Reinhard and the shooter, stunned, and felt my collar yanked hard. I stumbled and almost fell over but then was running, with Dwight ahead and Günter behind, round the side of the crowd in the shade of the building, heading for the gate.

The commotion had got the attention of most troops and police, so the surging crowd pressed again. Dwight shoulder-barged the other way and in his slipstream we kept moving, solidly, making ground. Getting through the pressed gate was difficult but Dwight beckoned with his hand. I shook my head not understanding.

"Gun! Give it here."

I did. He held it up, fired once into the arch, and a few people pressed aside to let us through. I was back in the west, and stooped, hands on my knees, coughing, wheezing for breath. Günter too was a sweating breathless wreck. Only

Dwight stood calm, unhindered, trilby still on and untouched.

After a while and some regained composure, Günter said. "I'm going back to Hamburg."

Dwight sniggered but I trembled violently. I'd have done it. I was doing it. The judgement remains the same.

I could hear a drunk protester shouting "Louse!" at the Soviet troops over my shoulder. Günter suggested a beer, now I was a disarmed civilian again.

I nodded, "Something stiffer."

Günter looked questioningly at Dwight.

"Sure." He aimed a damning glare at me, "Now my duties are complete."

"You louse," I heard again. More specific and nearer now. I turned. A man in dirty clothes with few teeth was staring at us. He only had one arm and was dressed too warmly for summer, which usually meant no abode.

"Are you talking to us?"

The man pointed at Günter's back. I tugged his arm and Günter turned.

"Hermannplatz."

Some dawn of recognition was coming over my brother. The man's face was filth-smeared, his eyes dim and yellow. "Left us for dead. Left me for dead."

Günter muttered, "König?"

"You know it's me. You louse!"

"I didn't leave you. I was picked up."

"Oh. Got a lift?"

"You don't understand." Günter was now having a bit of personal turmoil and a mild stammer. "The NKVD took me. I was in the same state as you."

"You weren't, you liar." Unconvinced, it faltered König a little.

"What happened to your arm?"

"They caught me stealing potatoes and put it through a threshing machine. A fair price for ten potatoes. I'm philosophical." His shattered teeth grinned nastily.

"I'm so sorry König."

After a tense silence, his slushy mouth resumed. "And what did the NKVD want with Captain Bebel?"

"Threats and recruitment. The usual."

"Why you?"

Now Günter had pause, and in that the man König must have seen guilt. He came towards Günter with his one good arm drawn back. "You damned louse!"

Dwight had to step in because Günter clearly wasn't defending himself. He caught König's flailing arm.

"Alright kid. You heard what he said. Günter didn't leave you for dead, he was picked up. Now if you're not gonna be peaceable you'd better scram. He's had enough excitement."

There was strain and tension in the locked arms. The American grip. This jaundiced casualty looked Dwight up and down fuming, his mouth twitching. His anger apparently undimmable.

Günter wouldn't catch his eye, as König looked over Dwight's shoulder. König's body relaxed. He turned and walked away, and without turning back, called, "Left us for dead, Günter."

We sat in Tiergarten, a band playing old time swing with old timers swinging on the bandstand. Gingham and headscarves. The old and - now we were rebuilding - a few young men with the women. I'd given Dwight back his holster and he kept his jacket on while Günter got a tray and I sat shaking in shirtsleeves.

"You're a damned fool Otto." Dwight was deadly serious. "I knew you were a hothead, but not that..."

I didn't say anything. Eventually. "Who shot him?"

"Special operations."

"What! CIA?"

"No, East. Interior."

"Why?"

"You'd have to ask Günter."

"I'm asking you."

"Here he is now."

The tray landed. I took my brandy, downed it, and took long slugs of the beer. A few moments later I'd stopped shaking, and felt the warmth of the sun again.

"Why did they shoot him Günter?"

"Eh?"

"Your lot."

Günter was silent, translated that silence into long gulps of cold beer for a while, and finally said: "They thought Reinhard was a spy. I assume Detlef saw you or Dwight and thought one of you was the contact. When he stepped out of the line, he must have thought you'd disappear and lose him. That's all I can think of."

Dwight looked up, indignant. "So I could have taken a bullet for being his contact?"

"Don't look at me. I didn't shoot anyone!" Günter protested, and began chewing his lip foggily.

The music played on; the sun and alcohol softened edgy day.

"Sorry about the spiking."

"I'm an addict now, living on the streets."

"I'm trying to say sorry Dwight."

"And I'm saying don't sweat it."

Another silence. But it was still fishy to me. "Why do... why did they think he was a spy?"

Günter cleared his throat. "I may have had something to do with that."

And in the warm evening I felt a little of my damnation shift off my shoulders, migrate a few feet away.

And he was right, wasn't he, the one-armed yellow St. Peter at the gate of Berlin: our cracked and disabled Heaven. I had left them for dead. All in 16th Panzer Division, the Ram. For whom I had guardianship. Fled, imprisoned, fragmented and gone. Who was left to forgive? Who was left to blame, entropy?

I put the key in the door but it was already unlocked; must have been in a frenzy when I left. But on opening the door

Ange's little floral holdall had been dropped in the bare living room. "Ange?"

"Honey, I'm home!" came a call from the bedroom.

When I walked in, she leapt onto her knees and then squealed in pain, falling back again.

"Hon, you're not due out. Did you discharge yourself?"

She pointed at her leg. "Time off for good behaviour. You'll have to come to me I'm afraid. I can't leap into your arms."

I smiled. God I was so happy to see her. I lay down on the bed next to her and pushed my hand into her black nest of curls. She rolled onto me. I saw the crutches against the wall. "What's the prognosis then?"

"You absolutely stink of booze. But you're not drunk."

"That's the prognosis?"

"It's my prognosis."

"Come on Hon. What do they think?"

"They think I'm a miracle, like the Virgin Mary."

"So no long-term problems."

"I knew you'd ask. Yes, there will be." She huffed and fell back.

"But nothing a well-supported dancer can't get over. You know... if she has a permanent partner. Always."

"You lunkhead, you can't dance." And she punched me softly.

EPILOGUE

Tempelhof in September. Unloading Skymasters. Unlike Skytrains with their sloped bays you can back a truck to a C-54... flour, sugar, meat, dehydrated potatoes, dairy. Real coffee. Unloaded in twenty minutes it leaves me dizzy. Coal sacks fall from Superfortresses which simply can't land.

Before work we stand with the children at Tempelhof fields, watching the dot-lined horizon. The kids' faces are intensely happy, trying to spot giveaway sprinkles from the cockpits: magic candy parachutes.

> Herr Bebel,
> Excuse my contacting you out of the blue and I hope this letter finds you thriving. I write on behalf of Albert Speer.
> Despite his straitened circumstances, Albert has expressed a strong wish for the olive branch to be extended in re. your testimony at Nuremberg.
> Quite used to the pressures which interrogation...

Yes, blah blah...

> ...agreed that you conducted yourself admirably in his support under Counsel Flächsner. (The defence

counsel forewarned Albert of your presence, and his good fortune to have snapped up Mr. Westwood's documentation before the prosecution could.)

He wished me in particular to say that you and he were aligned in indicting the regime, while skeptical about intelligence shared inside it. He is flattered to think you are 'of one voice' regarding his simple role as designer of buildings, of armaments to protect the nation, and in organising the so-called 'war-machine' to run efficiently - as any German handed ministerial portfolio would have done.

We still fondly recall your dextrous Bach recitals, your schnaps and dear Frau Bebel's hospitality. I trust she is well?

Albert has also instructed me to enquire as to your position at *RIAS*, and also your partner's contacts at *Der Tagesspiegel*. As you may know, Spandau...

I dropped the letter, lifted it, read the signoff: Rudolf Wolters. *Of one voice? ...Snakes.* Dora, Muna, coughing skeletons pushed in shit barrels. Have you forgotten? Worse than snakes: the transparent skin sloughed by snakes. I could see the phrase 'broadcast potential' lower down. How do they even know all this?

I felt like scrawling immediately asking the pair not to implicate me in post-Nazi apologies or any post-Reich associations whatever, and indeed, not to even implicate my poor letterbox or telephone in their chicanery.

"Anything in the mail, Hon?"

I was chewing my nail, skull wedged in the headboard.

"Just a guilt-wracked maniac with blood on his hands. The usual."

"You should stop hanging round with those."

"Mmm."

I was in a cafe when I heard the radio news, heavy rain cleaning the trees: in response to Allied imposition of statehood in the west, East Germany, including Eastern Berlin, were now also a state.

Both claimed my flag but Stalin or Pieck stuck an emblem in theirs: wheat for peasants (farmless), compasses for intellectuals (they'd defected) and a hammer for industry (Joe shipped all that home). A new Dark Ages, but with shiny mega-weapons.

I limped through Potsdamer's high balconies and grotty plazas - the socket-eyed centre of black markets, where the flowers bunched and migrants bartered, the stalls hastily bagged when VoPos came, banknotes vanishing. But I saw a nose I couldn't fail to recognise; my heart started flapping. It couldn't be true.

"Marianne."

"Angie!"

"Grab that girl!" A dark man was running towards us. "The thief. Grab her."

Marianne made to dash away. I held her wrist, a wash of euphoria in my brain: alive, kicking, yelling, smiling. *Kolompár was someone else*. I squeezed her madly. "Kolompár was someone else!"

I turned. "How dare you!" I shouted at him.

"What?"

"My sister is no thief."

"She steals cigarettes and petrol from my stall each day."

"Of course she doesn't." I manoeuvred Marianne behind me. "You have a case of mistaken identity."

"No mistaken identity. Her face is well-known and the traders won't leave their stalls. Look at her, how could you mistake her identity?"

Sorrow twanged my heart like Otto's chords. What Marianne had won was won in Ravensbrück. "Then we'll come to an arrangement. If I promise she'll never visit the market again."

"I'm owed."

"She'll be gone."

The man flung his hands in the air and walked away.

"Where are you living Marianne?"

"Around."

When I got home, accompanied with a twelve-year-old with holes in her face, olive skinned and sandy of hair, deep-set eyes at once defensive and opportunist, suspicious of all and everything, Otto looked at me wide-eyed in panic.

"This is Marianne."

He lobbed his gaze rudely over her head in terror. "Marianne. ...That's a nice name."

"Otto will teach you the guitar, and I'll teach you to dance and write German and cook."

Otto realised this wasn't casual brunch, and reached out for a table for support. Like I'd set up scaffolding for a decade of his life.

"Just for a while," Marianne said, warily.

"Just for a while."

She took her two little bags and wondered where to put them.

"There's a room for you. Through there."

Marianne walked to it and looked back, with a degree of doubt. Otto'd regained his balance and lit a cigarette. He wouldn't look me in the eye, knowing if he did he'd sealed his fate. One day he'd have to meet my maternal gaze.

Two apples had vanished from the sideboard.

Printed in Great Britain
by Amazon